ISBN   978-1502464071

Cover art by Mark Watts

CW00840183

Again, for Josh and Emily Watts

"Families are made in the heart."
(C. Joybell C.)

Ben Blake is on Facebook at
https://www.facebook.com/benblakeauthor

Follow Ben's blog at http://benblake.blogspot.co.uk/

Or email him at ben.blake@hotmail.co.uk

Also by Ben Blake

The Risen King
Blood and Gold (Songs of Sorrow volume 1)
The Gate of Angels (songs of Sorrow volume 2)
A Brand of Fire (Troy volume 1)

Troy

Volume Two

Heirs of Immortality

Let us hasten – let us fly –
Where the lovely meadows lie;
Where the living waters flow;
Where the roses bloom and blow.
Heirs of immortality.
Segregated, safe and pure,
Easy, sorrowless, secure;
Since our earthly course is run,
We behold a brighter sun.

Aristophanes

Book Three   The Thousand Ships

Caesura

It was a lonely little town on the coast, by the middle of three bays. The smallest of them, not much more than a nibble taken out of the land. But now it was home to all the kings of Greece. Aulis was where the fleet assembled.

It was still assembling, in fact, though it already seemed to the gaping onlookers that every ship on the Greensea must be here. The bays were packed so tightly that hulls scraped against each other whenever the current raced in the Strait of Epirus, making a noise like a knife scraping on bone. Beyond the bay and the Strait lay the island kingdom of Euboea, and masts rose in thick clusters there too, in two more inlets where the current swirled but did not drag – or at least, not heavily.

Ships had been coming and going for some time, in fact. Some had even sailed in the winter, which only fools dared, hugging the coastline where sea monsters were less likely. They had come laden with grain, mostly, and olives or figs in amphorae sealed with clay. Or wine, the soldier's most loyal friend, able to chase away his fears and soothe his hurts. The supplies had been carried up the hills and stored in hastily-built warehouses, or in vast tents made of sheets of canvas sewn together. The structures had climbed the hillside, spread along it, then spread further. The new city was larger than Aulis now, guarded by grim men in helms and cuirasses.

With spring the ships had come in numbers, this time laden with soldiers from all of Greece. I was there to meet them; Thersites, teller of tales. Where else could I have chosen to be? For the moment, Aulis had replaced Delphi as the centre of the whole world.

Agamemnon was first to arrive, as befitted the High King. He brought thirty ships at first, though more followed in fives and tens, bringing additional supplies. His brother was next, red-faced Menelaus still maundering into his cups, but he had sixty ships with him. Nestor brought eighty from Messenia, Agapenor sixty from Arcadia, Schedius forty from Phocis. Boeotia itself, on whose coast Aulis stood, provided more than seventy, led by King Leitus. Others provided far fewer, the small realms doing

4

what they could. Poor Odysseus, the shepherd-king of Ithaca, could muster only twelve hulls.

The same number came from Salamis, where all this trouble could be said to have begun. With them came a surprise. Huge Ajax would not lead them to Troy after all; that role went to his father, a man so monstrous fat it seemed the galley which bore him wallowed under his weight. Telamon glowered at anyone who glanced his way, and sweated in the spring sunshine like the pig which had gored him so long ago.

Very late, on the first day of the Festival of Dionysius itself, a final fleet sailed into the Strait. There were scores of them, ninety perhaps, and every sail was painted with a double-headed axe in black, with crimson eyes. Everyone recognised it: the *labrys* symbol of the kings of Crete since Minos' time. Aulis townsfolk and soldiers from varied lands came out to watch them approach. There was no room in the bays by then; the Cretans were forced to beach on the Euboea side. An hour later a single ship detached itself and sailed back across, to join the others in the central bay close to Aulis, where the other kings waited.

I saw it set out, by chance. As it ploughed across the Strait I made my way back into the town, to the palace Agamemnon had ordered built over the winter. The kings had been meeting there to discuss strategy and routes, all the dull detail of how to bring a thousand ships safely across the Aegean Sea to Troy. I'd sat through several afternoons of such debate and found nothing to interest me. But that approaching sail changed everything.

I suspected there would be drama, today.

Chapter One

The Son of Dogs

Agamemnon had brought a huge pavilion, rooms and rooms of canvas that billowed in the spring wind. There was a small entrance hall and then a big space that served as a *megaron*, including a long hearth down the middle built of stone slabs bracketed together with bronze. Coals burned deep within it, adding a smoky warmth to the air.

Beyond that, all Odysseus knew was that there were many more rooms. It was all anyone knew: Agamemnon kept his sleeping arrangements secret. His men surrounded the pavilion day and night, guards with the Lion of Mycenae etched on their cuirasses. Any man trying to reach the High King would have to pass them, and then who knew what else inside as he blundered around trying to find his quarry before the alarm was raised.

At the far end of the *megaron* was a dais with a chair – a throne, really – and before it was a table. Today it was covered with papyrus, three whole bull hides stitched together with great care. On them was drawn Troy, and the Plain west of the city.

Odysseus had been assured the map showed Troy as well as any Greek knew it. Down to the last sand dune and braid of the Scamander River, the mapmaker had promised. That was all very well, but every season changed the land. Streams ran dry in hot summers, trees were felled by winter storms. At Troy the Scamander flooded in spring, when the snow melted on Mount Ida; who knew where the river's braids lay now?

The men gathered around the table were talking as though the map really could be relied on. They were fools. Nothing was ever what you expected it to be.

Most of the stronger kings of Greece were gathered around the table. Menestheus was beside the High King, speaking little because his slow speech was so often interrupted. Nestor stood across the table, also speaking rarely, though when he did everyone stopped to listen. Agapenor nodded his head at every word Agamemnon spoke, of course, and Thalpius pointed things out on the map and explained them in his rough soldier's voice. Diomedes was there too, taller than most and marked by his bright blond hair.

A little way off stood Menelaus, not drinking today but still florid, the servants staying clear of him as much as possible. Tales of his bad temper had spread.

Odysseus had stationed himself some distance away, close to the edge of hearing. Most of the smaller kings had, such as Ialmenus of Locris, Leonteus of Pieria, Pheidippus of Calymne. And one other, astonishingly: Telamon of Salamis was here, reclining on a sturdy divan across the hall, his bulk overhanging the couch and sweating profusely. Odysseus hadn't seen him in years. He gave the fat man a polite nod, not really sure what else to do. Telamon nodded back and mopped sweat from his face.

Odysseus leaned against a stone pillar – pillars, in a tent! – and turned his attention back to the kings around their map. They'd stopped talking while he was distracted though, and now Agamemnon had his head bent to listen to a servant whispering in his ear. Odysseus caught the word "king" and then *"labrys"*, which was enough to tell him Idomeneus had finally arrived.

"Bring him here," the High King said brusquely, and then checked himself. "No. *Invite* him here. And send word to my wife to join me, with our daughter Iphigenia for company."

Odysseus was careful not to meet Agamemnon's stare. The other kings had found things to occupy them too, straightening folds in their *chitons* or leaning forward to study the map. They all knew of Idomeneus' demand, now. Some secrets were too large to keep. The Mountain Boar had shown the nerve to make demands of the High King, which set a bad precedent and might lead to worse trouble, in days to come. Certainly Odysseus expected the Cretan to find himself short on friends during this war; nobody would like what he had done. Or they'd be envious that he'd done it first.

"Where were we?" Agamemnon asked. The messenger hurried away, towards the anteroom.

"Down to two possible landing sites," Thalpius said briefly. There were few graces to the man's speech, though he was properly respectful to the High King. "The eastern beach of the Bay of Troy, or else Cradle Bay, across the Plain to the west."

"That's no choice at all," Diomedes said. "The eastern side is a bad as the southern strand of the main Bay. The problem is the same: when the *Meltemi* wind blows it will pin our ships tight to the coast. If that happens when a Trojan attack reaches the strand, we'll face disaster."

7

"They won't reach the strand," Ajax snorted.

Diomedes shook his head. "The Trojans are formidable, my friend. Or else why does it take all Greece to challenge them? And their city is right above that eastern beach. They could issue from the north of Troy – the Sea Gate, or the Citadel Gate, either one – and be upon us in those marvellous chariots almost before we could prepare."

"That's true," Agamemnon said, nodding.

"Also the eastern beach is steep," Menestheus put in. "The Trojans may have added defences." He paused, and for a change nobody spoke into the gap. "Wooden forts, perhaps."

"A distinct possibility," Diomedes said. "Especially when you remember who we're dealing with here."

"Yes, we know," Ajax said. "The Trojans are formidable. Can we –"

"Hector," Diomedes said.

It was strange, how a single name could bring such stillness to the room. Ajax glowered at the king of Argolis, so like a Trojan himself with that tumble of golden hair, but he didn't speak. All around the table faces tightened and throats were cleared.

"Hector will have to be dealt with," Diomedes said into the hush. "He is to Troy what Achilles is to Greece. We can't ignore him, or plan around him, because he stands square in the path of all we're trying to do."

"Then we'll send Achilles to kill him," Menelaus said.

Diomedes laughed. "Really? Since when did Achilles go where he was pointed, like a hunting dog trained to obey? Since when did any of us? Besides, I'm not sure even Achilles could kill this man, hand against hand."

"You sound afraid," Agapenor said.

There was a pause.

"I have no need to prove my mettle," Diomedes said, ending it. "But speak to me of fear again, my lord of Arcadia, and I will show you with my blade which of us has reason to be afraid."

"Stop it," Agamemnon said. Diomedes already had a hand raised, forestalling the words.

"I don't fear Hector," he said, now in a more normal tone. "But I'm not sure I could kill him. I'm not sure Ajax could, or Achilles. Hector is *very* formidable. We shouldn't fool ourselves over that."

"I'm not sure I could, either," Ajax admitted. The words might have been dragged from his lips.

Diomedes nodded. "With Hector to lead them, the Trojans are more than capable of reaching the strand of the Bay of Troy. We'd do better to land at Cradle Bay. Yes, I know it's four miles or more from the city, and it means we'll have to cross the Scamander to reach Troy. But the Trojans will also have to cross it to reach us, and on those sand dunes their chariots won't work very well."

"I agree," Nestor said. Menestheus nodded assent.

"Very well," Agamemnon said. "We will land at Cradle Bay. I intend to send the fleet across in three waves, each taking a different route. The first will head north from Aulis, passing by Scopelos and Panagia Islands, to seize Tenedos isle off the coast of Troas. The second will pass by Scyros and –"

He never finished the sentence. There was a sudden babble of raised voices from outside, clearly audible through the canvas walls of the pavilion, and then the flap was thrown back and a woman strode into the room, her face contorted with rage.

Odysseus saw that expression and faded back a step, slightly behind the pillar he'd been leaning on. Battle was one thing, and a noble calling in its way, but fighting a woman was different. As for this woman, there had been tales of Clytemnestra's temper even before she married Agamemnon, when she was still hardly more than a girl in Sparta. Menelaus could drink all day and not rival her fury. Odysseus didn't intend to bring it down on himself.

That she was furious was beyond doubt. Her face was black with it, her fists clenched at her sides and the muscles of her neck standing out in ridges. Behind her scurried a young girl, one Odysseus had never seen but placed at once because she shared Clytemnestra's firm jaw: Iphigenia. She was fifteen but looked younger, her body not yet developed. It was hard to believe she was niece to Helen, whose beauty was known around the world.

Odysseus was about to look back at the High King when another figure entered. He was a boy, looking a little older than Iphigenia, and he skulked along the edge of the tent as though afraid to come fully into the room. Much like himself, Odysseus thought wryly. He thought he knew who this was: Orestes, heir to Mycenae and the High Kingship. Agamemnon hadn't asked for him to be brought, which might be why the youth held back.

9

Interesting that he seemed more afraid of his father than eager to see him.

"Is it true?" Clytemnestra demanded. Her voice was harsh as a raven's croak. "You sold our daughter to the pig of Crete?"

Agamemnon stared at her. "Watch your tone, wife. This is not a private room where your temper will be tolerated."

"Is it true?" she shrieked. Several of the kings flinched back from the sound. "It is, I see it in your eyes. You son of dogs!"

So it had been possible to keep Idomeneus' demand secret, after all. At least from the women. Odysseus wondered how it had been done; bribed guards, probably, and careful control of who was allowed to visit the queen and who wasn't. Behind her mother Iphigenia looked terrified, her eyes wide and white, and no wonder. No girl wanted to be wed to a man from beyond Greece. Since Minos' fall Crete had been Greek, true, but that was just a claim. In the villages people would still hold to the old ways, of double-headed axes and labyrinths, and the sacrifice of children to appease gods in the shape of bulls.

Crete was very far from the heartland of Greece. Iphigenia would never see her home again.

"What would you have us do?" Menelaus demanded, from two steps behind the map table. "Accept what that woman-prince from Troy did? Duck our heads and walk meekly away?"

"You would know about princes who are half woman," Clytemnestra snarled, "being one yourself."

Odysseus winced, and Menelaus came forward with a growl in his throat like an enraged hound, but the queen gave them no time to speak. "What would I do? I would do what should have been done long ago, before Greek merchants began to suffer, before Egyptian and Phoenician traders seized our markets in the Euxine Sea. Send Hesione home. It's only your foolish men's pride that stops you doing so even now."

"That will not be possible," Telamon said.

His voice, once a warrior's stentorian battle shout, had become breathy and nasal with the years. With the increasing fat, more accurately. Still, it brought every eye to him, even stilling Clytemnestra's rage. He savoured the attention for a moment and then said, "Hesione is dead. She passed to Hades three weeks ago."

"Dead?" Diomedes wore a small smile. "How did she die?"

"In her sleep," Telamon said.

"Of course she did," Diomedes said flatly. "I expect the chirurgeons, much to their dismay, could do nothing?"

"Just so," the fat man agreed. His little eyes never moved from Diomedes. "You can imagine my anguish."

I believe we all can, Odysseus thought. Scanning the faces of the kings, he didn't think any one of them believed Hesione had died peacefully. Telamon had killed her, or had one of his men do it for him, unless he'd simply lain on top of her until she smothered. He glanced at Ajax and found the big man's face impassive. There would be no help there.

"So my child is betrayed," Clytemnestra said. Her tone was lower, but rage still whipped through the words. "You will have your war, and sacrifice Iphigenia to achieve it. I say it again, High King of Greece," she was sneering now, "you are the son of dogs and pigs. I pray the gods fill your mouth with dust and your eyes with Night itself."

"Father," Iphigenia said. Her voice trembled.

Agamemnon's broad face had turned the red of roof tiles. "Guards. Take my wife and daughter to the women's quarters and confine them there. If they try to leave you will tie them hand and foot."

"Father," the girl repeated.

Agamemnon didn't look at her. "Orestes. Yes, I know you're skulking there. Come out where I can see you."

He did so, a slender youth with his father's brown hair and his mother's thrusting jaw. That at least changed the shape of his face, so he lacked Agamemnon's broad peasant's look; a bull, as people said when the High King couldn't hear. He had to pause to allow Clytemnestra and Iphigenia to be escorted past, the queen holding her head high but the girl on the verge of tears. Orestes looked at the floor until they were by and then advanced into the middle of the tent.

"You're growing into a fine man," Agamemnon told him. "I think you're too clever to ruin it now by siding with a fool of a woman, aren't you?"

Orestes nodded. "Yes, Father."

"Make sure you remember that while I'm away," Agamemnon said. "Because I will be back, Orestes, and in glory. Depend upon it. In half a lifetime of conflict I've never lost a war yet. Why, I remember when…"

11

As Agamemnon began a long-winded reminiscence of his youthful bravery, a voice spoke in Odysseus' ear. "Did you see him wilt when his wife raged at him? Our High King is no lion after all."

It was Thersites, who always seemed to find a way into the councils of kings, or inveigle his way onto a couch when captains met to discuss tactics and drink wine. Odysseus couldn't make himself like Thersites, or trust him either, no matter what Menestheus said. There was a spark in the hollow-chested man's eye that spoke of more than mere cleverness. Cunning and guile, and perhaps a hint of mischief too. It was that last, particularly, which held Odysseus's tongue.

"He is lion enough when it matters," he said. He wasn't about to speak ill of Agamemnon to a man like Thersites. Starlings murmur together it was said, and what they murmured had a nasty habit of being repeated until it found its way to the wrong ears.

"Will he be a lion on the beaches of Troy?" Thersites asked. "Or does he roar so loud because he has no teeth?"

Odysseus turned his head to study the man. "Why not come with us and see for yourself?"

"Oh, I will," the bard said amiably. "I can hardly tell the tale of this war unless I see it for myself, now can I?"

He chortled and withdrew, leaving Odysseus to shake his head. Nestor was looking over, he noticed, a slight frown on the older man's face. Maybe he didn't trust Thersites either. Well, there would be more important things to consider in the coming days than one crippled storyteller.

"… left them crying out behind us." Agamemnon was winding up his story. "We didn't take any heed of their pleas, Orestes, and neither should you, when your mother tries to turn you against me. She will, when the fleet has sailed. You be sure you remember where your loyalty lies."

"I will, Father," the lad said. His smile looked sincere but his words were colourless, empty of feeling. Odysseus wondered whether anyone else had noticed it and then thought *I will wager Thersites did.* Trustworthy or not, the bard really was clever.

"Then go," Agamemnon told his son. "Talthybius, I want it announced that tomorrow my daughter Iphigenia will marry king Idomeneus of Crete. I trust you to ensure she will be there."

The king's Herald, a thin man standing among the pillars opposite Odysseus, bowed his head. "I promise it, my lord. There are… certain ways of guaranteeing compliance."

Odysseus shuddered inside. *What beasts we men can be, and we Greeks worse than most.* He didn't know what ways Talthybius meant and didn't want to, but he was sure the Herald would be as good as his word. Talthybius might not be the bravest of men, and he was much too weak to fight, but his loyalty and efficiency were beyond question.

"We were discussing the fleets," Agamemnon said. If his herald's words had disturbed him he gave no sign of it. He bent back over the map, and the kings gathered close again to peer as his finger began to trace out the routes the fleet would follow.

13

Chapter Two

The Promise of Ares

The ships came up the middle of the Euripus Strait, sails down in still air, oars shining as they dipped and rose.

The water was crammed with vessels all the time now, most of them supply craft loaded with amphorae of flour or figs, rowed by half a normal crew to make room for more cargo. The kings had ordered that all ships must move only northwards, to prevent collisions. The new arrivals passed them easily, a triple line of hulls that forced others to veer aside, sometimes dangerously close to the opposite coasts of Greece and Euboea. They kept their formation until a single ship broke off and turned towards Aulis, and the bay already jammed with masts packed like olives in a jar.

Its hull was dead black, layers of pitch without ornamentation of any kind. As it approached Greek soldiers came onto the slopes of to watch: Boeotians and Argolids, Cretans and Ithacans, Thessalians and Elids and Achaeans. From somewhere down by the shore a chant rose, was taken up by others, spread along the shore. After a time others began to echo it from the Euboean side, creating a resonance that seemed to shake the stones.

"Achilles! Achilles! Achilles!"

The single black ship bore down on the beach, towards a narrow space between two others. There wasn't room, the oars would splinter and then the hulls would grind together and split – but the rowers shipped their blades at a shouted command, smooth as olive oil, and the galley slipped into the space and grounded its prow on the strand.

As it did so several figures hurtled over the rail, leaping from deck to shore to land with knees bent and spears held high. They formed a curving line, shields so close they almost touched; no other soldiers in Greece could have matched the manoeuvre. Only the Myrmidons could do it. At their head stood a tall man in golden armour, blond hair spilling from beneath a golden helmet. The man whose name was being cried to the skies.

"Achilles! Achilles!"

"Well," Nestor said, watching from the hillside quarter of a mile away, "he does like a dramatic entrance, doesn't he?"

*

Isander reacted somewhat differently.

He'd been down on the strand when the Myrmidon ship headed in, one of a line of men carrying grain sacks from a galley to the store tents further up the slope. Someone had seen the incoming vessel and muttered that he thought it was black, the hull certainly looked black, and then all at once heads were coming up and work was forgotten. The name *Achilles* leapt from mouth to mouth and then became a chant, without any prompting that Isander saw. He put down the sack he was hefting and turned.

The Myrmidon ship grounded right beside him, so close he could have taken two paces and then touched its hull. Just before it halted ten armoured men sprang over the prow, one of them armoured and helmed in gold, and Isander thought his heart would stop from shock and elation.

Achilles glanced at him and Isander looked hastily away, unwilling or afraid to make eye contact. The blond man was much larger than he was, but even with his feet half buried in sand he seemed on the verge of dancing. Danger came off him like sweat from a weary horse, a scent that seemed to shimmer in the air. Isander caught just a glimpse of sea-green eyes, chill and as deadly as spume when the storm blows. He felt suddenly cold.

Then the sense of oppression passed, and he risked looking up again. Achilles had turned back to face the throng of men pressed around him, lifting his hands for silence. Sunlight gleamed off the bronze vambraces on his forearms. The crowd didn't quieten though, instead only changing their chant. "Troy shall fall! Troy shall fall! Troy shall fall!"

Arms punched the air with each cry. There must be two thousand men on the beach, Isander thought, perhaps twice that number. The roar made the ships tremble where they rested on the sand. Achilles stood in the midst of it all, arms still raised, smiling benignly as he waited for quiet. Finally the chanting faded into murmurs and restless shuffling. Achilles hadn't moved.

"Yes, Troy will fall," he said, and his smile flashed out like sunlight sparkling on sea water, "now I'm here to make sure of it."

15

The throng bellowed approval. Standing by the ship Isander felt himself frown a little. The other great captains of Greece would not like that comment at all, when they heard of it. Diomedes and Ajax, even Isander's own king Thalpius, would grind their teeth in anger at being so belittled. Agamemnon himself wouldn't be too pleased; the High King had planned all this, brought the kings together without mishap, and he was sure to say that was why Troy was in danger now. Not because one more warrior had come, however renowned he was.

Isander was inclined to agree. All the talk among the men was that the Trojans had the best chariots in the world, and a phalanx of men in the Apollonians who were the match of any. Against that the Greeks had numbers. They weren't going to win through the brilliance of their heroes, but through the weight of their massed spears – if they were to win at all.

But it was hard, watching Achilles gleam in the sun with the adoring crowd all around, to remember that he was just one more warrior, or to believe it. He looked like half a god at least, and he'd proved himself more than most men with his raids on many far coasts, these past ten years.

The crowd shifted, making room unwillingly, and two men stepped out from the ranks. *Speak a name and the Fates hear,* Isander thought as he recognised Ajax and Diomedes, the former towering over Achilles and the other just as tall and golden. There was a sudden tightness in the air and the mass of men went quiet, sensing it.

"I was starting to think you'd stay on your island while the war passed you by," Ajax said.

Achilles laughed. "And miss the fun?"

"I think if you want fun, the island is where you should be," Diomedes said. "There will be little enough on the plains beneath Troy's walls. Unless you think you can crack them open in a day or two?"

"Perhaps not as fast as that," Achilles said.

They were like strange dogs in a yard, Isander thought, each sniffing at the others and trying to decide if he should bite. They smiled, and their tones were light, but the amiability never reached their eyes. In the battle these three would be enemies just as much as the Trojans, each of them determined to garner so much glory that the others would have to admit they'd been bettered, all the days of their lives when talk turned to Troy. And

16

it always would. Whatever happened, whether the Greeks took Troy or were driven back into the sea, men would speak of this war for generations on end.

"Achilles is our talisman," Nikos said later, when the three friends had eaten and were seated around a fire. He kept his voice low; the camps were all crowded now, teeming with men sleeping in tents or under cloaks propped on sticks, and there were always ears to overhear. "But he wants fame above everything. *Kleos,* honour won in battle that lasts beyond death. I'm afraid he might be more divisive than helpful."

"He can have all the glory he wants," big Gorka said. "As long as he makes the war short, so I come home alive."

"Truly said," Nikos agreed, though he was smiling where Gorka had merely been grim. "Let Achilles win fame to rival the gods! All we ask is a short season of war, a pretty scar to show the women, and enough plunder to give us ease in our old age."

"Old age," Isander echoed, and snorted. They were young enough yet that decrepitude seemed hardly possible, a thing so distant that it might as well not be real. Infirmity came to other men; it would never come to them, strong and hale as they were. At least, it wouldn't come through the passing of years. It might be brought on them by battle, a severed limb or crushed hip leaving them hobbled and frail. But that was why they needed Achilles. The shorter the struggle, the less chance they would be maimed, or worse. If even death was worse than being crippled. Isander wasn't sure it was.

He would not have thought this way half a year ago, he knew. Naïveté had sloughed off him since he came to Olympia, and that went ten times since the army had begun preparing for war in Troy. Isander could still hardly credit it, even now. The youth who'd left his parents' home in the country seemed almost a different person to the one he was now. It was, he thought, almost as hard to remember when he'd been younger as it was to imagine being older. There might be something almost of philosophy in that.

A figure emerged from the darkness, making them all tense a little when they saw it was Axylus. The muscular man hadn't been as aggressive of late, perhaps because the three friends were full soldiers now, not recruits anymore. Still, none of them trusted him. He noted their wariness with a twist of his lips, but still hunkered down to speak to them.

17

"Have you heard?" he asked, his voice a murmur. He was being careful of lurking ears as well. "There's a Hittite in Troy. An ironsmith."

Isander felt his belly plunge. "Truly?"

"So it's said," Axylus assured him. "That sly dog Nestor has had people sniffing in the city for months, it seems. He knew there was a Hittite there but not why. Now he does."

"But the Hittites never let their ironsmiths go," Nikos protested. "They guard them like their own daughters."

Axylus shrugged. "Don't tell me, lad. Tell the Trojans if you think it's unfair. Me, I reckon when Nestor says something, he's got good reasons. Don't be having nightmares, now."

With that sardonic parting shot he rose and moved away, stopping at the next fire along to speak in a low voice to the men there. Presumably he was passing on the same information, which made his earlier murmur more an affectation than a serious effort to keep a secret.

"Do you think that can be true?" Isander asked. "It can't be. Can it?"

Nikos plucked a stalk of grass and chewed it for a moment. "I don't know. The Hittites really do guard their ironsmiths closely, so it seems unlikely… but Axylus is right. Nestor wouldn't say this unless he was sure of it. I'm afraid it might be true."

Gorka stirred, shifting his weight. "Probably is. Doesn't make much difference if it is. Iron making takes time."

That was true. But the Hittite might already have had that time; they didn't know how long he'd been in Troy, after all. In any case, a dozen iron swords could be enough to make a difference. They were stronger than their bronze counterparts, and so could be made with longer blades that carried greater weight, and sheared through armour more easily. Or so it was said. Fables had been told of iron swords for decades, though few Greeks had ever seen one. Isander was half surprised that Heracles had never been ordered to gain possession of one by Eurystheus, as one of his great Labours.

Well, the Greeks were going to see iron swords now. They knew that for sure two hours before midnight, when word ran through the camp that Agamemnon had given the order to sail.

*

18

Two mornings later horns blew on the mainland side of the strait, echoed after a moment from the Euboea shore.

Leonteus snapped an order. The kings had drawn lots over who should launch first, in the end. Attempts to discuss it rationally had degenerated into shouting matches three times, however Agamemnon cajoled and threatened. It was the gruff king of Pieria whose name had come out of the bowl, so now it was his men who strained to lift the prows of their ships and push them out to sea. They shifted slowly at first, with a grinding sound as pebbles rolled under the hulls, and then picked up speed. Men grabbed for ropes to haul themselves up, or splashed through the water to snatch at them. Those ships quickest to launch sprouted oars at the stern, where they had room.

One vessel had jammed in the gravel of the beach. Nestor pointed it out and chortled.

"Those men will have prayed half the night not to make such fools of themselves with the whole army watching," he said. "I suppose no gods were listening."

"Let's hope," Odysseus said, "that they weren't listening to Calchas this morning, either."

Nestor grimaced. "Small chance of that. Every eye in the world will be on us today, with the launch of this fleet. And the army it carries. Mortal or god, everyone will be watching."

That was true enough. Ships were putting out from the far shore now, dozens of them, and there would be more in the other bays, out of sight. Some three hundred vessels all told, and it wasn't even a third of the total. Odysseus had hardly believed the numbers at first. Even when he climbed the promontory north of Aulis to gaze across the Euripus Strait, so he could see the hulls crammed together in all the bays, he hadn't really believed it. Only now, watching so many masts move towards open water, did he really know it for truth.

Every god would have gathered, on Olympus and beyond. The Trojan gods would be aware of the fleet, on their own sacred mountains and in their rivers, their woods and glades. Naiads and dryads, even Nereids in the sea, would have stopped their work and games to watch. Which meant that Calchas' words this morning would have been heard, and noted.

Raging Ares promises us victory on the beaches of Troy, the Seer had said. His words were passed to Talthybius, on an outcrop of rock nearby, for the herald to repeat to the army at large. He was a thin man, but the voice that issued from that chest could crack rocks and shiver bronze. *The first man ashore shall ascend to immortality, and dine with the gods on Olympian ambrosia.*

It had taken the soldiers a moment to work that out. Odysseus and Nestor had exchanged glances in the grey light before dawn, each aware of exactly what the words meant and looking to the other for confirmation, out of habit. The entrails of a slaughtered eagle owl said that the first man to set foot on Trojan land was going to die. *Ascend to immortality,* indeed: it was a good turn of phrase, but unlikely to fool the army for long.

"Still worrying over that?" Nestor asked. "Don't be the first man on the strand and you have nothing to fret over."

That wasn't what had Odysseus concerned. He could imagine the Greek fleet milling about offshore, every captain and oarsman unwilling to lead the rest to landfall in case the promised death fell on their own head. The watching gods would mock them without mercy then, and the Trojans hardly less. Odysseus could hear their laughter already.

"I have to go," he told his friend. "Keep yourself safe, old man. I'll see you on the beach of Troy."

Nestor clasped his forearm. "Pup. I knew how to stay alive in a fight before you were even in swaddling." His smile faded. "Stay back from the worst of it if you can, Odysseus. Let the young men and hot-bloods bear the first burden."

"I thought I *was* a young man?" he asked, trying to capture a little of their usual levity. It didn't work, even on himself. He let go of Nestor's arm and went down the pebbles to his own ship, its crimson prow bright in the light from the just-risen sun. Men in plain chitons waited in lines on either side of the prow. He nodded to some, shook the hands of others: Ithacans knew each other, most of the time, and their king knew almost everyone.

Arion was there, watching the Pierian ships move out of the bay. The oars paused as they waited for other vessels, already in the channel and heading north, to clear out of the way. He glanced at Odysseus but didn't speak, or bow. Other kings would mock the Ithacans for that, of course: say they had no idea how civilised men should behave. Well, manners didn't seem important when your arm was up to the shoulder in a sheep's arse, your hand fumbling to straighten the unborn lamb so it could be squeezed out. Odysseus had stopped being angry about what other men said a long time ago.

Except that perhaps, if he could find a way to win a little respect in this foolish war, he might be able to change the way people thought. He was surprised to find he still cared about that.

The horns blew again, a second wave of blasts that ran along the coast and across the water. It meant the bays were clear for the next ships to launch: Talthybius had planned this well. He was much more than a mere herald, in truth. Odysseus nodded to Arion.

"Brace, lads," the captain said. He stood back, organising the operation while Odysseus took his place in the lines, fingers digging into a lip where one of the ship's planks overlaid another. It was good for the men to see their king working alongside them, just as he did back home.

"Cut the lines!" Arion ordered.

Two axes thumped down, shearing off ropes that had been wound over a high bar and then around posts driven into the beach. Over the past few days they'd been tightened, then tightened again, lifting the nose of Odysseus' ship a few inches out of the grit. Now the twin lines of soldiers threw their weight into the suddenly released ship, starting it moving before it thumped back down on the strand. When it did so it was already sliding, the rumble of stones accompanied by the groans of straining men.

"Board!" Arion called. The men snatched at ropes and nets, swarming up the hull to the deck above. The ship wallowed, drifting a few feet back towards the shore. Odysseus was one of six or eight men who scrambled to the stern and unshipped oars, dipping them hastily to keep it from grounding. After a moment the vessel began to move outwards again. The two axemen flung themselves at trailing lines and began to haul themselves in, hand over hand.

Odysseus waited for other soldiers to reach him, then relinquished his oar and went up to the steering deck, right at the aft end of the ship. Arion joined him there, wet to the thighs and sporting a red weal on his right palm where a rope had slipped across his skin. Together they looked back at the beach. Already Nestor was lost among the crowds of men, one figure indistinguishable among so many.

21

"The next time our feet touch land," Odysseus said at length, as the ship began to turn her prow towards the strait, "it will be on the soil of Troy."

Chapter Three

A Woman's Place

It had been easy, really. The man's habits were well known. A word in the right ear, a few drops of something unscented in the wine, and the rest was as inevitable as Fate.

The woman's room was in a corner of the upper floor, squeezed beneath the tiled roof. First door on the left at the top of the stairs. Nashuja would have worried about creaking, but these steps were stone, leaving no sound to give him away. He waited until the small hours of the morning anyway, a time when the men would be sodden and snoring, and the women they'd bought for a night deep in the sleep their labours had earned.

Then he went up the stairs, opened the door and went silently into the woman's room.

She was lying on the near side of the bed, half on her back and half on her hip, as if she'd frozen in the midst of trying to rise. Which might well be true. One arm hung down so the fingers trailed on the floor, and though her night shift covered her Nashuja found the sight somehow indecent. He went to her, only a pair of steps, and lifted the hand back to her side. It was then, leaning close to her, that he noticed her eyes were open, and following his movements.

That was not what he'd been told would happen.

The eastern drug he'd put in the wine was supposed to leave anyone who drank it unconscious. Nashuja had been assured it was so, but the whore was quite clearly awake. He stared at her for a shocked moment and then, with a thrill of fear, turned his attention to the man.

Eliade lay on his back by the wall, an arm across his chest and the other thrown towards the woman he'd been sleeping with. He wasn't asleep now; his eyes were open too, the irises turned right into the corners so he could peer at the intruder in the room. Nashuja must be little more than a shadow to him, but the man would have to be a fool not to realise that his drugging and the visitor were connected. Still, if he could have moved more than his eyes he would have risen by now. There was no reason for concern.

Nashuja hesitated even so. He'd expected to find both man and woman oblivious, the poppy drug sending them into a slumber so deep that neither would wake before noon. Instead he found a quarry wide awake and looking at him, with a terrible knowledge in his eyes.

"I'm sorry," Nashuja said. The words escaped before he could stop them, and he regretted it at once. Showing such hesitation made him appear weak. But of course it didn't really matter, because Eliade wasn't about to seize the moment and escape with his life. Nashuja stood up and pulled a knife from his belt.

It was the woman who made a thin moaning sound, as though she was afraid the blade was for her and she was straining to move. Eliade's eyes found the glint of the blade and then came back to Nashuja's, and there was nothing of fear in them. It was hard not to respect a man who faced death with such aplomb, even when he'd been duped and doped into helplessness.

Nashuja found himself giving the other man a nod. Then he leaned across the woman, and bracing his left hand against the wall he thrust the knife between two ribs and into Eliade's heart. He pushed himself upright again and looked down at the woman.

She made another keening noise, like a frightened bird. He ought to kill her, he knew. But he hadn't actually been ordered to, and Nashuja was not familiar with killing. He'd never needed to before, and he didn't want to take another life if he could avoid it. Mercy counted in a man's favour when it came time for his shade to travel the dark paths down to Hades. If the woman remembered him when she woke it would only be as a shadow in the dark, he thought, a faceless spirit who came with death and yet passed her by.

Nashuja turned and went back the way he'd come, down the stone steps and away into the streets of Halicarnassus.

She would talk, of course. Eliade's body would be thrown into a shallow grave in the morning, but nobody would mistake this for an accident, or a sudden ailment in the night. Everyone would know he'd been murdered. Nashuja's paymasters wanted it that way.

*

There were new things wherever she looked. The city, most of all.

24

Troy took her breath. She had seen the great cities of Greece, Sparta on its plain and Mycenae crouched on its hillside like a malevolent animal, unsleepingly alert for a sign of weakness. She'd seen their walls, made of great irregular stones fitted carefully in place, and once had believed there could be nothing more massive in the world. Not made by men.

Perhaps Troy had not been, then. Gods may have laboured here, or titans, or Cyclops bellowing to one another in their work. And yet the stones of the wall were simple rectangles, half a foot high and three times as long, mortared into place in curving rows. Mortal masons made houses of such things. There was no need here for immortals, or creatures of legend, but only for men and the techniques they used all over the world.

But on such a scale! From the plain below the walls and towers of Troy seemed to split the sky. Even from near the top of the ridge that impression held. If anything the walls were even more majestic up close, looming like cliffs yet as graceful as the flight of birds. Helen ran out of words to describe them. She was transfixed until Paris took her hand and smiled at her, a reassuring look, and brought her back to awareness of herself again.

They came into the city on a wave of acclaim, the populace crowding both sides of the avenue to chant their names. He, the wastrel prince, loved by all but trusted by few, until now. And she, the Argive queen brought in payment for Hesione, beauty for beauty, blood for blood. Except that she had come willingly, of her own choice. The Trojans would know that, she thought, they would have been told, and it made them cheer all the louder because it told them they were not Argives themselves. They were better, a worthier people, more refined and cultured than the long-haired barbarians across the sea. They took for justice, not for greed, and only then when granted permission.

The chariots carried Helen up the avenue, past houses built in ovals, like pebbles in sand. Through a great market square, festooned with awnings and rich with a thousand scents, splashed with colours brighter than she'd ever seen. Higher they climbed, coming at last to a great gate set in another wall, and they drove into the Pergamos where the palaces were, the temples, the great council hall of Troy where decisions were made. Somewhere here was the Palladium, the wooden effigy of Athena herself, one of the few deities Troy and Greece shared. It was said the city could never fall while it remained whole.

She wouldn't see that today. The chariots came to a halt outside a palace at the western end of the citadel, the greatest of them, and home of the king. Priam's residence, as it had been Ilos' long before, when the city was young. She and Paris joined hands, lifting them high, and ascended the steps together, hearing the cheers still pounding from the streets outside. They followed a herald along corridors and up short flights of stairs, until they came to the throne room and the Scamandrian guards on duty swung open the doors.

They were waiting inside, all the people Paris had told her about as they journeyed towards the city. Some had names she'd known before, back in Greece: Priam, his hair white but eyes still chips of blue; Hecuba, past her prime now but with the shadow of beauty still lying soft on her cheekbones. Antenor, who she'd seen once in Sparta, now measuring her from his place beside Priam's throne. And Hector, sandy-haired and intimidatingly big, whose name alone was enough to send Greek warriors into grim, muttering glooms. Beside him was a striking woman with white beads braided into her hair, who could only be his wife Andromache. Her eyes narrowed slightly when Helen came into the room.

Others she could only guess at. The woman with straggly hair and a too-long nose could be Creusa, and that made the thoughtful man beside her Aeneas. Strange to think that a family which had produced such handsome men as Paris and Hector should also birth a Creusa. A man with callused hands might be Lycaon, the third-born prince, and the startlingly tall man was probably Laocoon, the Seer. The rest of the faces blended together, too many of them seen too quickly, so she couldn't tell them apart. Helen concentrated on walking across the tiled floor, a little overwhelmed by the beauty of the blue-and-gold panelling, the cedar-wood ceiling, the grace of the courtiers as they bowed. Since fleeing with Paris to the east she'd seen mansions and temples to make a Greek architect blush, but the royal palace of Troy was something more, something finer.

"My father," Paris said. He knelt, hands flat on the floor as he bent to touch the tiles with his forehead. "I have come home, and with me stands Helen, formerly queen of Sparta."

26

They knew that already, of course, and their eyes had already been on her before her husband spoke. It was only when she was named that Helen bowed, as much as she was able to in the tight wrap skirt that was favoured here. She couldn't kneel wearing that, of course. When she straightened she found almost everyone still studying her, Andromache with ill-hidden curiosity, Priam and his wife with no hint of their thoughts at all.

"Brother!" Hector said. His voice was deep and rich, seeming to echo even in the room. He came down the steps from the dais as lightly as any dancer. "Stand up, and let me look at you!"

Helen began to turn, feeling a vague thread of concern. Beside her Paris rose though, a smile coming to his features as his elder brother approached. He spread his arms in greeting.

Hector punched him hard just under the ribs, muscles bunching in his bicep as he drove the blow in. The air went out of Paris with a rush and he staggered; Helen thought he might have fallen, had Hector not caught his shoulder to steady him. She opened her mouth, temper flaring.

"Let it pass," someone said in her ear. The hand that rested on her shoulder belonged to Hecuba, and though she wasn't smiling her tone was calm. "This was decided some time ago."

Paris was clinging to his brother, unable to speak. His face had turned almost purple as he fought for air, breath hissing through the narrow gap in his throat. Hector leaned forward until his mouth was beside the smaller man's ear.

"If Troy survives the Argives and I one day become king," he said, letting the words carry, "then next time you endanger the city by flouting all our plans, it will not be my fist in your guts. It will be my sword. By Ipirru of horses and Athena's shield I swear it, brother."

He stepped back. Suddenly bereft of his support, Paris stumbled to his knees again, still wheezing. Nobody else in the room had moved, except Hecuba. Princes and advisors stood and watched Paris fight for breath. Priam hadn't even glanced at him, Helen realised: the king's attention was all on her, had never wavered, and now finally he spoke.

"Be welcome to Troy," he said. "I won't pretend we're glad to see you here, not as you come. We never intended for you to marry my son. You were to be a counter for exchanging, that's all."

27

She lifted her chin. "So a Greek would speak, my lord. In my homeland women are game pieces to be played with by men. I had been told things were somewhat different in the more civilized lands."

There was a silence.

"They are different," Antenor said, in the cultured voice she remembered. "Were they not, you would have been brought here bound and weeping, and then kept in chains like a dog. As Hesione was."

She swallowed. This was very difficult, heavy with emotion. "Do you expect me to be grateful to you for that, Councillor? I am, I assure you. Almost as much as I'm grateful for the warmth of your greeting."

"She is clever, at least," another man said, over tented fingers. His ears stuck out like a sheep's.

"Any daughter of Tyndareus would have to be," Antenor said. "He was sly, that one."

"Would he have brought war against Troy?" steeple-fingers asked, with a hint of asperity. "Or do you think he would have agreed to our bargain, as you thought the other kings would?"

Antenor turned slowly to face him. "I have admitted my mistake in that, Ucalegon. You know it. You know I offered to resign my post as well. There is no more I can do."

"You can continue to advise me," Priam said, "as you've done so ably for so long. One misjudgement doesn't change that. I won't let you resign. Besides," he added, "I'm not even sure this was a misjudgement at all. The cursed Argives *should* have bargained. Even when Helen left Sparta of her own will, her husband and his like should have accepted an exchange."

"My *former* husband," Helen said, with emphasis, "would never have bargained. Nor would his brother the High King. They never do. Agamemnon takes what he wants and Menelaus always follows along behind. Everyone in Greece knows it. I'm amazed that you didn't."

There was a silence, every eye on her, and then Priam said, "You know them well, those Argive kings."

It wasn't a question, and the implication was too obvious to miss. "I do, my lord. I'll be glad to share that knowledge with you, and your Councillors, as part payment for your taking me in."

28

"Of course you will," Priam said. In the middle of the room Paris managed to get to his feet. He was still faintly green. "For now though, I need to discuss certain matters with my advisors, and I wish to properly welcome my son. My wife will attend to your needs."

"Come," Hecuba said. She made a sign towards the dais and Andromache stepped down to join them, moving with an easy grace in the tight wrap skirts Helen still found confining. Helen thought the other woman was about her own age, a little taller perhaps, with a black-haired beauty which might not match her own but a poise which more than made up for it. Andromache didn't glance at her once.

Helen looked back at her husband, now able to stand reasonably straight, but Paris wasn't watching her either. She turned and followed Hecuba, past a statue of a god with upraised hand and through a hidden door, and into the bowels of the palace.

*

"This is the women's place," Hecuba said.

It was two hours later. The sun had begun to slip westwards, down towards the high wall of the Pergamos on that side, topped with crenellations in a jagged line. Back home – back in Greece the men had compared those battlements to teeth, so often it had become trite to say it. The analogy didn't seem apt to Helen now. Not in this place.

They were sitting on wooden benches in a wide garden, cleverly designed. The flagged paths turned in gentle curves around acacia trees, or juniper, with a single oak tree in the middle. Helen had seen larger, but this one had been lovingly pruned and teased, until its branches spread out in a wide fan with shade beneath, a blessing in the heat of summer. Tulips and crocuses grew in clusters, and fritillaries with their nodding heads of purple and white. The air was rich with scents and the hum of early bees.

"Women's place?" she asked.

"Men don't come here," Andromache said. She'd lost some of that wary look, but she still held herself a pace away from Helen, as though afraid to touch her. "Except for servants and priests, men are forbidden."

29

"And they accept that?"

Hecuba nodded. "Of course. They could force their way in, but it would break Troy. The lesser cities would be horrified, and the temples here would refuse to deal with the king until he had restored the garden, and made atonement. For this," she added, musing, "the penance would be very great, I think."

"As it should be," Andromache said, resuming the tale. "Helen, women here are not powerless, as they are among Argives. Here the queen arranges her children's marriages and deals with the temples, on each city's behalf. The king collects taxes and pays for civic projects, and he runs the army. Each has their own area of authority."

It was what Paris had told her. What she'd seen, too, in one city after another as the two of them had travelled north through storied lands she had never thought to see. Miletos with its Minoan murals, Caria itself, Ephesus and the great library facing the sea. Lydia, which was called Maeonia here, then Mysia, and the dye shops of Sardis, in the shadow of Mount Tmolus. Wonder after wonder, and women holding power in all of them.

But Helen had never believed. Not truly, not in her soul. She had made love with Paris in orchards and gardens, in bedrooms with shuttered doors thrown open so the sound of the sea rolled in; once even on a rooftop, under the stars. She'd heard his whispered promises and yet not allowed herself to think them true, not for her, not in this world. Perhaps in another, a part of paradise set aside for women, or a place remoter yet, one unknown on earth even in myth. Somewhere, but not in Troy, and not for her.

"This is Elysium," she said.

The other two women exchanged smiles, and Hecuba laid a hand on Helen's arm. "Not quite that. But close. Now let's sit, while I have servants bring wine, and I will begin telling you what a princess of Troy needs to know."

"And let us hope," Andromache said, "that there is something of Troy left to be known, after the Argives have wreaked their vengeance for what you have done."

Helen felt the words like a barb, and the more so because she'd been so happy a moment before they were spoken. But they were true, beyond questioning. Whatever Troy was, paradise or no, it was in peril because of what she had done. She opened her mouth and then closed it again. Hecuba's fingers tightened on her arm.

After a moment Andromache made a pushing gesture with one hand, as though to cast away what she'd said. A conciliation, perhaps. Wordlessly the three women turned, as one, to gaze at the western wall of the Citadel, beyond which the Argive ships were sailing towards them.

*

South and east of them, near the feet of Mount Ida where the woods began, another woman wept.

Oenone's tears were hot but brief. Everything seemed brief to one such as she, who had lived so long she might be thought immortal. The slow unrolling of time was enough to prove she wasn't, that the years added weight to her existence as they did for all mortals. But the flakes of time lay light on her shoulders. She might live another ten thousand years and not weep in any of them.

Somewhere in the forest around her a dryad began to sing. A moment later another joined in, the notes rising into the twilit sky.

Oenone stood at the edge of her pool, knee-deep in water, and looked towards Troy. She had shared her soul with Paris and once her kind did so it was done forever, irrevocably. She could feel him there now, sense his heart. There was a woman with him. A foreigner, though that meant little to her. The whole world had belonged to her people once, in a past so distant she could barely remember it, when she and her brethren had been free to roam where they chose and the earth had never known mortal men. People today called them the Golden Race and told fanciful tales of their deeds, in the days before the gods came to Olympus and the world changed.

They were more than mortals though, and some had a touch of the foretelling of gods. Oenone was one who did.

"The day will come when you need me," she whispered. The words were like a vow. "When you need me and no one else will do, and that day I may turn you away, son of Troy."

The dryads were still singing, ten or a dozen of them now she thought. Oenone sank back under the water and rested there, letting the song soothe her as the night grew dark.

Chapter Four

The Bones of Bats

It had been a strange childhood, in many ways. Always, from the very start, there had been an awareness that she was the spare, the leftover, of no importance to anyone much except her parents. But oh, they had loved her. She remembered that, too.

"We are tied to a great family, you and I," Mother had said once. She was combing out Penelope's hair, which fell down her back in an auburn curtain. "But not too closely tied. Your father is not the king but the king's kin, and the weight of queenship won't fall on you."

Father. Icarius of Sparta, brother to King Tyndareus, captain of his armies and beloved of the troops. But more than that he was her papa, who picked her up when she ran to him and spun her around, and hugged her tight every evening so she went to bed feeling warm and safe inside.

In the days there were lunches by the river, the Evrotas which ran so clear and bright from the hills. There were games with the other children, and lessons in the tutor's rooms, or in the shade of orange trees in the garden. Sleepy afternoons when the heat grew heavy, then draughts or dice in the evenings with Mama, and Papa too when he was home.

In the days there were her cousins, too. Clytemnestra had a livid temper even in adolescence, so Penelope was always careful around her. It was almost a relief when the older girl was sent away to be married, taking her waspish tongue and cutting jibes with her. But Castor remained, training to be king one day. Helen was there too, a few years younger than Penelope, born to her parents late almost as an afterthought. When a toddler she was ordinary enough, pretty in a toothy kind of way, clumsy as all small children are. Penelope remembered when that had begun to change, her own uncertainty as adults began to look at Helen in a different way, with something in their eyes she had been too young, then, to understand or put a name to.

She knew it now: longing, and envy. Even when Helen was eight, or ten. Men eyed her and calculated when she would be old enough to wed, while women saw that burgeoning beauty and cursed Aphrodite in their hearts. Everyone was aware of it. Sometimes kings visited for no obvious reason, happening to be in the area – as though they owned the farmhouse down the road, and had popped in to borrow a cup of olive oil or a knife. They always managed to steer the talk to Helen though, and then Penelope knew that was why they had come. They were fishing for the chance to see for themselves if the stories of Helen's glory were true.

They were, of course. They were prepared, but even so those kings would stare when Helen entered, stunned sometimes into silence. It wasn't just her beauty, though that was a part, a large part of it. It was how she moved, the fall of her hair, the coy look up through her lashes from violet eyes. She was a rose so vivid no one ever saw the thorns.

Now they had. The barb that was Helen had led to war, and Penelope's mother had been proved wrong: the weight of queenship *had* fallen on Penelope. Not in Sparta, true, but windy Ithaca to the west, remote land of sheep and steep hills. But it was no weight, most of the time, for it meant she was with her husband Odysseus, and she was as warm and safe as she had ever been in Sparta.

Until the war took him away, and she had to carry the kingdom herself, alone.

"I know you have nothing but boys and old men," she said. It was an effort to keep her voice calm, but she thought she managed. Odysseus almost never shouted, and she'd seen that men responded better to his persuasion than to anger. Her father had been the same, and Tyndareus the king as well. Fear made people follow, but they fought better when they agreed.

"Boys and old men," she said again, regaining her line of thought. "I have the same, Idmon. All the warriors have gone to Troy. We have to manage as best we can with what we have."

"And the pirates?" the man standing before the throne asked. "If they come in numbers against us?"

"What will you do," she snapped, forgetting calmness, "let them ravage the sheep pens and take the women while you stand aside?"

He looked startled, then dropped his eyes. "No, my queen. Of course not."

"Then I don't see why you're complaining," Penelope said. "What do you think I can do? Wave my hand and make warriors rise out of the ground, as though I had sown dragon's teeth in the soil?"

She looked around the audience hall. Another eight or nine men were waiting to speak with her, which was about all the little chamber could hold without feeling awkwardly crowded. "I'll wager my supper that half of you have come here today with the same plea, or close to it. You need more men, more help from Same, to hold your towns secure. I will tell you what you already know: there are no more men to be had. No more help to give.

"But in Ithaca, when a storm rages on the mountains you go out into the wind and rain to fetch in the lambs. When pirates prowl the coast you ready your bows and prepare to make them pay a price. You do *not* whimper like frightened children and come begging for help. Need I say more?"

Idmon had the grace to look embarrassed. The lord of Zacynthos would never have come to Odysseus with idiocy like this, never. He'd have known he would be mocked without end, mostly in that gentle way her husband had, but Idmon would have felt every word as a knife. Well, let it be a lesson to him, and the other men now shuffling their feet behind him. The little towns across the islands had to look to their own defence for a time, until the army (and the king, if mercy knew their names) came home. In the meantime Penelope had too much work to do for her time to be wasted this way.

The merchants had been asking to meet her for three days now. Yesterday they'd sent three requests, and two more this morning – *another* thing which would never have happened if Odysseus was in the palace. The traders wouldn't have had the nerve to push him so hard. Meanwhile there were temple rituals to be performed, and sacrifices to be slaughtered. Sometimes Penelope held the chalice in her husband's name, standing where the king should stand. For other rituals she held infant Telemachus up and pressed his tiny hand to the goblet, or the altar, when a male presence was needed. All to ensure the little Ithacan fleet reached Troy in safety.

Troy. The very name made her tremble with fear now.

In addition to all that, the dry stone walls at the south end of the island needed repair, which meant taking two hundred townsfolk up the hillside for a day, including whole families, and making an event of it. The women would prepare snacks and the youngsters carry the smaller stones, while the masons and farmers muttered and judged and then laid the wall so hardly a crack showed. But that meant taking people away from other work, most of it needed; or at least half the town would always claim as much. And all this just when pirate ships had begun to slink along the coasts, for the first time in years.

This would not happen if Odysseus was here.

But that begged a question: why was it happening now? Why did the people of Ithaca think they could press Penelope harder than they could her husband, make demands, sent increasingly strident requests?

The answer was simple enough. They didn't see her as holding authority here, even as her husband's delegated proxy. Probably they thought of her, even if only beneath the surface of their minds, as the daughter of a foreign king, an outsider, more used to a gilded court than the simpler realities of life in little Ithaca. Well, it was true, she couldn't argue with it. But she couldn't let the belief persist, not if she was to do as her husband had asked.

"Keep them safe," Odysseus had said. Almost the last words he spoke to her before boarding his crimson-prowed ship, to set sail for Aulis and the gathering of the army. "All of them, I mean. All my Ithacans."

My Ithacans, *she'd thought, noting even then the proprietary phrase. Odysseus really did think of the islanders as his responsibility, to be guarded and protected with all the strength of his arm. And the cunning of his mind, which in his case was rather greater. "I will."*

"And most of all, take care of our son," Odysseus said. "Whatever comes. Without you I will die, but if he is lost my soul would shrivel on the road to Hades, and never reach the black waters of the Styx."

It was the same thing, of course. If Ithaca was kept safe then Telemachus would be secure as well, blatting in his crib in complete ignorance of the perils that lurked around the islands. And he *would* be guarded: she was determined on that. When he was older she would tell him of the dangers that threatened in his infancy, and he'd listen with the wide-eyed excitement of every small boy, but he wouldn't understand. Not really. And that was good, because it meant he'd never sensed the threat when it was real, and upon them.

She could deal with both things, she realised. Keep her son safe, and deal with the Ithacans' doubt at the same time. She'd always been quick, and Idmon was still standing in front of her looking embarrassed while all this poured through her mind, and she spoke.

"Niobe." She knew her servant would be behind her, and within earshot; she always was. "Bring me a bow. We're going to show these brave men how to defend themselves."

Idmon blinked. "You can't shoot a bow."

"Then it's time I learned," Penelope said.

*

She was with Telemachus, enjoying the afternoon sunshine on the west porch, when Niobe came to her.

"My lady." The serving woman wrung her hands as she spoke. "There has been… there's something you should hear."

Penelope laid the child down in his crib. Fear had clutched her at Niobe's words, terror for her absent husband and for her infant son, who would be left fatherless and alone should the worst happen. Another man would become king here and Telemachus would lose his birth right, be cast out to make his way as best he could. Everyone would know him: the son of Odysseus, heir to a high Fate but now living a tin destiny, no more significant than any man. The prospect made her shiver under her cloak.

It didn't occur to her to be afraid for herself until later.

"What is it?" she asked. Her voice was quite calm. "Is there news from the east, and the fleet?"

"Not exactly," Niobe said. She was normally a curt, capable woman, but now she looked like a dead soul's shade, drained of colour. Penelope thought the evening light might stream right through her if she stepped into its rays. "It's… it's Solymi. He says he must speak with you."

That explained her loss of composure, then. Solymi put most of the women in Ithaca into a state of trembling terror, just by walking into a room. Half of the men too, come to that. Penelope, raised in more sophisticated Sparta, had seen worse than him even as a child – but not much worse. She felt the hairs prickle on her arms.

Solymi was a Seer. Such people were found everywhere, of course, even in towns so small even Agamemnon wouldn't think them worth fighting over. People had their superstitions wherever you went. Fall asleep under a cypress tree and it will steal your mind; put pepper on your tongue to break the habit of cursing; drive away crows before they can bring bad fortune down on you. Here in island Ithaca it was believed that fish guarded wisdoms known to no man, and that carrying bat bones in a pocket brought good luck. Penelope had taken to doing so herself. There was often truth in folk beliefs.

Or in the words of Seers.

"Send him in," she said.

With Niobe gone, Penelope looked down at her sleeping son again. After a moment she lifted the crib and carried it to a bench on the far side of the porch, where the moving sun still cast its light. She told herself it was so he could enjoy the warmth, not because Solymi was coming. Not at all. The man was unsettling, but he was no killer of children.

She shook herself. What did she fear he might do, eat the boy? Niobe's unease was affecting her, that was all. She turned back to the doors and there Solymi was, smiling at her with half his face.

The other was a ruin of white ridges over red scar tissue, without even an eye. Raw-looking skin had spread over the empty socket. The ear on the same side was only a nub, and his hair grew in patches, like wiry grass on the hills. Seen from the right Solymi looked perfectly normal, a man of advancing years not worth a second glance. Seen from the left he was a monster. It was enough to make a person believe those stories of a beast below the palace of Knossos, half man and half bull, a living punishment on Minos sent by the gods. Penelope couldn't remember the king's sin now. It didn't matter.

"You have words for me?" she asked.

He nodded, still smiling with the half of his mouth that worked. His one-eyed gaze went past her to the crib, and before she could stop herself Penelope moved to block his line of sight. He noticed and the smile flickered, becoming both bitter and resigned. And grotesque, but then it was always that.

"Your words?" she prompted. Best to get this done so she could feel clean again. "What are they?"

"I have seen a beach," he said. The words were slurred, distorted by the slackness on one side of his mouth. "Through my unseeing eye, you might say. A beach filled with men."

Fear leapt in her again, like bile in her throat. "Troy?"

"Perhaps," he said, "though I have not seen the city."

Solymi liked to spin his tales out, make a listener wait for every scrap of information he had gleaned. This was all he had, the only time he could get people to look at him for longer than it took for revulsion to cross their own, unscarred features. Penelope understood it and pitied him, but she had no patience for it, especially now. She made herself take a step towards him.

"No games," she said. Her voice was still calm, still controlled, but there was a thread of iron in it now. "Tell me what you know, Seer, or I will take your other eye and condemn you to the dark."

He glared, but after a moment he spoke again. "I saw a beach with armed men ranged along it, backed by dunes. Horns were blowing. Out to sea ships were approaching."

"The fleet?" she whispered.

His one eye never blinked. "Hundreds of ships, with the sun high above, and crows cawing in the air."

It could only be the Greek fleet, approaching the foreign shore already. Penelope felt her self-control waver and she willed herself to stay calm, though she couldn't prevent a shiver running up her back. She was suddenly too hot. She turned to face east, hardly aware of what she was doing, staring through the wall and across all of Greece to where her husband was.

The war was beginning.

Chapter Five

Arrival

The Greensea was almost perfectly still that morning. There was no wind: even the *Meltemi* had died down, for the first time in two weeks. Snow might still lie on the higher slopes of the Thracian mountains, to the north, but no breeze brought the sharp scent of it across the Hellespont to the Plain of Troy.

On the western side of that plain soldiers worked in groups of eight or a dozen, digging out ditches in front of wooden palisades erected over the winter. Left to itself sand filled the makeshift moats in barely a week, which meant constant work to keep them deep. It had been a long month, waiting for the Argives to attack. Word kept coming east on trader's boats, telling of vast preparations being made in Boeotia, but the war galleys had not appeared. The soldiers worked with shovels, their spears close by but unneeded.

Antenor and Pandarus believed the Greeks would land to the north, at the Bay of Troy. It was Hector who'd insisted that defences be built westwards too, around Cradle Bay, and Aeneas supported him. So here the palisades were, looking out over a calm sea in which only two sails moved, as far as the keenest eyes could see. One was moving west, dwindling into the far distance; the other inched north, probably bound for Imbros or Samothrace. Neither seemed to be part of an invasion fleet.

Beyond Cradle Bay, further down the coast, three chariots stood outside another palisade, this one made of stakes so tightly packed that they were more truly a wall. Rooftops crowded within, and voices rose in a near-continuous roar of acclaim.

"You may," Heptolamus said in an undertone, "have to hit someone before they quiet down."

"Perhaps I should hit you?" Hector asked.

The charioteer snorted. "Not my first choice."

Everyone in Leris had turned out to see the prince of Troy. That meant the best part of a thousand people, now. The town had grown a good deal in recent years, transforming itself from a fishing village into a large settlement almost worthy of being called a city, with its own troop of soldiers and a barrack hall to house them. Even so, the inhabitants still called themselves

Trojans, and they looked to the great city on its hill for leadership and protection.

Not that Troy could offer a great deal of either, if the Argives came. The city lay only a dozen miles away, but if the Greek soldiers seized the beach that would be too far, much too far. No sortie would be able to reach Leris and relieve it. Nor were there enough soldiers to hold a line between the two towns. Troy needed to throw the invaders back into the sea before they gained a foothold, or else retreat to their strong places and wait for the storm to pass – which meant Leris would be left to survive alone. If it could.

These people knew that. And still they cheered, as though Hector had come bearing the thunderbolts of mighty Tarhun in his hands, ready to smash the Argive ships into splinters before they even approached the shore. He could hear his name being chanted somewhere in the din, but the crowd couldn't catch the same rhythm at the same time, and it kept breaking apart into a chaos of yells.

"Nobody adores you more," Hector said, still quietly, "than people who are afraid they will fall without you."

"Then these folk should revere you as a god," Heptolamus said. "You, and Aeneas and Pandarus. Sarpedon too, if he comes."

"He'll come. He's my mother's sister."

"Include him, then. That makes four captains who stand between the Argives and the gates of Troy. It's not a time for Lycaon's diplomacy or the queen's careful planning. This is a time for strong spears."

"If the Argives come."

Heptolamus smiled thinly. "They'll come."

There wasn't any real doubt of that anymore. The stream of reports of the preparations at Aulis had silenced those who thought the Greek kings could never work together, that their plans would founder on mutual distrust and old hatreds. Agamemnon had forged them into a single force, at least for the moment. Not long ago Priam had believed the High King less of a danger than his father had been; too sullen, too bitter, too self-absorbed. So had Antenor, the most trusted of Priam's advisors. They didn't believe that now, and neither did Hector. Bitterness and pride could be potent forces, driving a man to achieve things beyond a more balanced personality.

It was said, on both sides of the Aegean, that the gods worked in such men. Sometimes to raise them up, sometimes to cast them down. Sometimes both. There was no way to tell if they were doing so now, and whether Agamemnon would be raised or destroyed. Perhaps both.

Perhaps Hector would be destroyed.

"Quiet, you dogs!" he bellowed, suddenly out of patience with the crowd. His voice carried above the crash of battle and it carried here, like the roar of mountain thunder on a clear day. "I said quiet!"

One final diminishing din, and then the throng went still. Not silent, perhaps: there was too much excited shuffling for that, and here and there a cry that no one took up. But it would do. Hector wasn't a man who lost his temper easily, and he hadn't now either, but it helped for people to believe you could snap. He'd learned that long ago, from his father.

It seemed he'd learned most of the lessons in his life from Priam. Except those he'd learned from his mother.

"Your warehouse is full," he said. "The spring means you won't run short of water. And you've strengthened the palisade and dug out the ditch, so you're as prepared as you can be. I'm proud of you."

That gained a cheer, as expected, but Hector had a hand raised to calm the crowd again before it could do more than start. "But if the Argives come – and they *will* come, depend upon it – your defences won't keep out a determined assault. Ten thousand Greek soldiers will pour over the stakes like a river overflowing its banks, and Troy is too far away to help."

Now he had silence. Every eye was on him, every person stock still. He made sure to be relaxed, not to let the tension he felt show.

"When you see the Argive sails, send your children to Thymbra," he said. "Every boy too young to fight, and every unmarried girl: all of them. Thymbra is harder to reach, and there's an escape route up the Scamander gorge besides. Keep them safe.

"But Troy won't forget you. We're too far to help directly, but by all Ipirru's horses, we'll make them pay for setting foot on our soil. They'll wish they had never set sail but by then it will be too late." The crowd had begun to scream again, and he raised his voice back to its battlefield bellow. "And while Greek meat is fouler than Trojan, our crows will grow fat on their corpses!"

They roared at that, stamped their feet and shook their fists in the air. Soldiers on the steps of the warehouse rattled spears against their shields in the traditional approval of a Trojan fighting man. They would know the truth though, even if the folk in the square didn't; pretty words were all Hector had to offer. If the Argives gained the beach of Cradle Bay then Leris was lost, too remote and ill-defended to stand a chance against the hordes which would be thrown against it. The attackers would never leave such a threat behind them when they turned towards Troy, on the far side of the plain. Leris would be doomed.

Unless the Trojans could meet their enemies on the beach and throw them back into the sea. That was possible. No fleet such as this had ever sailed, or tried to force a landing on a hostile and defended coast. They might overwhelm the Trojan barricades or they might collapse into chaos, ships colliding as they tried to reach the beach, soldiers left thrashing in the water. The few who made land would be shot down by Trojan archers and their galleys set alight.

It was a pretty picture, but the truth was that Hector didn't know. *No fleet such as this has ever sailed.* He thought only the Fates knew what was to come; for mortals and gods, there was no way to tell.

"Come on," he said to Heptolamus. "I want to get to Thymbra before noon, and then back to Troy before –"

The noise of the crowd changed, became uncertain. Hector heard it, the way he heard a change in the sound of battle even in the midst of it, and he broke off. He remembered the moment ever after, standing on the steps of the warehouse of Leris as the mood altered to one of sudden fear, and he turned to look west and saw a thin tendril of smoke rising far out to sea, like a beacon or an augur of dread.

"Tenedos," someone cried from the throng. "Tenedos is burning!"

"Heptolamus!" Hector bellowed, and from distant Troy he heard the first, tardy clang of the alarm bell.

*

42

The dress had a tight bodice, higher cut than those Greek women wore, back home. *In Greece,* she amended; Troy was home now. Then she corrected herself a second time, because on this side of the sea her people were called Argives, a term that reeked of disdain and contempt, but with a thread of fear too.

Helen had always thought of the Greeks as a fine, civilized people, the match of any around the Greensea. But she'd begun, in her few weeks in the city, to realise that the Greeks – Argives – were seen by the world as something between wolves and vultures, part marauder and part scavenger. She had the start of an understanding of why, as well. It was hard to meet the orphans of Myrmidon raids without it.

But for now what vexed her was the uncomfortably tight bodice, and the hem of her wrap skirt that trailed on the floor. That was *much* longer than she was used to, and she kept almost tripping as she walked. Andromache moved with an easy poise, hands at her sides and gripping the skirt with only two fingers. It looked effortless, even though Hector's wife was heavily pregnant now and walked with a sort of waddle, like a very fat duck. Helen still couldn't match it.

And black pearls had been sewn into her hair, so the thread was invisible and the gems flashed in the light. It looked striking, but Helen could feel the weight of them and had to keep fighting the urge to lift a hand and run fingers through her curls. She even had to leave them in while she slept, which woke her when she shifted her head on the pillow. It seemed this was how noble women lived in the civilized east. Helen could have done without it.

"Are you paying attention?" Andromache asked.

Helen's hand paused halfway to her hair. They were sitting in a room in one of the temples of the Pergamos, the citadel of Troy, supposedly to be lectured on the workings of the various priesthoods. There had been a number of such days recently, at Hecuba's orders, in an effort to accustom Helen to the city as quickly as possible. Some days were interesting, others plain dull. Unfortunately this was one of the latter.

She lowered her hand, trying not to feel self-conscious. "Of course I am."

"Then what did Laocoon just say?"

Andromache didn't like her. There were probably good reasons for that, given what Helen had brought on Troy through her flight from Menelaus, but she had long ago grown used to the fact that most women hated her anyway. It was a consequence of her beauty; men stared at her with their tongues hanging out, and women narrowed their eyes and nursed envy in their hearts. It had bothered Helen as a child, though her concern had vanished when she was given the choice of her own husband. Women in Greece did not have that power. If the price of it was jealousy, it didn't seem so high to Helen.

Still, Andromache ought not to imply so openly that Helen was lying. Even though she was.

Beauty was not her only weapon, though. Her father had not raised his girls to be fools, so Helen only smiled slightly and said, "What matters more, I think, is what he carefully does *not* say."

"I suppose that means something," Andromache said.

"It means that Laocoon doesn't like me, and is trying not to let it show," Helen replied. "It might be better to have it out in the open now, before the poison of secrecy goes to work. Don't you think?"

She directed that last at Laocoon, sitting on a stone bench facing the two women. Stone benches were the only seats in the temple anteroom, though an acolyte had brought a cushion for Andromache. Even sitting the Seer was very tall, and as thin as a reed. Helen thought he must only be able to eat three bites at a time without his narrow stomach bursting.

"I think you are here to learn how to deal with the temples," Laocoon said. "Might we proceed with that?"

"We might," Helen said. "Although my husband is the youngest son of the king, of course. Not the eldest. Hector, Troilus and Lycaon would all claim the throne before it came to my Paris – and even then, I suspect one of the other lords of Troas would lay claim to it in his place. Aeneas, perhaps, or noble Pandarus from his eyrie at Zeleia. There's ambition in that man."

"Who are you to speak of ambition?" Laocoon snapped. He made a visible effort to bite back the words, but too late, and once they were spoken his head twitched like a bird's. His lips thinned with the effort of not speaking.

"Now we're getting to it," Helen said. She was tired of all this; tired of being the object of stares and whispers, tired of

44

accusations both spoken and silent. "You think I came to Troy out of ambition?"

Laocoon's head jerked again. "It doesn't matter why you came. You are here, and the Argive army will follow."

"I see," she said. "So no doubt you knew nothing of the plan to abduct me from Sparta, before Paris sailed. And had you known, you would no doubt have argued eloquently against it."

"I knew," he admitted. "Antenor believed the Argives would trade Hesione for your return. I deferred to his judgement."

Helen let herself laugh, genuinely amused. "And in case that plea doesn't excuse you from responsibility, you've decided to hate me? I'm surprised, master Seer. I would have thought you'd know that events rarely turn out the way we expect, however careful the planning."

"Stop this," Andromache said. She'd pushed her weighty body into a more upright position, sitting forward on her bench. "Both of you. Helen, you must know there are Trojans who blame you for the army being mustered across the sea, and they'll go on blaming you."

She did know that, and knew as well that there was nothing she could do about it. Andromache and Laocoon had simply been there in front of her, and not concealing their dislike well enough. Helen wondered suddenly if Laocoon had seen a vision of the struggle to come. He was a Seer after all, and reputedly the best not only in Troy but in the whole western coast of Anatolia. They used carved bones here, and the entrails of chickens, which was strange to her but seemed to work. She should have wondered this before.

She managed a smile, and thought it looked natural enough. "Of course, sister. I only wanted to clear the air."

Andromache's eyes tightened at being called *sister*. She couldn't argue with Helen's right, since they were sisters, at least through marriage. But she didn't like it. These Trojans really were not very good at hiding their feelings. It would make life easier here if they all turned out to be the same. Andromache turned back to Laocoon and drew breath to speak.

The door behind them banged open before the words could form. It slammed off the wall and bounced back, but missed the man who burst into the room, almost running in his haste. "Do you – have you –"

45

"Paris?" Helen said. His hair stuck out in clumps as though he'd been pulling it in bunches. He was the colour of wet dough, and his eyes had a wild look to them, as though he'd encountered a goddess and barely escaped with his skin. "What are you doing here?"

Laocoon had risen to his full impressive height. His skin had gone grey, like old dust settling on parchment.

"Smoke from Tenedos," Paris gasped, and just then the tocsin began to ring. Heavy notes clanged out over the city. Laocoon stared for an instant and then ran for the stairs, Helen and Paris right behind him. Andromache levered herself halfway to her feet before falling back with a curse.

Helen barged into the narrow stairwell just behind Laocoon, but ahead of her husband. There was time for a flash of astonishment at that; it would never have been possible in Sparta, or anywhere in Greece. She was freer here than ever before, and already growing used to that. Then she was racing up the stone steps, falling behind Laocoon as the tall man took the stairs two or even three at a time. Paris' breath rasped behind her. They burst into the sunshine of the roof to find the Seer already at the low surrounding wall, standing rigid as a mast as he stared westwards.

Helen took a step towards him. All at once her legs felt heavy as stone. She could see past Laocoon now, to a sky broken by a single thin plume of smoke, south and west of Troy. Where Tenedos was. Her throat felt tight. Paris took her hand and she shook him off, almost angrily.

Another step.

She saw a wide strip of sea, between the parapet and the sky, and in it masts sprouted like terrors in the night. Hundreds of them. A thousand, perhaps. She made a small noise, a sound of sheer fear that was nothing like a word.

Menelaus had come. He had come for her, and brought with him all the might of Greece, their ships and soldiers and kings, to take her back. Or kill her. She supposed that was more likely, now. Whoever won this war, a lot of the Greeks down there would die beneath the walls of Troy, and those who lived would not take kindly to seeing Helen live afterwards in Sparta just as she had before.

Her heart thumped. She wouldn't live in Sparta again, come what may. She offered a prayer to Aphrodite to guard her from

46

that and only then remembered that the goddess wasn't worshipped here in the east. It took a moment for Helen to remember that in Troy it was Arinna who presided over the heart, wife of the supreme god Tarhun. Helen sent a benediction to her as well.

"Fate preserve us," she said finally. More masts were still appearing from the haze of distance. "They did come. I never really thought they would."

"I'm sure that will be a comfort to the women whose sons die for you," Laocoon said.

There was no reply to make to that. The three of them watched the approaching fleet for a moment longer, and then without words they turned and went back inside.

Chapter Six

The Palisades

"We are Greeks!" Axylus bellowed. He stood near the stern, facing along the length of the galley and the lines of men hauling on oars. One hand braced him against a rope that ran up to the square sail. "There are no warriors in the world better than us. We have the best armour, the best training, and the best bronze blades!"

Isander leaned into another stroke and felt his heart lift. It was true; Greeks were the finest fighting men on the Greensea. Others might match them in Assyria, or far off Qitan in the east, or in lands yet undiscovered across the Ocean, but nobody in the known world could stand with them one-to-one and triumph. No one – and yet a small, fugitive voice in the back of his mind whispered *the best bronze, perhaps… but the Trojans have iron.*

He was already hot, and sweating hard inside his armour. Spear, sword and leather shield rested in niches beside his bench, but he didn't need them yet. He pulled on his oar again, cutting the blade deep into the water, and this time felt an imbalance in the cadence of the rowers. Isander had been slightly ahead of the rest. He made himself wait a beat, pulled again, and found himself still too fast. He armed sweat quickly out of his eyes and looked around.

Everyone was still pulling at their oars. In the seat in front of him Gorka's back muscles flexed and relaxed, but perhaps not as much as before. Or as fast. Across the aisle and forward Nikos was the same. All the men Isander could see, two thirds of the soldiers on the galley, were pulling just a little less hard, a little less rapidly. He wondered if Axylus had noticed.

"Remember your training," the big man shouted, "and if the gods smile on you, you will survive."

Evidently not, then.

The ship's captain let go of the rope and strode along the plank that ran down the middle of the narrow warship, still yelling. "When our keel grinds on the beach, muster at the prow. Jump ashore only when there are twenty men together, I will *gut* any man who leaps too soon! Then form the shield rank as fast as you can! The Trojans are filth but their archers can shoot. Don't give them a target!"

48

Isander eased his rhythm a little more. The galley had slowed perceptibly now, the foam flowing past his seat thinning to a mere smear on the water. The ships alongside weren't pulling ahead though. They were slowing too, and suddenly Isander remembered words spoken on another beach and he thought he understood why.

The first man ashore shall ascend to immortality, Calchas had said, back at Aulis, *and dine with the gods on Olympian ambrosia.*

That was what Talthybius had said, more accurately, relaying the words of the Seer in his own sonorous voice. It hadn't taken long for the soldiers to realise what it meant. Whichever Greek first set foot on the Trojan coast would be killed, and dwell in the gods' halls before sundown.

"Olympian ambrosia is all very well," Nikos had murmured, in the ship later that day, "but you'd still be dead."

The soldiers were thinking of that now, as they drew closer to Cradle Bay and the Trojans waiting there. And they couldn't even see it. Oarsmen faced towards the stern, pulling always towards their own backs, and now they wondered if they were too close, about to be the first ship to rumble onto stones and come to a halt on the coast of Troy.

Isander could hear a voice calling from the next ship, a galley hardly more than fifty yards away. "- form a shield rank as soon as you hit the beach! Give them nothing to shoot at!"

That was Socus, captain of the armies of Elis, shouting the same instructions that Axylus had already given. But his vessel had slowed too, and now began to wallow in the water as oars stilled completely. And then someone near the stern of Isander's ship let go of his oar and stood, actually stood right up and turned to look forwards, towards the beach ahead.

"Ares' teeth!" Axylus roared. "Sit your ragged arse down, you son of dogs! And pull!"

But nobody was pulling, at least not more than a desultory tug on the shaft of his oar. Another man stood, then a third. Isander could see men standing on the other ships as well, craning to peer at the waiting beach. He half rose, just enough so he could twist around and see for himself. The beach was still three hundred feet away, probably more, and made of sand not stones. Axylus had told them confidently that it was all pebbles on Cradle Bay.

49

Tree trunks had been half buried in the sand, their sharpened points aimed outward, and so low that water lapped around them. Any ship trying to beach must run the risk of impaling itself, and then would be pinned helplessly in water too deep for armoured men. Behind the beach sand dunes formed a steady line, twenty feet high or more... and dotted with wooden palisades on every crest, like the mountain holds of bandit chiefs back home. Above those walls Isander could see moving figures. Trojans.

His belly swooped, bile rising to his throat.

"Row!" Axylus yelled. His hand slapped the side of Isander's head, making him reel. "Row, you sons of whores and goats! Did you come all this way for fear to rule you? Will you tell your wives you set your eyes on Troy and slunk away like cowards?"

Isander thought of Meliza, his red-haired love, waiting for him back in Olympia. She had whispered to him on the pillow, the last night they had spent together before the army left for Aulis. *I always swore I would never wed, but come home alive from Troy and I might, my young lion. I might.*

Axylus was striding along the ship, snarling and slapping as he went. Men began to turn back to their oars. Isander hesitated a moment longer, and then sunlight flashed in his eyes and he turned his head to see a city shining on a hill, its towers rising and rising as though to hold up the sky itself.

He froze, unable to tear his gaze away.

Nothing men built could be so proud. The Trojans must be beloved of great gods indeed, and terror clutched at Isander with hands of cold slime. He shoved it down, gulping.

"For Meliza," he said aloud. He would go ashore for her, and then leave it to the gods whether he saw her again. He bent to seize his oar and began to pull, as others around him did the same.

Before the oarsmen could resume their rhythm another galley cut through the narrow gap between Isander's and Socus'. There was nothing to tell who captained it, or which land it came from. But the soldiers were hauling at their oars like men taken by demons, and chanting as they went; *hai! Hai! Hai!* Even Axylus turned to look, his rage forgotten.

Then Isander saw a man in silver armour near the stern of the new ship, a lithe figure with tumbling golden hair, and suddenly he did know who this was after all.

It was unfortunate, more than anything. If Agamemnon had the brains of a squirrel he would have had Calchas read the entrails away from the main army, just in case the omens were bad. But no, that wouldn't do for the Great Bull of Mycenae. He had to have it done publicly, so the army could see him presiding over it all in that ridiculous rainbow armour, and as a result the soldiers were too afraid to set foot on the shore.

The first man ashore shall dine with the gods on Olympian ambrosia. That was what Calchas had said, or words very close to it. A foolish thing for a man to announce, especially one as experienced at reading omens as Calchas was. It would have been easy for him to pause for a moment as though examining the butchered animal, and use the time to think what to say. He needn't even lie, just choose his words better. *The first man ashore shall win glory everlasting,* or something like that. It would have been true enough, and the ships would have raced each other all the way to the shore.

Instead they hesitated, each waiting for another to take the lead. Even Agamemnon had slowed, somewhere in the dense cluster of vessels to the north. At this rate ships would start to collide with one another as they lost headway and the waves began to push them around.

From the shore he could hear jeers, derisive laughter. The Trojans were *laughing* at them.

Someone had to seize the initiative, had to dare the gods to be as good as their word and take the life of the first man to stand on Trojan soil. Or sand, anyway. It might as well be him.

"Pull!" Diomedes cried. The beach was close now and he pulled his helmet over his ears, tightening the strap with a quick tug. "This is for glory! For Argolis, and the tales of the storytellers!"

His men roared, on this ship and the one following hard behind. Thenelus had the command there, a friend since youth, and now captain to the armies of Argolis. Diomedes gave him a grin and the other man made a pushing gesture with both hands, urging Diomedes on.

Of course this wasn't actually about glory for Argolis at all. Glory, yes, but for Diomedes. Ajax was on a ship somewhere with his father, and Telamon these days was a ball of lard weighty enough to slow any ship. Certainly there was no sign of him that Diomedes could see. And Achilles? He'd been given the task of taking the island of Tenedos, which would be vital as a supply base for the Greek armies if the war dragged on for more than a few weeks. It was an important duty, and one which gave Achilles a command of his own, free of the High King. He'd snatched at it, beaming with triumph over his rivals, not yet realising that it also got him neatly out of the way. He would not be there when the beach of Troy was taken. What songs would be sung about him?

The storytellers would speak in their resonant voices, fingers plucking the strings of lutes, and it would be the name of Diomedes they invoked.

"Look!" the helmsman cried.

Diomedes whirled. For a moment he could only stare, almost choking as rage threatened to overwhelm him completely. There was a ship ahead of him.

Then he burst out laughing, amused despite himself. He should have foreseen this. Of all the lords of Greece, this was the one most likely to understand first, and then to act.

"You sly fox," he snorted, half in admiration. "Oh, Nestor, I'd eat your heart if I didn't like you so much.

"Pull" he shouted again, still laughing at himself inside. "If we can't be first ashore, by the gods we'll be second! Pull!"

*

The Argives are here.

That one thought hammered in Hector's mind as the chariots flew north along the road, just behind the dunes. It made it difficult to think. He'd known they were coming, had heard the stories of their muster from a score of ship captains, men with no reason to lie. None were Trojan; their own people didn't go to Greece these days. But some were Phoenician, some Carians with no love for the Argives, and one had even been Egyptian, a man with skin so dark it glowed like the reflection of the moon on still water. The tale they told was always the same: the Argives were mustering in Boeotia, at a port no Trojan had ever heard of much less seen, and their victim was to be Troy.

May Tarhun hurl lightnings to burn Paris to ash where he stands. It was a regular curse for Hector now, one he'd spoken to

52

himself so often it had lost some of its edge. *May Ipirru's heavenly horses trample him for eternity, day after day, crushing his skull and liver with their hooves.*

This wasn't helping. He relaxed his hands on the rim of the chariot with an effort of will. The sand dunes blocked his view of the sea now, and he didn't know where the approaching ships were. Close, of course, but not ashore yet; he would have heard the sounds of fighting if they were.

"Faster!" he shouted.

Heptolamus shrugged. "Going as fast as we can."

Hector swore and thumped the rail.

The road flashed by. They were already driving so fast that the other two chariots with them in Leris had been left well behind, visible now only as a twinned plume of dust. Twice a wheel had struck some unseen obstacle and Hector's feet had left the car's rattling floor, though Heptolamus only swayed slightly and gave a little grunt. Sometimes Hector thought his friend was touched by gods, able to read the packed earth of the road ahead and react to it before his mind even noticed what his eyes had seen.

People had begun to stream out of Leris before the chariots were well out of the gates. Not just the children either; everyone was going, except the men who'd fight on the palisades. Women, oldsters who couldn't fight anymore, children. Probably a lot of youths would stay, boys really too young for war but who were needed now the assault had come. Hector might have argued against that but there was no time, no time.

The chariot burst out from behind a stand of lotus and tamarisk, their long leaves forming a barrier that had hidden Troy from view. In front of them the plain swarmed with soldiers, lines and companies hurrying towards the beach of Cradle Bay. Some hadn't yet reached the fords over the Scamander, even; Hector knew at once they wouldn't arrive in time. Others, the leading troops, had come to the place where the plain's rich earth gave way to sand and then dunes. Those at the front wore the white and gold lacquer of the Apollonians, a sight which made Hector smile with pride. The Apollonians were the best, which was why the other companies strove so hard to beat them.

They rarely managed to.

"Get fresh horses and come back for me," Hector said. He unclipped his spears from the side of the bucking car. "And find out where Aeneas and Pandarus are, if you can."

Heptolamus leaned closer to the prince, without taking his eyes from the road. "You want me to leave you on foot?"

"Chariots are no use in this sand," Hector said. "Anyway, if it goes well I'll never leave the palisades."

"And when does battle ever go well?"

Hector grinned and hoisted his shield. "It goes well enough for me to still be alive. Oh, and tell one of my brothers to order half the men guarding the Bay of Troy to come south. They'll be too late to help in the battle, but they might be needed to cover our retreat."

Heptolamus nodded, his attention still all on the road. He reined in and the three horses slowed to a canter.

Hector threw himself from the car, angling sideways to miss the packed earth of the road. He landed on top of his shield in soft sand, spears clutched in the other and under the shield, so he didn't stab himself when he rolled. He came to his feet at a run, feeling a bruise already starting to rise on his left arm where the rim had dug into his flesh. He noticed it only peripherally, his focus now on the coming battle as tightly as Heptolamus concentrated on the road.

Shouts came from beyond the dunes, a steady cadence that made no sense. *Hai, hai,* or something like that. It wasn't a Trojan cry and Hector slogged up the dune towards a palisade at the top, his feet spraying sand as he went. A young soldier heard him and turned, his spear rising, only to lower it in visible relief as he recognised the prince.

"My lord, the Argives –"

"I know they're here," Hector said brusquely. Habit made him put a hand on the youth's shoulder as he passed, softening the harsh words. He went the last few yards and looked down over the wooden defences he'd ordered built, to the fleet now bearing down on the beach.

Had he not seen battle for the Hittite King, he thought spit might have dried in his mouth. Hector had never thought there were so many ships in the world. They filled the sea, lines and ranks of them spilling all the way to the haze of the horizon, so many that he doubted they could all find berths. Cram them together on the strand like olives in a jar and some would still be left bobbing on the waves. That many galleys meant the Argives had emptied their land, and soon the beach would be thick with screaming Greeks and their weapons.

But Hector had fought at Emar, when the Assyrians had brought legion after legion of spearmen marching onto the field, following lines of chariots with spikes glinting from their wheels. They'd poured onto the field for hours before the muster was complete – and they had been beaten, of at great cost. The Hittite king had rewarded him for his valour that day with an ironsmith to bring home to Troy, a gift never given before. He'd fought at Rhyinia against the Egyptian hordes, less well trained and armed but even vaster in numbers, and every one of them eager to die for their god-king. Before even that he'd been on the field of Kantassa, when Urhi-Tešub's cousin had tried to seize the throne and instead had seen his army butchered. The cousin had ended as a flayed, whimpering remnant, tossed into a bath of salt water to drown; Hector couldn't even remember his name.

Troy's name would not be forgotten. He would not allow it, however great the foolishness of Paris, whatever hosts the gods saw fit to send to these shores. His own name could fade for all Hector cared. One man's fate meant nothing. But a city, a culture, a place of beauty and laughter and love… that must endure. Through any storm.

The lead ship was heading straight for him, he realised. Foam sprayed from its prow in curtains.

"This is destiny!" His voice boomed across the dunes, over the mutter and rattle of men preparing to fight. He had no doubt that it boomed over the water too, into the ears of the Argives. "The eyes of the gods are on us. Fight well, Trojans! Fight for your city, your wives and daughters, and leave this sand awash with the blood of invaders!"

The men roared, as he'd known they would. Away to the north a tall man behind another dune-top palisade nodded approval in a manner so familiar that Hector was almost sure he was Aeneas. But there was no time to be sure. Hector planted one spear in the sand and hefted the other, waiting.

The Argive ship ground on the sand. An armoured figure sprang from the deck and landed in knee-high water, pausing for a moment to steady himself. The hesitation was a mistake.

Hector hurled his spear, the throw driven by rage and all the power of his heart.

Chapter Seven

The Sons Who Die

He jumped from the galley a moment too soon, before the keel had grounded on the sand. The ship was still moving and that threw him off balance. A younger man might have been able to compensate; Nestor thought he could have done it himself, twenty years ago. Even ten. As it was he landed in shallow water and stumbled, his old knees groaning on the edge of balance.

A spear took him in the throat. He felt his eyes go wide with shock.

Someone was standing next to him. Nestor turned his head and there was Eurydice, the wife of his years, the fire of his heart. She was smiling. There was no grey in her hair and she was smiling, the way she had when they were young and unafraid, and the world was theirs.

"Come." He remembered her voice, warmth and welcome alike, and a shiver ran through him as he heard it again. "I've waited for you, my love. Come with me to black Styx, and the Orchards of Elysium beyond."

He tried to speak but couldn't. He understood; the spear in his throat. But at the end her voice had changed, become something like slithering mud in the dark, and the arms she held out to him were as thin as bones. He was afraid. Eurydice closed her fingers around his own.

Nestor fell backwards. He was dead before he hit the water.

*

Diomedes went over the rail of his ship into a hail of arrows and stones. A spear clanged against his round shield as he landed, luckily just a glancing blow. A full one might have knocked him over before he could steady himself. A moment later he was crouched behind the shield, with his men locking theirs against his in a wall of metal and leather. Missiles still poured down on them. Someone cried out and went down, leaving a gap that was quickly closed.

"Advance!" Diomedes cried.

The knot of men pushed out of the water, up onto the beach of Troy. Those at the sides trailed backwards, their shields turned to offer protection from the side. Thenelus' galley grounded to the left and more soldiers leapt down. The Trojans shifted the focus of their barrage, aiming for the men who hadn't yet formed a shield wall, and several soldiers fell. The patter on Diomedes' shield grew less. He peered over the top.

Timbers shrieked as a third ship crashed into one of the sharpened tree trunks the Trojans had placed on the beach. Diomedes heard cries, grunts of sudden pain as men were flung against their oars. There would be broken ribs there, lungs pierced by splinters of bone, men killed or maimed before they even lifted a spear. It wouldn't be the worst of this day. He ordered his shield group left, to join with the new arrivals there. More ships were landing, more soldiers springing into the water and onto the sand. More were dying. He ignored them.

Ahead were two dunes, both steep, both made of fine sand. Climbing those to the palisades at the top would cost a lot of lives, even before swords could be unsheathed. The alternative was to force a path through the lower place between the forts, while the Trojans hurled stones and whatever else they had down from the heights. Diomedes didn't like the thought of that at all.

"The hill on the left!" he shouted. That was slightly lower, the slope perhaps a little more gentle. "Straight for it!"

He was already growing hoarse. That was what shouting in battle did for you, but it couldn't be helped. The shield group began to advance, every man staying tight to those beside him, their shields forming a solid wall. Some still went down though, caught by an arrow to the shin or a stone to the helmet. When that happened the line close instantly, before the Trojans could redirect their aim. The band left a trail of bodies behind them as they scuttled forward, some moving, others still forever.

The priests said that sometimes, if the light was right, you could see the shades of the dead leave their bodies and begin the long, cold journey to the river Styx, and the black water that burned. Diomedes thought he had done, once, when his men slaughtered bandits in a high valley in the north of Argolis. It had been almost twilight then, the heights bathed in sunshine but the valley floor deepening into dusk, and the light had had a strange quality, like reflections from mountain lakes in winter. Today was brighter, the sun burning overhead, but something of the same quality hung in the air. Diomedes didn't have time to look for shades though. Perhaps later, if he was still alive.

They were climbing the dune. The hail of missiles grew thicker, battering on their shields. Diomedes felt a stone strike his shin and then roll away, deflected by the greave he wore. More Greeks were joining the ends of the formation, hurrying up from newly arrived ships to replace fallen men. Diomedes peeked over the top of his shield again, gauging the distance to the wooden stakes.

"Ready!" he cried.

Sand slipped under his sandals as he pushed on. They were closer now. Closer… and close enough.

"Volley!"

As one, his men lowered their shields and turned, so they could throw their own spears. In that moment of exposure half a dozen were hit. But a shower of spears fell on the Trojans behind their wall, and behind them the Greeks rushed in against the palisade.

A Trojan thrust a spear at Diomedes' belly. He evaded it and jabbed back, the point going just above the man's cheek guard and into his eye, deep enough to kill. He jerked once and went down. Next to him a Greek soldier dodged a blow but stumbled against the sharp stakes of the barrier, and a second later another Trojan stabbed him through the armpit and he collapsed, spraying blood and shrieking in a voice like a woman's.

Diomedes vaulted the barrier and two Trojans rushed at him. He grinned through the gap in his helmet and went to meet them.

*

The Argives were too many. Aeneas knew that just looking at the size of the fleet, still coming in towards the beach even though so many ships had already landed. Several ships had struck the stakes and now floundered twenty yards off the beach, their captains trying to organise the oarsmen to bring them around again. They'd manage it in the end, as long as no other ship crashed into them while they manoeuvred. That had happened, a little way to the north, leaving one ship holed and sinking, the men aboard it hurriedly shedding their armour before they had to go into water deep enough to drown in.

Bodies were strewn across the sand. Almost all of them were Argive, but ten more landed for every one that fell. They'd reached the palisade in half a dozen places that Aeneas could see,

58

and they only needed to break through in one and the beach would be theirs. The best the Trojans could do was make them pay for it with blood, and hope the losses were too high for the Argives to bear.

This was only the first battle, after all. Here the Trojans stood behind flimsy wooden palisades; later, across the plain, they would shelter inside the mighty stone walls of Troy. Whatever losses the Argives suffered here would be repeated there ten times over.

Aeneas glanced south, to the dune where he'd caught a glimpse of Hector's white-plumed helmet. He couldn't see it now, but he was sure his friend was alive. It would take six gods and a rending of the sky to put an end to that man. And Hector was a good captain; he'd know when to sound the horns and retreat.

"Ship coming in," Leos said.

Aeneas shook his thoughts away. There hadn't been a landing on his section of the beach yet, but Leos was right, a ships was approaching now. One of many, in fact, running in at speed. As he watched the oars were pulled in and the lead galley nosed between two long stakes, brushing one with a screeching sound until it grounded on the sand and was still.

A *huge* man leapt down, tall and massive across the shoulders. He carried an oblong shield with a bronze rim that must be incredibly heavy. Aeneas almost expected the earth to shake when he landed. He knew who this giant had to be.

"Ajax," he muttered. Leos gave him a quick look, in which the fear had not been wholly concealed.

Ajax, son of hated Telamon of Salamis, the thief of Hesione. One of the great heroes of Greece, if the stories had any truth to them. Looking at him Aeneas could believe it. Other Argives were jumping down now too, one of them taking a place beside the titan, tall but less bulky than Ajax, wearing a helmet of boar's tusks.

Boar's tusks meant a noble. Another noble from a Salamis ship had to be –

Teucer. Hesione's son, borne to Telamon against her will. And now fighting for the Argives against Troy, against his mother's land, in the name of an abductor and forcer of women. Aeneas felt heat rise in his face.

"Sling men!" he cried.

59

Ajax heard him, even over the rising crash of battle, and snapped orders in an accent so rapid that Aeneas couldn't follow it. Soldiers were still pouring down from the galley, and from a second one now too, but they made no effort to advance. Aeneas frowned. They were sitting targets were they stood, raised shields or no. What were they doing?

Men on the first ship were swinging a winch into place. A net hung from it. Aeneas couldn't see over the rail to what they were doing, but the Argives were still gathering around Ajax and his brother, and still making no move to advance.

"Loose!"

Stones and arrows showered down on the group of men. Most rattled off raised shields, but a few found their way through gaps and men fell, some in silence, others with cries or shrill screams. Still the Argives merely stood and endured it. Aeneas began to frown.

The winch swung out over the rail. A man clung to the netting, gripping with both hands and feet. A hugely fat man, sweating like a hard-run horse, in leather armour lashed around his girth and held there by bronze clasps. For a moment Aeneas didn't understand, and then realisation came in a flash of rage.

The obese man had been to Troy's beaches before. To steal, and abduct. This was Telamon.

Aeneas opened his mouth to order the missile men to change their aim, but there was no need. The Dardanians he led had realised too. Suddenly arrows began to fall around Telamon in a storm, and though they mostly skimmed off his armour the stones did not. Telamon cried out; Aeneas saw his mouth move, though the roar of battle by then was too loud for him to hear the man's voice. The woman-thief tried to twist aside but he was too big, the stones too many, and he only managed to tangle himself in the netting.

An arrow found Telamon's neck and stuck there. The fat man jerked. On the beach mighty Ajax let out a bellow of rage and started towards the dunes at last, realising the danger too late.

A sling stone hit Telamon full in the face. His head snapped backwards and when it came up again his features were a ruin sheeted in blood. Seconds later another rock hit his temple and this one dislodged him from the mesh, to fall with an almighty smash into the sea.

"Brace!" Aeneas yelled. He'd been too preoccupied with watching Telamon's demise to realise how close Ajax's body of men had come. The missile men had focused on the hated lord of Salamis too, letting his giant son have an unchallenged run up the dune. There were at least two hundred Argives in the band. Aeneas barely had time to join the line before they struck.

A volley of spears rattled on the palisade, or flew overhead. Some found a mark in flesh and men went down. A Dardanian riposte felled a handful of Argives and then the attackers smashed into the defences.

Men were screaming everywhere, buffeting each other in the sudden crush. Aeneas fought in silence though, as he always had. He took a spear thrust on his shield and stabbed back low down, to take the Argive climbing the palisade in the groin, where no armour protected him. The man let out a squeal and collapsed on his belly, and at once was dragged back by his comrades to get him out of the way. In the brief respite Aeneas saw Ajax simply *leap* the wall, smashing a hole in the waiting spears with his big oblong shield. A moment later his own spear darted and a man fell. An Argive slipped in on the other side and Ajax knocked him senseless with one swing of his shield arm.

This could get very ugly indeed if Ajax wasn't stopped. Aeneas started to pull out of the line, snapping for someone to take his place, and then had to turn back when an Argive threw himself over the palisade, much as Ajax had done. He was nearly gutted at once but managed to take Aeneas' blow just on the edge of his shield, so the spear point glanced aside. A moment later his answering jab lanced over Aeneas' shoulder. Aeneas turned his torso and slammed his shield to the left, striking the ash shaft and breaking the Argive's spear.

On his next strike the attacker caught Aeneas' spear between his body and shield and cut it with the sword pulled from its scabbard. It was a very clever move and it broke Aeneas ash handle as well. It was followed with a scything sword blow that had Aeneas backpedalling as he snatched his own blade from above his shoulder, parried, and after a feint lunged past the Argive's shield to take him in the throat and kill him.

As he struck he looked into his enemy's face, and the eyes looking back were very blue and very Trojan. Hair spilling from under the helmet was fair, an easterner's colour.

Teucer. Hesione's son.

61

There wasn't even time to swear. Aeneas' muscles shrieked as he pushed the sword point aside, to it took the young man in his shoulder instead of his throat. It went through the leather cuirass and deep into flesh and muscle. Teucer gasped and his shield sagged, the weight too much for the wounded joint.

"Brother!" Ajax bellowed, somewhere behind.

The boy was looking at him. Expecting to die, Aeneas realised. He pulled his sword back. "Get yourself out of the battle and back to the ships. I will not kill you today."

"I would have killed you," Teucer retorted.

Ipirru's balls, but he had a Trojan's courage. "And next time I may kill you. But today, for your mother's sake, you live. I have your word to withdraw?"

Teucer stared at him with undisguised hate. "My word."

That would do. Perhaps something could be arranged, later, that would spare this young man the carnage to come. Aeneas would let others decide that; he had his own horses to tame. He turned away, pausing to snatch up a fallen spear. Leos was fighting to his left, still holding the line of the palisade, though the Argives had broken through in some places. Their dead littered the wooden stakes though, and there would be many more beyond. Never mind that.

My own horses to tame. He went to meet Ajax.

The huge man was scything through the Dardanians, cutting a path to his brother. Aeneas was six feet tall, but this man overtopped him by inches and outweighed him easily. Aeneas was quick though, had used that to his advantage many times when training against the bigger, stronger Hector. He whipped in fast and in the first exchange he broke Ajax's spear and laid a long gash along the big man's bicep, almost to the elbow.

In the second his own spear was splintered with dismissive ease, as though it was a stick of kindling in the hands of a child. Ajax drew a sword from his belt and slashed viciously, several times: the second blow split muscle above Aeneas' left knee and blood flowed at once as he wobbled.

Aeneas drew his own blade. It glinted in the light and he saw Ajax notice, saw the man's eyes go wide. This was iron, one of the first blades made in Mursili's new foundry by the wall. Aeneas had practised with it every day, growing more and more used to the different weight and balance. He stabbed at Ajax and turned the move into a cut instead, so his sword hammered into Ajax's and cut a deep notch into the bronze.

"Fight me without that gaudy thing," Ajax rasped. "Fight fair."

Aeneas grinned like a wolf. "Shrink six inches and maybe I will."

The great titan of a man snarled and rushed him, trying to knock Aeneas down with the oblong shield and then stomp him. The gods knew he was big enough to do it. Aeneas slipped aside and landed a skidding blow on Ajax's hip, enough to slow him at least and maybe to draw blood. But he wasn't quite quick enough and that big shield caught his shoulder and sent him staggering, which was when horns began to blow just to the south.

By the time Ajax slowed his rush and turned, Aeneas had already moved away. The quick blasts of the horns signalled that the beach was lost, and all Trojan forces were to retreat east to the Scamander and beyond. More horns began to sound, some to the north now, as the message spread.

Hector had said the Argives wouldn't pursue, since their objective this day was simply to establish themselves on the coast. But Aeneas didn't plan to test that by waiting. The archers and slingers waited now behind the dunes, ready to cover the withdrawal. Aeneas shouted for his men to rally around him and they began to comply, breaking off combat all around the breached palisade.

"Coward!" Ajax roared. He struck sideways as a Dardanian fled past him, almost splitting the man in half. His notched bronze sword broke and he hurled the useless hilt at Aeneas in fury. "Stay and fight me. Trojan coward!"

"I'm no Trojan," Aeneas shouted back. "I am Aeneas of Dardanos. Remember my name."

He would remember it with honour, if there was any justice. Ajax had lost his father today, the hated Telamon killed by flung rocks and salt water, but he might have lost a brother too. Only Aeneas' mercy had prevented that. Perhaps Teucer would tell him so, and the first bridge would be built between the warring sides. Sometimes such bridges offered a way to end the fighting, while both armies were intact. And if not, Aeneas had still done the right thing. He couldn't have faced going back to Priam to say he had slain the son of Hesione, the last link the old king had to the sister lost so long ago.

A knot of Argives came down the dune in pursuit, and were met with a barrage of stones and the archers' last remaining arrows. Three fell in a single volley and the rest retreated. Hector was right again, it seemed; the Greeks weren't going to follow. Aeneas turned and led his men east.

*

There hadn't been much fighting, in the end. The Trojans manning their dune-top palisades had pelted the arriving Greeks with missiles, but they'd been too few to cause real damage. The first handful of ships had landed enough men to drive up the sand and capture the forts, and the Trojans had blown horns and retreated onto the plain.

An arrow had struck Isander's shield rim and whined away into the sky, and Gorka had been hit by a stone right in the middle of his own shield. It had made him grunt in surprise and effort. Nikos had avoided harm altogether, and that was it, the worst of the landing on the beach of Troy. They had been so afraid of it and in the end, by the time they came ashore, there was nothing to do.

Further north it had been harder. Isander could see the bodies that littered the beach, tiny black shapes against the sand. Above dark specks circled in the bronze sky, waiting their chance: crows. There were always crows on a battlefield. Isander had always known that, and never truly understood what it meant until now. Not in his guts. He wished he hadn't thought of that analogy.

He sat down on the beach, trying to breathe evenly. His hands might stop trembling if he could.

"Aren't we following?" Nikos asked, not far away.

"I reckon, once Socus is here." Axylus sounded the same as he always did, brash and sure of himself. The scar on his forearm stood out lividly as he wiped sweat from his brow. "Can't just let them slip away. If we catch them by the fords over the river we might hurt them badly."

"We will not be following," someone else said. The voice held such a tone of command that Isander lifted his head to look at the speaker, but he didn't look like anything remarkable. Fairly tall, with well-made but plain cuirass and shield. "They'll have archers waiting at the river. We would lose a lot of men and kill too few to justify the price."

"How do you know they'll have archers?" Axylus demanded.

The man shrugged with one shoulder. "I would. So would Diomedes, or Achilles, if I know them at all."

"You know them?" Axylus' tone was suddenly diffident. "Who are you, then?"

"My name is Odysseus."

Axylus hesitated, seeming to want to speak but thinking better of it. Probably he was biting back a snide remark about the peasant-king of Ithaca, who everyone knew was hardly better than a farmer… except that he knew Diomedes and Achilles, and the other lords of Greece besides. Gorka turned to study the ordinary-looking man, and Nikos' eyes were suddenly thoughtful.

Odysseus came over and sat on his heels next to Isander. "You all right, son?"

Isander nodded. His hands still fluttered like dying birds.

"I was the same, my first time on a battlefield," Odysseus said quietly. "You know what my father told me? He said that everyone is the same. Even men like Achilles, and Heracles himself I imagine. Young men all hear the tales the storytellers weave, and they all see the glory and imagine the cheers. But when you're really there, when the arrows are real and the next one might end your life and your eyes will fill with night… then it's different."

"Achilles felt this way?" Isander asked. His mouth was full of bile.

"Everyone feels this way," the king said again. "There's no shame in it. The shame would be to feel nothing, because a man like that might as well already be dead, and someone so hard-hearted would go straight to the darkest plains of Hades in the end, don't you think?

"Remember how you feel now," he said, not giving Isander a chance to speak. "But don't let it affect you. There will be harder fighting than this before the war is over."

"At the walls," Nikos said.

Odysseus looked at him. "At the end, perhaps. If we stay the course. But on the Plain of Troy, before that."

"But the Trojans fled. Will they face us in the open again?"

"This was sand, lad. On the Plain their chariots can wreak havoc among us, and the Trojans know it. In any case, Troy has allies." Odysseus gestured eastwards, towards the climbing hills. "Mysia, Maeonia, maybe even Hattusa. When they come, the numbers will change. We'll have work, when that happens."

Isander looked north, to where Troy sat atop its hill in the sunshine. Four or five miles away. He thought of trying to force a path to it in the face of swarming chariots and swallowed.

"Herald coming," Gorka said. His first words since this morning, when the three friends had clasped forearms and vowed to see one another in the evening, when the battle was done. The rest of them turned to see a lone man scrambling across the coarse sand, the branch of an olive tree tied diagonally across the front of his cuirass. He slipped and nearly fell, recovered, and came on more slowly until he reached them, panting in the heat like a weary dog.

"My lord Odysseus?" he gasped out.

"Yes," the king answered. He must be asked that a lot, Isander thought. Odysseus was such an unimportant lord, and looked so ordinary, that people must always mistake him for a common man. He didn't seem to get angry about it, if he ever had. "What's your message?"

"King Diomedes sent me to tell you," the man puffed, "that we lost Telamon of Salamis today. He was killed by sling stones and arrows as he was being lowered from his ship."

"He tried that in battle?" Odysseus shook his head. "Well, he never had much more sense that old Theseus, I suppose. Too caught up in those dreams of glory. He's small loss to us. Although if I'm asked," he added, with a sidelong look at the friends, "I'll deny I said that."

"Nestor of Messenia was also killed," the herald said, rushing the words as though afraid what would come of them.

Odysseus went very still. Looking at him Isander saw his eyes turn hard, chips of flint in soft ground, and he wondered what had changed inside him. Suddenly Odysseus didn't look ordinary at all. He looked like the sort of man who made monsters flee and gorgons tremble at the mere rumour of his approach. After a moment Isander stood and went over to the Ithacan king, and hesitating only a moment he put his hand on the king's shoulder.

"Thank you, lad," Odysseus said. But the words were flat, and beneath them ran a current of hot rage. The king turned and walked back down the beach, towards the camp his soldiers had begun to lay out under the prows of their ships, and as he went Isander thought he began to weep.

Chapter Eight

The Sound of Hammers

Hector came through the gate stained with blood from his nodding white plumes to his greaves. In two places there was more than blood; Andromache was afraid that the spatter on his shoulder was brains. None of it seemed to be his, thankfully. He was all dust and blood and he looked terribly tired, but he stepped down from the chariot and slapped Heptolamus on the back, without any obvious sign of injury.

Outside the Pergamos the city was in turmoil, the sound of its unease a constant mutter. Sometimes a wail would go up, the sound of a wife mourning a husband or a mother her son. She tried not to listen.

"Love," he said to her. She smiled but made no effort to touch him; all that filth would ruin her gown. Even the sight and smell of it made her nauseous, but this deep into her pregnancy almost any strong scent did that. Hector turned towards his father, standing on the steps of the Pillar House with a cloud of servants and advisors around him. There was a stoop to Priam's shoulders that Andromache hadn't seen before. It seemed to have appeared since this morning – since the afternoon, in truth, when the Argive ships had been sighted and the tocsin began to ring.

"The beach is lost?" Priam asked.

"It is," Hector said, and then, "*Where is he?*"

Everyone heard the change in his tone. That was not how a man spoke to his father, or a prince to his king. Priam looked at his eldest son and said nothing.

"Hector," Hecuba began.

He never looked at her. "Paris is the one who brought the Argives to our shores. But today there was no sign of him as Trojans fought and died. Did Paris fight? Was he in the palisades?"

Still Priam didn't reply.

"Then I ask again," Hector said. "Where is he?"

"I believe he is in his chambers," a new voice said. Antenor moved out from the group around Priam. His voice was as suave as ever, but tension had etched lines around his eyes and mouth, as new as Priam's stoop. "But I regret I must correct one thing you said, my lord prince."

There was a pause, and then at last Hector asked, "What thing?"

"That it was Paris who brought the Argives here," Antenor replied. "It was he who led the raid on Sparta, true, but I was the one who plotted it. If there is blame here then it lies on me more than any." He turned to Priam. "I have failed the city, and I've failed my king. I wish to resign my post as advisor."

"No." Priam didn't hesitate. "One misjudgement does not destroy the work of years. I have told you this before. And besides, the Argives *should* have bargained. You know it. We just didn't realise we were dealing with madmen."

"It might destroy that work," Antenor said softly. "Everything I've done in your service will be made nothing, if the Argives breach our wall."

"And how will they do that? The wall will hold."

"I ought to resign, even so."

"You need my consent and I refuse it," Priam said. "And I need you, old friend. I do not wish to discuss this again."

Antenor bowed his head. Outside the citadel wall the cries of the city went on and on.

"Paris is a prince of Troy," Hector said finally. "He led the raid on Sparta and he's needed now, when the city is threatened. The people must see their princes fight. Whatever the truth of your words, Antenor, Paris has a duty you do not and I will see that he does it. By all Ipirru's horses I will!"

Troilus, the second prince, hadn't fought today. But that was because he was leading the men who herded two hundred horses to the slopes of Mount Ida, where Argive raiding parties couldn't reach them. The bloodstock had to be preserved or Troy would fail even if it won this war. As for Lycaon, Priam's third son, he was on his way to Hattusa – perhaps there already – to ask the Hittite king for aid. An army might come, or might not. It depended what other dangers Urhi-Tešub was facing, on other borders.

But Paris was here, in the city, spending most of his days and all his nights with the woman he had stolen away from Menelaus in Sparta. Organising the defence had been left to Hector and the men he trusted, Aeneas and Pandarus for the most part. That might be excusable. But staying in his rooms while men were slaughtered in battle was not. Hector was right.

She rubbed her lower back, where the weight of the baby pained her most. She felt so slow now, so ungainly, but her mind still worked. Someone was going to have to speak in support of her husband and that was a wife's work. She drew a breath.

Priam spoke before she could. "Paris is in his chambers, yes. I will have him brought to us."

"No," Hector said. "I will go to him."

He turned and strode away, following the base of the citadel wall towards the palace where Paris lived with his pilfered bride. One of the Apollonians guarding the king actually moved as though to follow him, before remembering his duty and stepping back into position. Perhaps he wasn't sure any longer whose hands held power in Troy.

Neither was Andromache. She kneaded her back again and then pain shot through her with such force that she couldn't stifle a moan. Hecuba was there in an instant, calling for servants to help carry Andromache inside. It was impossible to protest, or even to speak. Each breath seared in her lungs.

The baby is coming. It was the last coherent thought she remembered for some time.

*

An Argive fleet had entered the Bay of Troy some hours after the main battle to the west. It had scouted the shores and then left again, without landing any soldiers. But by then the damage was done. Hector had made it clear that the secrets of the ships of Colchis must not be handed to the Greeks.

By the time the first ship nosed down from the Hellespont, Phereclus' boatyard had been set ablaze.

He supposed he understood. Greek ships couldn't pass the strait to the Euxine Sea, but Colchian ones could. The Argive sailors quailed in terror rather than dare the strip of water between Naxos and Locri, in the far west, but that was just choppy water to a Colchis vessel. A few eastern captains had even sailed the length of the Greensea and ventured into the Ocean itself, where waves could rise as high as the mast and a gentle swell could break a ship's back. Some of them had come home again.

But it was hard, to see all his work burned down to the sand. Every hull, every plank and half-shaped bench. Nothing remained for the Argives to pick over and guess at. Nothing of what Phereclus had hoped to achieve, here in this high city on a strange sea. It was always so; craftsmen built and warriors destroyed, in a cycle that might have had no beginning and surely would never end. The artisans usually appeared again after the fighting died down, to rebuild what they could and rediscover what they must. That might not happen here. Phereclus was the only man in the west who could build those Colchian ships.

He didn't like looking at the ashes of his efforts.

"More charcoal," the smith said. Phereclus couldn't remember his name. But he hurried to obey, because already he'd learned the necessity to be quick in the foundry. He grabbed a shovel and scooped up charcoal from the pile at the back, carried it back to the furnace and poured it through the rectangular gap in the back. The flames inside seemed to choke and died back slightly. It was still ferociously hot in the room though, as it always was; Mursili insisted on the fires being banked overnight but almost never put out.

"Good," the under-smith said.

He was a man of few words. Perhaps none of them had included his name. Phereclus thought of him as Ring-man, because of the three concentric circles tattooed into his forehead. It was a motif found in Colchis too, one that denoted a bronze smith seemingly all across the world. The circles represented the sun, a tiny piece of which lived in every forge-fire. Or so the guild back home said. It made as much sense as anything.

Ring-man was the only bronze smith in Troy who'd agreed to help Mursili make iron, and to learn from him. The rest had curled their lips and walked away, despite Priam's pleas. The guilds had enough power to defy the king at times, if they stood together. Only Ring-man had broken that unanimity. Phereclus thought he deserved to have his name remembered for that alone.

The smith thrust an unfinished sword into the furnace. It was just a blocky piece of iron at the moment, more than two feet long but unsharpened, the way the swords came out of their moulds. Mursili was the one in charge of the casting, in a large room at the other end of the foundry. Though actually *in charge* was too timid a phrase: Mursili did all the casting himself, and shouted in his own language at anyone who interfered. Whatever the words meant, the Hittite language made them sound appalling.

71

"Going outside for a while," Phereclus said. Ring-man nodded without taking his eyes from the glowing sword.

The temperature dropped as he stepped through the door. Sweat beading on his forehead was suddenly cool. Phereclus took a bucket and went to his left, keeping the city wall at his side, although he knew Troy well enough now not to lose himself in the tangle of curving streets. A few moments brought him to a cluster of springs, clear water bubbling out of the earth and into stone channels which guided it into wells. From the other side excess ran out under the wall, which was where horses were allowed to drink. Phereclus washed his face, removing the worst of the charcoal and sweat, then went to the wells and filled the bucket. He drank thirstily, then topped it up again.

A sound from above made him raise his head. Soldiers were patrolling the wall, right at the top of the second section, some thirty feet above his head. Dusk was coming on. "Anything to see?"

The soldier looked down. "Nothing much. They're keeping to their side of the Plain for now."

Their side of the Plain. This morning it had been owned by Troy, just as much as Bramble Hill or the Chiblak valley. Tonight the Argives held it. Hector had said the quickest way to victory was simply to throw the Argives back into the sea, and it hadn't happened. There had been too many, and now the call was going out to Trojan clients and allies across Anatolia. There would be another battle, a bigger one this time, and when it came as many of the Trojans as possible would be armed with iron.

Phereclus walked back to the forge, carrying the full pail of water. Anyone working in the heat of the smithy dehydrated fast, and needed a constant supply of clean water to drink. Washing wasn't much use, once the charcoal and ash had been ground deep into the skin. All they did was rinse their faces and wait for the end of the day before reaching for the soap. Building ships was hard work, and dirty, but Phereclus had never been this filthy.

Mursili was waiting when he got back. The ironsmith dipped a clay cup in the water and drained it in two gulps, refilled it and downed half of it again. When he wiped sweat from his brow he left black streaks behind. "Thank you. I'm always thirsty these days."

"That's because you hardly leave the foundry," Phereclus replied. "Everyone must rest, my friend."

The Hittite shrugged. "I can rest when the Argives are gone."

He passed the cup over and Phereclus drank. Perspiration had popped out on Mursili's face again, and more trickled behind his ears. The long chiton he wore was stained with it. Usually at work he wore a leather apron over the top, which protected most of his body from burns but did make him sweat like a blown horse. Phereclus passed the cup back.

"Do you regret coming here?" Mursili asked. "To Troy?"

Phereclus' lips quirked. "Ask me again after the war. You?"

"Hattusa is going to fall," Mursili said. "Everyone there knew it even before I left. We've lost too many battles, too quickly. I've traded a doomed city for one under threat, that's all." He drank again and added, "But Troy shouldn't look for aid from the Hittites."

His Luwian had improved enormously in the past few months. Phereclus remembered when Mursili first came to Troy, and communicated mostly by sign language and eruptions of bad temper. His accent was too strong for him ever to be mistaken for a native, but he was fluent enough to be understood even through the ring of hammers and the constant rumble of the furnace.

He had overcome his discomfort with tall women, too. The two men had attended the same reed houses, on several memorable nights. It was a pity they were working too hard to spare the time anymore.

"The battle at Sinjar will finish us," Mursili said. "The Hittites, I mean. We lost thousands of the Golden Spears and more than half the chariots. It would take a generation to replace them and Assyria won't grant us the time. Their army will be back, and Hattusa will burn like from wall to wall."

"So you're glad you came?"

"By all the gods, yes," Mursili said. "Since my childhood I've seen nothing but Hattusa, and then only one part of it. The quarter filled with smiths and tanners and masons, all jammed in together so their noise and stink doesn't disturb the rest of the city. Coming to Troy was an adventure. And there is a glory, a beauty, in this city. Don't you think?"

"A grandeur," Phereclus said, without thinking.

"A grandeur," Mursili agreed. "You see? We believe the same. Troy is worth fighting for."

73

"But we aren't fighting," Phereclus said. "Men died on the beach today. We stayed here, where it's safe."

The little man nodded. "We stayed here, but we fought. With every blade we make, we fight. Hector wants to arm the Apollonians with iron swords, did I tell you that? A whole company given my blades. Imagine what they will do to the Argives when that day comes."

The Apollonians were the best of the soldiers of Troy. The other companies denied it, pointing to their own claims to glory, accumulated over the years like polish on a shield. But it was the Apollonians whom other armies feared, and it was they who Trojan boys dreamed of joining, when they grew old enough to wear the white and gold lacquer on their armour.

Phereclus thought of them equipped with iron swords slung on their backs. They would meet the Argives with spears first, the way soldiers always did, and as the battle developed those spears would be broken, one by one. The two sides would find themselves fighting with blades. And then the Apollonians would chop through their enemies like a wind through leaves. The Argives wouldn't suspect it at first, would not think the struggle could turn so quickly. When it happened they might panic. Phereclus had seen enough sudden terror in sailors to know how quickly it could happen when the wind was howling. Or when it changed.

And the Apollonians would have Hector at their head. The hero of Emar, veteran of Kantassa, a man feared across the known world. A man who knew the damage iron could do, and how best to inflict it. Which he would do. There was a hardness about captains of men, a detachment that allowed them to make choices that sent men screaming to their deaths.

Phereclus didn't want to be part of this war. He wanted to build ships; that was all he'd dreamed of, since he was a small boy. Ships to sail to faraway ports, load their holds with exotic cargoes and strange spices, and then sail home with tales of wonders seen and miracles performed. He wasn't a fighting man, but that was what Troy needed now. Not new swords, as much as more men to wield the old ones, and kill with them.

He owed something to this city. He would pay the debt as best he could, and try not to moan at the Fate that chose him.

"If we fight by making blades," he said to his friend, "then let's set about making them."

74

*

Scamander's braids gleamed in the setting sun, sending arrows of light into Periso's eyes were he stood on the tower. On the west bank the Plain of Troy was eerily still. No wild horses roamed the grass, or stood in sleepy herds as they waited for darkness. Many had been gathered to the east side of the river, behind the fords with their defences of walls and earthen banks. The rest had been sent further afield, to Mount Ida or east to Tereia. In normal times that town wouldn't be considered a safe place to corral the most expensive horses in the world. Now it was the safest place they could find.

Night came.

Dark fell first on the Plain, sweeping across it from sea to river and beyond. Briefly the tops of the willow and tamarisk along the Scamander remained lit and then they dimmed too. The towers above the Scaean Gate were still bright though, bathing in the red light of late evening as Ipirru drove his sun-chariot down behind the Ocean in the west. It was a sight Periso never tired of. He leaned over the wall to watch the line of darkness advance up the masonry, rushing higher until it fell over him and the day was gone.

"Stop hanging your arse out like that," Hyrca said. "One of these days you'll tip right over, if an Argive doesn't shoot you first."

"The Argives are all over by the beach," he replied.

"You don't think they might have sneaked an archer or two close to the wall? Just for a look?"

Periso considered that, and then stepped back onto the parapet. Hyrca gave a snort of amusement.

Behind them the stables were settling down. They were full of horses too, these ones trained and calmer than the wild *tarpans* now grazing on unfamiliar pastures to east and south. They had seen a lot of work today though, smelled a lot of blood, and they were only now growing calm. Almost all those horses had come back to the city through the gate where Hyrca and Periso stood watch, the Horse Gate as people usually called it. They would go out again the same way, when the time came to challenge the Argives again.

75

Those Argives were building a camp across the Plain, using wood from the Trojans' own defences to make a wall. Now as night came down lights began to gleam from Cradle Bay, dozens of campfires visible through gaps between the dunes. Sometimes the light breeze shifted to an easterly and Periso could hear the sound of hammers, or of faint laughter. It made him sick with fear and tremble with hate, both at once.

That is our land, he thought as he stared at the fires through the miles between. *Our sand and soil, and we will take it back from you, however mighty you think you are.*

"We'll be part of the fighting, next time," he said. They hadn't been today, he and Hyrca. They had driven their chariots to cover the retreat from the beach against a pursuit that never came, and neither had seen an arrow fired at them or a spear thrown. Periso had veered all day between relief and disappointment. It was only now, hours later, that he was calm enough to understand that today had been a good day.

He was still alive.

"We'll be in the midst of it," Hyrca agreed. "With Apollonians in the back of our chariots, I don't doubt."

That was almost certainly true. It was the Apollonians who spent most time practising with the charioteers, honing their skills of balancing and bracing while also casting spears, and all as the cars were driven at speed. Soldiers and drivers rarely worked together for long, so they were used to accommodating different partners and never grew too comfortable. Casualties were low among drivers but high among the fighters, and chariots themselves were often damaged beyond repair. A new car never felt the same as the old, to charioteer or passenger. Men had to be able to adjust straight away.

Hector was the exception, as he so often was. He and Heptolamus had been a team for years. But then, the normal rules didn't apply to Hector. You took him on his own terms, and trusted in his skill to bring you through.

Periso did trust him. When the counter attack came he would drive alongside the prince, part of the assault on the Argive camp that would break them and hurl them back into the sea on flaming ships. Chariots didn't work well on sand, and the Greeks were building a wall around their tents, but that was all right. Hector would find a way.

He stared at the firefly lights and listened to the sound of hammers, all night long.

Chapter Nine

A Shadow at the Fire

"We will take his body home," Thrasymedes said. "Bury him in the gardens of the palace he built. My father's shade will like that."

His father's shade was beyond caring now, walking the road to the black river of the Styx, beyond which all the souls of dead men dwelt in Hades. The Fields of Tartarus for the cruel, amid endless punishment; or the Asphodel Fields for those whose good and evil balanced out. Only the very best, the virtuous and indisputably good, were granted a place in the paradise of the Orchards of Elysium. That was where Nestor should be, if there was any justice. If the promises of the gods meant anything more than the sigh of wind.

The first man ashore shall ascend to immortality, and dine with the gods on Olympian ambrosia, Calchas had promised, back in Aulis. It would be pleasant to believe that, to picture Nestor drinking at Zeus' right hand, but Odysseus couldn't make himself believe it.

He'd come through the battle for the beach only to find himself numb at the end of it, like an amphora drained of wine and now empty, useless. Nestor was dead. Odysseus had thought of him as a father, which was hard on poor Laertes who'd actually sired him. But there it was; nobody could control what the heart chose. He was grieving for a father now, by any measure that made sense, even though he had no right to.

Thrasymedes was Nestor's true son. And the young man was king of Messenia now, on this second evening of the war. He looked startlingly like Nestor had, before age greyed his hair and etched wrinkles in his skin: taller perhaps, but with the same curly brown hair and big eyes that made women swoon. He was almost as good a charioteer too. But he wasn't as clever, or as shrewd, and not only because he lacked the years for wisdom to accumulate. It was easy to look at him and see not what he was, which was considerable, but only what he was not.

"I expect it will," Odysseus said. They were sitting around a campfire and he kept his eyes on the flames. He was afraid that if he met Thrasymedes' gaze the younger man would see his true thoughts, and he couldn't bear that.

78

"He's sharing a table now on Olympus," Menestheus said in his slow voice. "Eating with the gods... and deservedly so."

That was the prophecy again. Well, perhaps it was true after all. Certainly the first man ashore had been killed, just as Calchas had promised. The Greeks had won their victory on the beach of Troy as well, as foretold, and the two evenings since had seen hordes of bulls and rams sacrificed to Raging Ares in thanks. Odysseus could smell burned meat and wine in the air, over the tang of the sea, but it stirred no appetite. He'd eaten, but since landing food tasted dry, like the black ashes of a priest's fire.

The sorrow of the other kings had been obvious when they gathered in the rainbow-pattered pavilion before Agamemnon's ship, the day after the battle. Several had come to Odysseus to offer condolences, including some he wouldn't have thought would do so. Schedius, Leitus of Boeotia, even the newly-arrived Idomeneus, swaggering and cocksure now he'd secured his marriage into the Atreide line. Odysseus had answered with thanks and toasts, taking only small sips of wine for fear that more would make him maudlin. He thought a number of the kings felt the same way. Nestor had been a friend and councillor, and a second father, to many of them.

There had been much less grief for Telamon, and if it hadn't been for great Ajax glowering around the room on the edge of fury, the kings might not have shown any at all.

"He was a true Greek," Agamemnon had said at one point, speaking in the dead man's memory. "A warrior in his day, worthy to sail with Heracles himself, and not be forgotten beside him."

A warrior in his day. A cleverer man than Ajax might have noted the implication in that phrase, whether the High King had intended it or not. Telamon had not been a warrior for a long time. He'd stayed at home enjoying his notoriety and the pickings of his youth's pillaging, Hesione among them, while he indulged himself with wine and meat and grew so fat he could barely move. It seemed fitting that he should end battered to death in a net, while being lowered to join a battle his own pride and stubbornness had done much to cause.

Odysseus hadn't said that aloud. Ajax was looking for an excuse to start a fight. He'd tried to kill the man who led the Trojans in front of him and failed, even taking a nasty slash to his left arm that now was wrapped in bandages. That would not

79

have improved his temper. Now was not the time to provoke him.

"Who was he?" Odysseus had asked instead. He took care to keep his tone mild. Best pick his words carefully too. "The Trojan, I mean. The one who wounded Teucer."

"Does it matter?" Ajax snapped.

"It might, when we encounter him again. Anyone good enough to survive a clash with you is worth noting."

That had made the big man's chest swell even further than usual, of course. "I heard him called Aeneas."

Not a Trojan but a Dardanian, then. Odysseus knew the name, and a bit more than that besides. Aeneas had married one of Priam's daughters, tying himself and his city tight into the Trojan network. In Anatolia it was marriages which bound cities in alliance, not treaties, just as it was in Greece. There would be no shifting Aeneas, no chance to persuade him to stand aside or step back. Besides, the rumour was that he'd married Creusa for love, just as Odysseus had married Penelope after Aphrodite moved a shining finger and cost him his heart forever. Even with his own experience, Odysseus doubted the story was true. More likely it was Aeneas' friendship with Hector that had led to the match.

Aeneas was reputed to be able to trade blows with Hector and not be crushed in moments. It wasn't likely that Ajax knew that. Not that it made any difference; the giant would still have flung himself at any Trojan captain, just out of hot blood and pride.

Odysseus' mind was still working, taking new information and holding it up to the light, turning it to be examined from every angle possible. He was the thinker, using his brain the way other men used spears. But Nestor was still dead. No amount of thinking could change that.

Ajax had argued for an immediate assault on Troy. He had support from Menelaus, from Agapenor, and from Nireus of Rhodes whose land was so close to the Asian coast. The Trojans had been driven from their own shore and were dismayed now, he said, probably quaking in fear of a Greek attack. They knew the invaders were too strong. They would wait for allies to come and their own confidence to recover, and should be finished now, before either thing had time to happen.

Diomedes had stood up to answer.

80

"I'm forced to wonder," he said, "if your understandable grief has affected your eyesight, Ajax."

The new king of Salamis didn't know what he meant.

"Look out of this pavilion and you'll see Troy," Diomedes said. "Even now, at night. You'll see the hill of Hissarlik and the wall atop it, sprouting towers every few dozen yards. You'll see the battlements that march on either side of the gates. They are the biggest and strongest defences in the world. Do you really intend for us to assail them with only our spears?"

"It must be done," Ajax snarled. "What better time than now?"

He had a point, actually. The Greeks could range around the Plain of Troy for ten years if they chose to, and if they had the stamina for it, and the walls of the city wouldn't be an inch shorter. They couldn't tunnel under because a hole six inches deep anywhere on the plain struck water. They couldn't go through the wall because they had no weapon to pierce it. All they could do was go over, and waiting would make that harder, not easier, when Troy's allies began to arrive.

But Diomedes had a better point. Assault on the wall was madness, and would lead quickly to heavy Greek casualties while leaving the Trojans all but untouched. A few days of it and the Trojans wouldn't need allies; the Greeks would be so diminished that they would be driven easily from their beachhead, and the war would be lost. The number of defenders hardly mattered. Attacking the city was still a quick way to defeat.

That was clear to anyone who could think, and Odysseus' mind continued to analyse and calculate even in the midst of grief. He couldn't stop it, couldn't help seeing what others might miss. Couldn't help speaking, in this mood, seated by the fire. "The war is futile. Troy will not fall."

Words close to treason to the High King. Menestheus looked across the fire and didn't answer.

"You say we should sail away?" Thrasymedes demanded. "With the dust in my father's mouth still fresh? I thought you were his friend."

Odysseus raised his eyes to stare at him. "I was and am. I will keep his memory for all my days, and mourn him just as long. And I'll watch over you as best I can, Thrasymedes, as he once did for me. Even though you speak foolishness when your blood is hot."

The young man hesitated.

"But spilling more Greek blood won't do your father a bit of good." Odysseus gave him no chance to reply. "Nestor is dead, my young friend. Night has filled his eyes. We won't honour his shade by sending thousands more souls to pursue him down the road to the Styx."

"You really think we should go," Menestheus said. He stopped, seemed to chew his words for a long moment. "Speak it softly. Ajax would likely stomp you for suggesting it."

"Pounded by Ajax or pierced by arrows under the Topless Towers of Troy," Odysseus said, "it's still death."

"You know Agamemnon will order the attack."

Odysseus nodded. He did know that. Most of the Greeks had come here for *kleos,* undying glory won it battle, and the spoils of gold and silver that went with it. Kings or common soldiers, they all knew they could go home wealthy and feted, if only they survived. For most men it was a risk worth taking. There were thousands on this beach who would rebel at the idea of turning away now, when the hard work of getting here was done and fame lay within reach.

"You mean to leave anyway," Thrasymedes said. He sounded half awed and half horrified, but he must have at least some of his father's brains, to have understood so quickly. "Agamemnon will never forgive you."

"Agamemnon will be rotting on this beach," Odysseus replied, "or on the Plain of Troy. He planned this expedition with great care, everything from the fleet to supplies, to the number of soldiers each king could bring. He even gave his daughter away to guarantee the ships he needed. But he never considered anything beyond this point, did he? He's brought us to the walls of Troy. Now he doesn't know how to take us over them."

A figure emerged from the darkness around their fire. Odysseus had posted guards, so only friends would be allowed to approach, but he tensed even so. If Agamemnon learned of his intention to sail away there would be very bad trouble, and most of it would fall on Odysseus. But the newcomer was only Thersites, limping round-shouldered over the sand to murmur, "Achilles is here. He's speaking with the High King now."

82

The three kings exchanged glances. Odysseus could read the thoughts in the others' minds; Thrasymedes wondering if this news would change Odysseus' plans, Menestheus dourly sure that it wouldn't. He felt weary to his bones. Far across the sea his son was in his cradle, perhaps asleep, perhaps crying fit to scare the gulls. Penelope was there, trying to run the islands with the king away, and his heart ached for her almost as much as for Telemachus. Odysseus should be there with them, surrounded by love, not huddled on this windswept strand. He'd been lured away by necessity and the realities of power, but it was time to accept a different necessity and go home.

"There's something about that man," Odysseus said when Thersites had retreated. "Something in the eyes that says he knows more than he says. I can't trust a man like that."

Menestheus coughed into his hand. "Do you say so? I know another man *very* like it."

It was too much effort to glare at the man. Besides, he was right: men said the same thing about Odysseus. There was still something not right about Thersites though. He was attached to Menestheus now, more or less, but he still appeared sometimes at other pavilions, reciting his sagas for other kings. He seemed to hear everything first and choose who he told. Such a man could cause a great deal of mischief in a short time if he wished.

Well, it wasn't his problem anymore. Come morning he would give the order for his men to prepare the ships, but carefully, without letting anyone realise what they were about. The last thing they needed was Agamemnon storming down the beach in a rage. Better to slip away an hour before dawn, navigate the crowded bay and be standing out to sea when the sun rose, with too much of a lead to be caught before they came to Ithaca and peace. Agamemnon wouldn't give chase anyway. His men were needed here.

Odysseus could take Nestor's body home at the same time, if Thrasymedes agreed to let him. That would be good. He would lay the body at the prow, so the familiar sea breeze played on Nestor's skin one final time.

Kings and heroes were not supposed to fall at the start of an adventure. Perseus didn't fall when he faced the Gorgon. In the end Theseus might have died an ignoble, hollow sort of death, but before that he'd slain the outlaws of the land and defeated the mighty Minotaur of Crete, throwing down the kingdom.

Odysseus supposed that was why they were heroes. The men who died trying were not remembered.

Nestor would not be. The thought pained Odysseus, the ache sinking deeper into his heart. He needed to be home. He had to be, or else go mad on this Trojan beach, in a war he didn't want to fight.

"Achilles is coming to speak with you," Thersites said. He'd reappeared without Odysseus noticing, and was looking straight at him as he spoke. "And there are rumours that Agamemnon will call an attack on the river defences tomorrow morning."

"What rumours?" Menestheus demanded.

"Word from a man I trust," Thersites answered. He faded into the night again, his lame foot thumping on the sand.

That was why Odysseus didn't trust the man. Important news, delivered in bland words and with no explanation of how he knew. With evasion, even. But never mind that now: the other thing Thersites had said was far more important. Achilles was coming, for some reason Odysseus couldn't fathom. The guards wouldn't stop him, even if he approached with his blade drawn. They were there as much to keep other Greeks away as to keep out Trojans – a sad truth, that – but they would stand aside for Achilles.

The fire had burned down. Odysseus thought he must have dozed, as he mused on the heroes of ancient days. But he was awake now. He threw another log on the fire and sat straighter as footfalls approached.

Even on soft sand Achilles was light on his feet, eerily so. It was like watching a laden wagon that darted like a chariot. In the firelight his blond hair gleamed and his eyes were like a cat's, bright green and shining. He went straight to Thrasymedes and gripped his arm. "I was sorry to hear of your father's loss, my friend. He was one of our best."

"His shade will hear your words," Thrasymedes said. He sounded half strangled with his own awe.

"King of Attica," Achilles said to Menestheus, a formal greeting but not one that could cause insult. Then he turned to Odysseus. For a moment the two men only looked at each other.

"You came to Scyros to persuade me into this war," Achilles said finally. His voice was soft, almost lisping, another disorientation to the senses. "I didn't think your heart was in it, even so. You told me Troy's walls were everything the stories claimed them to be."

He nodded. "I remember."

"Do you remember the man who came with you?"

"Eliade? Of course."

"I'm sorry to bring you these tidings," Achilles said. "He was murdered, my friend. In Halicarnassus, by an agent of Troy named Nashuja. Word reached me on Tenedos yesterday."

The words faded to a buzzing in Odysseus' ears.

Eliade. A friend and companion for a decade, since they were youths together on Ithaca. When Laertes began to send his son to other kings for the summers, to gain experience and friends, Odysseus would return to tell Eliade of all he'd seen. The other boy had gobbled up the stories like sweetmeats, eager to see the palaces and rivers himself one day. Odysseus had promised that he could. The summer after he became king he'd set sail for the east, to trade and explore, and Eliade had captained the ship that took him.

A promise kept, trust repaid. It was how the world worked. You kept the faith with your family, with a few close and carefully chosen friends. As years went by you married your children to theirs, making one family of many, and there were no ties stronger than blood. Marriages made bonds between more than cities. That would have been Eliade's destiny. All gone now, all lost to him.

Nashuja had been trusted too, if not as much. He'd helped with trade deals in the east, been a reliable contact in Halicarnassus since that first summer long ago. And he was a Trojan agent. Not a surprise, in itself, though Odysseus hadn't known of it. Every man had to give his loyalty to someone. But now he'd killed an Ithacan, a known friend of Odysseus himself, and that could not be allowed to pass.

No king could afford to be seen as weak. If Odysseus let this go by the pirates would begin to circle, and rival kings would sniff at Ithaca's margins in the hope of plunder. It was not to be tolerated.

He wasn't going home after all.

"There are rumours," he said, choosing his words, "that we're to attack the Trojan river defences in the morning."

Achilles nodded. "Agamemnon will give the order at dawn. But I will not be there."

85

"What?" Menestheus asked, startled.

"The Myrmidons are to go raiding," Achilles said. "To Pedasos and Lyrnos, first, to reduce Troy's ally cities in the south. My ships are being loaded now." His lips twisted. "I think Agamemnon wants me far from Troy, so when the city falls he can claim the glory for himself."

There was probably some truth in that – quite a lot of it. The strategy made sense though. A few raids, a city or two burned, might be enough to make Troy's allies keep their soldiers at home, fearful they would be next. But sending Achilles was idiocy; he would be needed here, at the heart of the great struggle. Agamemnon had let his pride dominate his sense. Again.

Odysseus pushed that aside and tried not to think about the casual *when the city falls*. "You're wasted on this."

"I know that," Achilles said sullenly. "But as you told me on Scyros, sometimes we must do as the High King orders, however we disagree." He hesitated. "Patroclus is staying here, with my father and fifty Myrmidons. I want eyes I can trust on Agamemnon while I'm away."

"Trust mine," Odysseus said. "I will watch him for you."

Menestheus and Thrasymedes both glanced his way, but neither spoke. They would understand why things had changed. The murder of Eliade was too flagrant an insult for any king to tolerate. Even the lord of little Ithaca.

He thought of little Telemachus, bawling in his crib back home, and thought he felt a scar in his heart grow hard.

Chapter Ten

No Parley

The Greeks assembled next morning.

Isander's company of Elids was among the first through the new wall around Cradle Bay. They marched north, keeping the dunes on their left and the Plain on the right. The air was still and a morning fog hid the world from view: the Bay, the Plain, even Troy itself were gone.

Behind them came more Elids, and then the few companies of Salamis. For all their lack of numbers they were still led by Ajax, and that made them formidable. After that marched Achaeans and Laconians, Euboeans and Atticans, all the mustered splendour of Greece. The line went on and on, soldiers pouring onto the Plain like rising water. Here and there a chariot paced the warriors, each one carrying a captain in a boar's-tusk helmet. Ajax glowered from beneath his; the only other lord Isander recognised was Diomedes, distinctive in his silver armour half a mile back.

Thirty thousand men. It must be the finest army in the world.

The lead unit reached a stake driven into the ground and halted, then turned to face east. Company after company did the same and then they walked across the Plain of Troy towards the city. The fog began to burn off as they moved, and presently Isander saw Troy emerge from the mists like a city of fable, towers and turrets shining in the sun. His mouth was very dry.

The army approached the river Scamander and the earthworks beyond it, and stopped.

A man stepped from the ranks with an olive branch held high above his head, the sign for a truce. Agamemnon wanted to parley. Presently a man with nodding plumes came out from the Trojan side, a sword hilt sticking up above his shoulder from the odd scabbards they used here. He beckoned, and three chariots rolled out from the Greek lines and splashed into the river.

The sun beat down.

*

Menelaus had come to claim her back.

She recognised him in one of the chariots below. There was something in the set of the shoulders, the stance and posture, that told Helen this was her former husband even while the dissipating mist still half concealed him. It was inevitable that he'd be in the delegation; she ought to have realised that. With him was towering Ajax, a huge man who left no room in the car for a charioteer and so drove himself, and a man Helen didn't know. A slim fellow with brown hair. She wondered what he was doing there.

From above the Scaean Gate she could see clearly. The three chariots drove past Bramble Hill and to the ford of the river Chiblak, then on to the bottom of the switchback road that ran up to the Scaean Gate itself. The lords dismounted where Trojans waited for them. Hector, speaking for his father; Paris, shamed into leaving the city; and lastly Aeneas. They watched without moving.

Paris looked frightened, a lamb out of place amidst all those wolves. He was a bloodless sort of man, really, handsome and charming but with nothing beneath the smile and the words. He came to life only in the act of love. But then, a stronger man would never have allowed her to seize the initiative, that day in Sparta when he had come for her. If it had been Hector that day, or Aeneas, she would have found herself trussed hand and foot and carried back to Troy in a sack. With Paris she'd been able to take control. He was weak, a soft man in a hard world. Not the sort of man you'd expect to be a prince.

He was weak, but he was hers, and that had allowed her to escape the prison of her life in Sparta.

She still struggled to believe the Argives had come to take her back. It was madness, an overreaction beyond belief. Enough fog remained over the river to hide their army but she knew it was there, tens of thousands of men arrayed on the Plain ready to attack.

"This isn't my fault," she said, mostly to herself. Andromache gave her a sidelong look but said nothing.

Below her Menelaus removed his helmet and looked up at the city walls, measuring them. Red hair fell untidily over his eyes but he saw her on the wall. He checked for a moment, missing his stride, and Helen thought she saw his nostrils flare in suppressed rage. His fists clenched. Then he jerked his eyes

88

away, but his gait after was stiff and angry as he led the three Greeks to the waiting Trojans and stopped.

"You asked for parley," Hector said mildly. "Speak."

"Will you really risk Troy for one woman?" Menelaus asked. Demanded, really, his voice thick with fury. He might have meant to be diplomatic, but that moment's glimpse of Helen had roused his always-quick temper. "You know how strong Greece is. Troy cannot stand against all our might. We would crush you, take your city as we took your beach, and all for a whore who betrayed her husband and her home."

Hector quirked an eyebrow. "This is a strange way to begin a parley. Don't you have terms to offer?"

"For Helen?" Ajax growled. "The time for terms is past. You Trojans killed my father yesterday."

"Ah, yes," Hector said. "Your father. The abductor and raper of women. The stubborn king who brought war to Troy's beaches not once, but twice. It is twenty years too late for his shade, or his son, to complain that he found death here. It was long overdue."

Ajax snarled, and on the walls bows creaked as the strings were pulled tight. The big man hesitated. After a moment the smaller one, brown-haired and nondescript, put a hand on his arm to calm him.

"You wish terms?" Menelaus asked. "Then hear these. Troy will hand Helen back to me, and also this man," his finger stabbed at Paris, "who stole her from my palace. In addition the city will give half of its treasury to Greece, to compensate for the cost of this army. In future Greek merchants will pay one tenth of current taxes for use of the Trojan Road, and –"

He stopped there, because Aeneas was laughing at him. Ajax's snarl deepened and he took a pace forward, but then stopped as the archers on the wall drew their bows again. He had fought Aeneas on the beach, Helen remembered, each of them wounding the other. They were a contrast, one hulking and furious, the other whipcord slim and laughing out loud. The king of Dardanos wiped an eye with the heel of his hand.

"Forgive me," he said. "But this is a great deal to ask for one woman. Especially one you call a whore. For her you want Troy to prostitute itself to you? I think this is bluster. You haven't come to parley, but to threaten."

"Look at our army," Menelaus said. He swept an arm behind him, to where the soldiers he spoke of were still hidden by fog along the Scamander. "We are able to threaten, if we choose."

"And we to ignore it," Hector said. "My reply is terms of my own. We see your army; do you see our wall? You cannot conquer here. Take your army and leave, and you will live. Troy wants no war with Argives. Return Hesione to us, and we will halve Greek rates on the Trojan Road."

"Hesione is dead," Ajax snapped.

Hector stared at him. "How did she die?"

"We can guess," Aeneas said, before the Greeks could speak. His voice was flat. "Hesione died as the war began. I do not believe in coincidences that large. Telamon killed her, didn't he? To remove any chance of the other kings using her to bargain, I imagine. He saw women as tools right to the end."

The third man turned to study Aeneas. There was a wry half-smile on his lips and suddenly Helen knew who this was; Odysseus, the clever king of Ithaca. The one other kings called *chorikos,* the peasant. She hadn't seen him in a long time, not since he married her cousin Penelope, but she recognised that twist of his mouth. Aeneas noticed him and the two men weighed each other for a moment.

"Is this true?" Hector asked. His voice had gone quiet, as always when he was angry.

Ajax glowered. "She died in bed. She was old."

She had been around forty in fact. Hardly old. Even on the wall Helen could hear that lie.

"Get gone from here," Hector said. "There will be no parley."

"More Trojan arrogance," Menelaus said. He flung out a hand to point directly at Helen. "Give her to me!"

"Come take me!" Helen shouted. She took a step and stood half on the battlement, in full view of the Greeks below. The *Argives,* she reminded herself, people hated here like no others. She heard Andromache hiss in either vexation or concern. Probably the former.

Hector's voice was winter cold. "Get gone or I will have you shot like rabbits. You have nothing to say. Go. Now."

It was Odysseus who moved first. He turned and went back to his chariot without a word; he hadn't spoken once during the exchange, Helen realised. Neither had Paris, though in his case it was probably because all the spit was gone from his mouth.

90

Menelaus and Ajax stayed, glaring at Hector, but the prince made a sign and the archers raised their bows a third time. That was enough. The two big men went back to join Odysseus, turned their chariots, and drove back towards the Chiblak ford. Beyond Scamander Helen could see the Greek soldiers now, wraiths emerging into view as the mist thinned.

She could see the Trojan chariots too, almost a hundred of them drawn up behind a screen of elm and willow south of Bramble Hill, where the three Greek kings couldn't see them. She thought she knew what Hector planned to do.

*

They went along the wall as the Argive kings drove back to their army. Trojan soldiers were lined along the battlements, but not many; most were below, in the earthworks or the forces in reserve. Andromache kept looking west, assuring herself that the battle hadn't been joined, and that Hector was still unhurt. Five steps and a glance, five steps and a glance, all the way past Mursili's smithy and the clear springs inside the wall, past the Sea Gate and the barracks, until she and Helen came to Ilos' Tower by the Pergamos, where Priam sat in a canopied chair and gazed over the plain.

His advisors were grouped around him, Antenor and Ucalegon, Laocoon and even Cassandra, though hardly anyone ever listened to her. Antenor's son Helicaon would be out on the field, one of the unidentifiable men waiting to defend their breastworks against the Argive assault. Antenor looked terribly tense, but then, they all did, though they tried not to show it.

"Other women at last," Hecuba said, from a chair beside her husband's. "I was beginning to feel quite abandoned. Come, children, sit with me."

It rankled to hear Helen referred to as one of Troy's children. But Andromache was as adept at hiding her thoughts as any man – better than most, if the tight eyes around her were any guide. She arranged her skirt and sat on a lower chair to Hecuba's right, leaving Helen to take the seat further along. Precedence allowed her that much.

If Paris fell below then Helen would have nothing. No husband, no home, nowhere to make her welcome. She had made no friends in Troy. The people would likely toss her through the

91

gates to take her chances in the growth-thickened hills east of the city, at the mercy of wolves and whatever nymphs wandered there.

Everything Helen had depended on Paris. How ironic, that she should have thrown away one life and begun another, plunged the world into war, and yet was still reliant for her position on a man.

But then, every woman depended on her husband, even here in the east where there were certain paths to power for women to follow. Wife to a king, priestess to a god. It was a delusion to claim that the Trojan women were any freer than their Argive sisters.

Or a woman could be mother to a prince.

Astyanax was only a few days old. It was a short enough time that Andromache still felt drained and sore, as though every muscle in her body had been beaten with mallets. But her heart swelled whenever she thought of him, and the pain went away, for a time. This was the first time she'd left him alone. Hector needed her to be there to see him fight, needed to know she was watching and praying for him, and so she would be. Perhaps she depended on her man just as much as Helen did on hers – but Hector depended on her too. And Andromache loved Hector too, with a fierce and forceful surge in her heart, and she tightened inside at the thought that he might fall.

The Argive host began to move.

Hector clambered into an earthwork by the western braids of Scamander, overlooking the ford. At this distance Andromache couldn't make out his face, but the white plumes of his helmet were unmistakeable. The Argives would know him by them too, but that couldn't be helped; soldiers needed to see their captain. That was why she could pick out Ajax by his great oblong shield, or Diomedes in his shining silver armour, like a piece of glass glimmering in the dust. Or Agamemnon, clad in a cuirass painted with the colours of a rainbow; he was arrogant, that one, and as proud as a peacock with three hens to dominate.

She could see the companies of Troy, easy to make out in the bright lacquer of their armour. Scamandrians in red and black, Palladians in yellow, and now the green and blue of the Idaians, captained by Pandarus. It hadn't taken the lord of Zeleia long to come to Troy's aid. He had held his own in matches against

Hector, when they were younger men. It would take a good Argive to face Pandarus and survive to tell of it.

There were no Apollonians in the line. She turned her head and saw them, waiting on Scamander's eastern bank, with the chariots from Bramble Hill now streaming between them and into the gap between the river's channels. Earthworks and hills hid them from the Greeks' view.

The Argives entered the furthest channel of the river and missiles began to fall among them. Paris had been given command of the archers and sling men, probably because he was less likely to panic if he was behind the main lines. Most of the arrows and stones rained down near the fords, where the Argives were advancing fastest. Elsewhere they were forced to wade chest-high water, then climb a steep bank past thick lines of trees and undergrowth. She saw several slip and fall in the channel, and imagined them cursing.

Shouts rose now, and the screams of men in pain. Over it boomed Hector's voice, one she thought she would recognise in Hades itself. "Stand, Trojans! Stand! Today we make Ipirru proud!"

The lead Argives smashed into the earthworks. In moments the battle front had disintegrated into a mass of struggling men, Argives fighting to clamber up the earthen slope and Trojans struggling to force them back. The noise was awful, even a mile away. If she looked south Andromache could see Argive units stretching away towards the hills, until they faded into the last of the mist clinging to the river. She supposed there were more beyond that; there always seemed to be more Argives. But they wouldn't matter today. Thymbra town blocked their approach along the eastern side of Scamander. It would fall, if the Trojans lost today, but it would keep their flank secure.

Hector had told her that, last night as they lay waiting for sleep. She prayed he was right.

She prayed for Troy's allies to come soon, as well. Maeonians, Hecuba's people, and Carians from Miletus, so badly scarred by Argive ambition. Her own Cilician folk, from Thebe-under-Plakos, and above all the Hittites from the east, repaying the debt they owed Hector and Troy itself, source of the horses they prized so highly. Horses now crammed into tiny pastures around Bunarbi, or on the slopes of Ida, to keep them safe.

93

"They're breaking through," Ucalegon observed. He'd put the tips of his fingers together as he often did, making a tent over which he spoke. "In the north, and across the upper ford as well."

"At heavy cost," Antenor said.

"They can afford to pay a higher price than we," Ucalegon retorted.

Priam stirred without looking away from the struggle. "He knows that, my friend. Leave it be."

They watched the Trojan line bend inwards, bit by bit.

*

"We can hold!" Aeneas screamed above the noise. "Stand fast! Stand fast, men of Dardanos!"

Not just Dardanians, Troilus thought. Trojans had found themselves mixed up with Aeneas' men now as well, both groups fighting madly to hold the northern ford. There were a lot of Argives pushing against them though. The earthwork had been built to defend from all sides, so if overrun it could still be held amid a sea of enemies, and they'd nearly reached that point now. Argives had lapped around them to the south already.

"We have to withdraw!" he shouted to Aeneas.

The slender man ducked a spear thrust and stabbed in reply, the motion almost too quick to follow. An Argive gurgled and fell back atop comrades climbing behind him, knocking at least one of them over. "No! Stand!"

Troilus grimaced. Hector had given command of this area to Aeneas, so it was no good arguing. Those two knew war better than Troilus ever would, and they both said the same thing; if overrun, a group had a better chance of survival inside the bastions than trying to flee across the Plain. Standing was safer than running, however instinct might scream.

Troilus would have to trust them. He was more at home among horses than he was fighting men.

An Argive spear point skidded on the shoulder of his cuirass and across his upper arm, leaving a wide gash. Troilus hissed and stabbed back, but he was slower than Aeneas and the Argive now clambering over the bulwark ducked under it. He lost his grip on his shield though, and as he scrambled to retrieve it Troilus stabbed him in the thigh. He rolled away, back over the lip of the earthwork into the safety of his attacking comrades.

Most of the horses were gone now. Last year Troilus hadn't even been aware that three Argive kings were in the city until they were ordered to leave, but he noticed the absence of the horses. Oh, he realised that soon enough. The stables were fuller than ever, paradoxically, but the Plain outside was empty. He and Tanith had very little to do.

He supposed he loved her, his sweet Phrygian girl. Sooner or later his mother would find him a wife from one of the lesser cities of the Troas, Pedasos perhaps, or Tereia to the east. It was especially true now Hector was married, and had a son. Lycaon was wed already, to a Hittite princess no less, and even fickle Paris had found himself a wife. Which is what had caused this carnage, of course. Troilus didn't really see how that had been allowed to happen, but it was done now. No use complaining.

Married or not, he would ask Tanith to stay with him. He'd pay his wife the respect she was due, and give her the sons and daughters that would secure her position here in Troy. But when he wanted love he would go to Tanith, the innocent-looking girl who could make him feel and do such things… a man couldn't feel too harshly treated by life, if he knew a woman like her. Was loved by her.

The next Argive over the lip was a bear of a man, not especially tall but thick-bodied with muscle. He turned Troilus' spear thrust but then slipped on the earth and his own spear went wide. Troilus lunged, but the man got his shield up just in time to block.

Pain exploded in Troilus' leg and he collapsed, the limb unable to support him. Blood was pouring over his boot. Someone must have stabbed him in the calf, a cowardly trick he should have expected from the Argives. He swept his spear left to right, warding off anyone who might be coming for him.

"Troilus!" someone shouted. Aeneas.

"Down!" he yelled in reply. The pain was incredible, so great he couldn't see more than blurs. He swept the spear back again. "Here! Here!"

A week ago he had still been helping in the stables. Mucking out mostly, with the stalls all full and many of them holding double. But he didn't mind that. It was a good way to get to know the horses, which ones flicked their ears in irritations, which ones were calm, which kicked their back legs and could

95

kill a man if he wasn't wary. He wished he was still there. His lashing spear struck something and he heard a grunt of pain.

He wished he was with Tanith.

Something stung under his arm. That didn't hurt, oddly, but he knew what it meant. You killed a man by stabbing into the three points armour couldn't cover; groin, throat and the pit of the arm. Troilus had been waving his spear so wildly that the Argives couldn't get to throat or groin, but a spear had found his armpit. He could feel warm blood pouring, a flood of it from a severed vein.

Still no pain, but he couldn't hold the spear anymore. He blinked and the world came into focus. Argives were swarming over the earthen bank, driving the defenders back. Aeneas was shouting something nearby, but Troilus couldn't hear what it was.

There was a Greek standing over him. A young man, hardly more than a boy in fact, but he held a sword. That was all that mattered. Troilus tried to speak and couldn't.

The sword came down, to the throat this time. Troilus didn't feel it enter.

Chapter Eleven

The Chariots

Isander pulled the sword out, panting. Around him other Greeks pushed forward, clearing the bank. Gorka got up and came to stand beside him, joined a moment later by Nikos.

"Looks like he was an important man," Nikos said.

That was true. The dead Trojan's armour was very well made, layers of hardened leather painted over the top with blue and gold lacquer. Those were the colours of Troy itself, not just one of the soldiers' companies. Isander wondered who it was and decided it didn't matter.

"I claim this man's armour and gear," he said, raising his voice. His hands had been trembling all day but now there was a lull they were steady, and his tone was too. "Does anyone dispute my right?"

Several of the men glanced across, but none spoke. Gorka shifted his feet. "I nearly had him myself."

"Doesn't matter," a gruff voice said behind them. "The killing stroke was Isander's. The armour is his."

Thalpius came to stand over the dead man. The king of Elis was spattered with blood and dirt, and there was a deep dent in the top of his helmet. It didn't seem to bother him. "You know what those colours mean, lad?"

"Troy's royal house," Nikos said, before Isander could speak.

"Only the house of Priam is allowed to wear them," Thalpius said. Always gruff, tiredness had given his voice a rasp like a dozen wasps. "This must be a prince. Not Hector, or Paris. Maybe Troilus. Whoever it is, Priam will pay a big bounty to have his body returned." He turned a squint on Isander. "Well done, lad. You won your *kleos* here today."

He beckoned for servants to come and bear the body away. Isander watched and stood a little straighter, without really meaning to. Every soldier who had come to Troy did so dreaming of *kleos*, fame and glory won in battle that would last long beyond death. Almost none would win it. They would be killed instead, or at best would hack and hammer their way to survival, but go home as poor as they had started. But a god somewhere had smiled on Isander. Now even his king knew his name, and approved of him.

He would go home wealthy, and with a measure of fame. If he went home at all. There was still fighting to be done.

"You lucky dog," Axylus said, not unkindly. "I hope you're still humble enough to eat with us ordinary –"

He broke off, wheeling as a group of Trojans came storming across the earthwork, holding together in a mass as they drove towards the men now gathering the prince's body. Thalpius gave a loud war shout and leapt to meet them, his best troops closing around him. Isander whooped and threw himself forward.

The two forces crashed into each other without slowing. Shields clanged and men went staggering back, rocked by the force of the impact. Gorka smashed a man flat on his back and rammed his spear through the Trojan's belly, where his armour had broken away. The man shrieked like a dying turkey. Isander exchanged blows with a large man who drove him back, his spear hitting Isander's shield again and again, like a mallet pounding wood. Nikos tried to help but another Trojan engaged him from the right. The Elids were pushed back.

"Hold!" Thalpius screamed over the din. It was almost certainly what the Trojan captains had been crying, in the first moments of the battle. Isander didn't have time to appreciate the irony. "Hold your ground!"

A man emerged from the Trojan lines, wearing a cuirass lacquered in green down each side. Down to using his sword now, Gorka swung but the man ducked under the blow, incredibly fast, and getting his shoulder behind his shield he rammed into Gorka and sent him tumbling. Isander stared in shock; he hadn't thought even Ajax was big enough to throw Gorka aside like that. Certainly this slender man shouldn't be. But then Thalpius was turning, the green-armoured man snaking in to strike at him, and Isander screamed as he redoubled his efforts. The Trojan he was facing snarled and gave ground.

Thalpius stabbed at the Trojan captain, missed. The other man's spear licked out rapidly, twice, striking the top of the king's shield and then his already-dented helmet. Thalpius twisted, changing the angle.

Isander's desperate attack struck flesh – not a killing blow this time, but a deep wound to the arm. The Trojan backed away quickly, leaving Isander to turn towards his king. He took a step towards him.

Thalpius' spear found the Trojan's shoulder, but the cuirass held. Then the slim man shifted his weight forward and stabbed the king in the side of the neck and in the armpit, the two blows very fast. Thalpius stumbled. Isander screamed and threw his spear, but he wasn't set properly and it flew wide.

The green-striped Trojan rammed his spear into Thalpius' mouth. The point clanged as it struck the back of his helmet and he fell.

Isander realised he was screaming. He hurled himself forward, trying to draw his sword and strike in the same motion, and instead struck the king-killer with his shoulder. They were both knocked over, falling apart and scrambling up, the Trojan with grace and Isander more clumsily. He managed to get his shield up to absorb a ringing blow but the Trojan was already looking around, gauging the battle. He began to back away, calling out in his own tongue, and the Trojan force retreated with him.

"Ajax," Gorka said, gasping.

Standing, Isander saw the new king of Salamis approaching, some two hundred soldiers at his back. Enough to have overwhelmed the green-armoured man and his Trojans. Isander looked for the killer and couldn't find him, though he couldn't have gone far; men milled everywhere he looked, some fighting on the earthworks and some beyond, on the Plain between the river's branches. He realised he was panting for air.

"Where's Thalpius?" Ajax demanded as he arrived. "What –" His eyes fell on the dead king, and all the briskness went out of him. "Oh, but this is a heavy loss. Who killed him?"

"Don't know," Isander said. "A man with green stripes on his armour."

"Aeneas," Ajax snarled. "He and I swapped wounds on the beach." He lifted his left arm a little, as though to display the bandage on the bicep. "He wounded Teucer too."

"I've promised to give him better next time," the fair-haired man next to Ajax said. He carried his shield awkwardly, a little higher than was normal, and looking closer Isander saw that his left shoulder was heavily strapped under his cuirass. The wound Aeneas had dealt him must be serious. Isander wondered why the younger son of Telamon was back in the fighting so soon, and then realised; it was because of his mother. He was Hesione's son too, must have grown up hearing sneers about his Trojan

99

blood. This war was his chance to prove he was as good a Greek as anyone.

Aeneas must like that strike to a man's left shoulder. Ajax and Teucer both bore wounds from it, and Thalpius had taken a blow to the top of his shield on the same side. Isander decided to remember that, in case he found himself close to the Dardanian again.

"Give my body to the dogs if you don't," Ajax said, and the brothers exchanged grins like children.

Isander had won glory that would last all the days of his life, and more; then he'd seen his king cut down just yards from where he stood. He had a point to make on this Plain as well. His hands had begun to shake again but this time it was from anger. He wanted to find Aeneas and cut his throat, chop his dead body into pieces and throw them in the river for the turtles and fish to eat. The small voice that whispered he was no match for the Dardanian could be ignored. There was too much heat in his brain for him to listen.

"Who commands now?" Ajax asked.

Socus pushed through the ranks of Elids, his armour filthy with dirt and splashed blood. "I do."

"You claim the kingship?" Ajax said, eying him.

"I claim command in battle," Socus answered. "Only that. Kingship, we can sort out later."

"Then you'll accept my command?"

"For today," Socus said.

The huge man nodded. "Good enough. Then let's go down to that Plain and make them pay a price for a dead king."

Isander bent to pick up an intact spear from among the dead. It was lighter than his own but it would do. There were Trojans to kill.

*

Ajax paused before descending from the breastwork. He surveyed the battle lines to the south, eyes squinting against the sunshine. The morning's mist had burned away completely now and already the day was getting hot. If the fighting went on for long it would be torture.

"Diomedes has taken the other ford," Ajax said after a moment. "And I think that's Idomeneus who's got across as well,

100

down towards that poxy village. The man's a gorgon-faced pig, but he can fight, I'll grant him that."

Isander had spent the past few days hating the king of Crete, as most men in the army had. Idomeneus had demanded a price for joining the fleet – the High King's daughter in marriage, no less – had been given it, and then spent days with her while the first wave of ships sailed. Nights too, no doubt, when Greeks were dying. When he did arrive Idomeneus had swaggered around the camp as though he was the king of it all, and Agamemnon just a lesser lord who bowed to his will whenever Idomeneus crooked a finger.

He couldn't hate him now. Idomeneus was a Greek, and that made him a friend in Isander's mind.

"Come on," Teucer said. He pointed with his spear. "The lead companies are halfway to the other branch of the river. If we don't hurry all the good Trojans will be taken."

It was true, Isander saw. Some Elid companies were down there, mixed with other Greeks, all chasing the fleeing Trojans towards a thick line of trees and rushes which marked the eastern braid of Scamander. He started down the side of the earthwork without waiting for orders. Gorka and Nikos came with him, and surprisingly Axylus too, which brought the rest of the group down in their wake. Ajax clapped Isander on the shoulder when he caught up, smiling so that all his teeth showed.

Half a mile south of them there was another breach in the Trojan line, just above the point where the river divided into two streams. The Plain of Troy was too wet for much dust to rise when men struggled, and Isander could clearly see the gleam of Diomedes' silver armour. The king of Argolis had attacked the other ford and had obviously taken it, driving the Trojans back across the grasses in disarray. Between the two Greek breakthroughs the defenders were still in their breastworks though, still fighting to hold the line of the river.

"Shouldn't they be running?" he asked.

Gorka spat, puffing. "Let them stand and die."

"No, he's right," Nikos said. He raised his voice. "Captain Socus! Why aren't the Trojans leaving their positions?"

The new lord of Elis – the king, as like as not – slowed to look, shading his eyes. Ajax did the same. They were down on the Plain by then, their line of sight not as good as before, but they could see men fighting on the high earthworks easily

101

enough. Isander's brows contracted. The Trojans weren't even *trying* to escape to the city.

"Fools," Ajax snorted. "Ignore them."

"They expect to hold their positions," Isander said. He spoke without thinking, and was immediately aware that everyone had turned to stare at him. The day before he might have quailed under their eyes; an hour before, he might have. But he had killed a prince today. He kept his back straight and said, "The Trojans are planning something. They must be."

"Against thirty thousand Greeks?" Teucer said. "I don't believe –"

He broke off and they all turned once more, as one this time, to the sound of horns east of them.

The pursuing Greeks had come to an abrupt halt. Ahead of them hundreds of men had emerged from the reeds, Trojans in white and gold lacquer trotting in small groups. Isander counted quickly and made the units twenty shields wide and perhaps five deep, a hundred men each, and he could see twelve, perhaps fifteen of them. Apollonians. The best troops Troy had.

Between them were ranged chariots, and he felt his mouth go dry.

Scores of chariots, with three horses to pull each. It was an insane waste of good animals, something unthinkable in Greece or even Egypt, where quality horseflesh was so precious. In Troy it was plentiful; everyone knew the stories of the Trojan horses. They emerged from the trees and patches of rushes, pouring onto the Plain like wine from a spilled amphora. Isander swallowed hard.

"Bind my tongue…" Ajax said.

A single man was running across the grass towards the chariot, well ahead of even the most advanced Greek. With a cold shock Isander saw the white plumes nodding from his helmet and knew him; Hector. In all the planning of this war two things had come up over and again, two prospects which terrified the Greeks beyond all reason. Hector, and the chariots.

Both were here, and Isander was heading right into their teeth. He swallowed again and grinned at the men around him.

I killed a prince today.

"Are you going to let them slaughter our men?" he asked. With that he started to walk again, briskly but not running, giving himself time to catch his breath. He'd hardly gone ten steps

102

before a shadow fell over him and mighty Ajax's hand fell on his shoulder, for the second time in a few moments.

"Lad," the huge man said, "you have the heart to make a man of legends. Ares' teeth, but you do!"

Nikos looked as proud as a cockerel, and even Gorka managed a smile. They were all there, every man of the mixed company – Teucer, Axylus, even Socus himself – following young Isander the farm boy into the face of the storm. It was ridiculous, when you thought of it that way. He slowed his pace and gestured ahead of himself.

"Maybe I do, but you already have your legends," he said. "I'd be honoured to follow you into battle, lord Ajax."

The right thing to say, and to the right man. Ajax grinned and hefted his spear above his head, holding it sideways like the head of a hammer. "Into lines, my boys! Let's break some Trojan chariots!"

The men shouted agreement, hurrying to form tight ranks, as the screams ahead of them began.

*

The kid had courage, got to give him that. He must have a bit of skill too if he'd killed a Trojan prince – that, or luck, which was nearly as important. If he lived through the next couple of hours he might become someone of note. Someone to fear, even.

Not that Ajax feared anyone. Diomedes and Achilles each thought they were the best warrior in Greece, but Ajax stood in their company and was not overshadowed. Certainly he wasn't afraid of them, or of the Trojan lickspittle who'd wounded him the other day, Aeneas. Ajax had given as good as he got in that exchange. Let Aeneas fear meeting Ajax again, not the other way around. The bastard had killed Thalpius today, which was all he would be allowed.

Enough of such thoughts. Better concentrate on what was in front of him now. Ajax spared a glance for his brother, checking that Teucer was there beside him and he was all right. Shouldn't be in the battle at all really, with his shoulder bruised to Hades and back from his clash with Aeneas at the beach. But then, Ajax ought to be resting as well; his shield arm protested every time he lifted it, and that would only get worse. There were a lot of bruised and injured men in the fight today. Best leave well alone, and say nothing.

Teucer grinned at him, his fair hair flowing out from under his helmet. His mother's hair, and his mother's blue eyes beneath it. Trojan looks. There had been men who called Teucer a foreigner, until Ajax taught them better. He was seven years the elder, but he could hardly remember a time when Teucer hadn't been there, a pace to the side, running to keep up with his enormous brother. Or a time when Ajax had not waited so Teucer could keep up.

Enough, he thought for a second time. He focused his attention on what was happening ahead.

There were too many bodies in the way to see clearly, but it was obvious the Greeks were getting the worst of it. Ajax could hear the rattle of chariot wheels, and now and then caught a glimpse of one flying from right to left, men standing in the cars with spears in their hands. The Greeks were trying to form lines again, to reshape companies broken down by fighting and the hurried chase across the island between river channels. But they were hampered by missiles that began to fall among them again, from new Trojan positions at the eastern branch of Scamander. A captain in a plumed helmet stood among them, shading his eyes as he gazed towards the fighting.

A man near the front took a sling stone to his temple and collapsed, his head twisted halfway around.

"Slow to walk!" Ajax called. As he did so he heard another voice, this one booming over the battlefield like the cry of an eagle among sparrows. He didn't understand the words – they were in the liquid Trojan language – but he recognised the tone of a leader exhorting his men. And he knew who that thunderous voice belonged to. Hector was here.

It wasn't only the young lad who could kill a prince. And if Ajax killed Hector, *then* let Diomedes and Achilles bicker, because every man would know which of them was the greatest warrior in Greece.

The soldiers were still trying to organise their lines. Ajax saw a flash of white and gold and then the first of the Apollonians struck, their shields locked into a solid wall of wood and leather. Greeks were thrown back by the force of the impact, actually flung into the air to land atop their comrades, knocking more men off their feet. Trojan spears darted and stabbed. Another company of Apollonians smashed in, then a third. And the Greeks were running, some men throwing aside their spears and shields, voices raised in please for the gods to spare them. Ajax's lip curled in contempt.

They were twenty yards from the fighting. Ajax began to trot again, then levelled his spear and ran forward.

The men behind him followed smoothly, as though trained for it. They'd never worked together before, were from different kingdoms even, but they behaved the way brave Greeks should. The nearest Apollonian captain saw them and shouted orders but it was too late, far too late to respond. Ajax locked shields with the men on either side – he had to stop to do it – and they hammered into the easterners like a thunderbolt from Zeus himself.

Now it was the Trojans who fell. Ajax swung his shield and a man was hurled backwards, crashing into two of his fellows and bringing them down too. Isander bent to thrust his spear through the belly of the first; Ajax himself finished the second with a stamp on the man's windpipe. The Apollonians fell back, their neat ranks crumpled and bent awry.

A spear darted at Ajax and he broke it between his own shaft and his shield. For a moment the point was near his face and he stared at it in surprise. The metal was silvery grey, not the familiar bronze. That meant –

"Iron!" someone shouted nearby. "They have iron!"

"Stand!" Ajax shouted. Panic could take hold quickly here. "They're still just spear points!"

The Trojan opposite him grinned and drew a sword. That was iron too, longer than a bronze sword, and the spine of the blade was thicker. That might make it heavier than bronze, and slower. Ajax lunged quickly, but the Apollonian chopped the head off his spear with a single blow and then rang his sword against Ajax's oblong shield. The bronze rim shivered and he heard it crack.

His father had given him this shield. These weak easterners had killed Telamon with arrows, like cowards.

Roaring, Ajax pulled out his own sword and attacked. The Trojan parried his first blow and on the second Ajax's bronze blade was sheared right through, four inches above the grip. But he didn't stop. He shoved his damaged shield into his enemy and then thrust the jagged stump of his sword straight into the man's face, as hard as he could. Bone crunched and the man's arms went wide as he fell, the broken blade still sticking up from his mouth until he hit the ground and it was knocked loose.

"We need to stop this right now," Ajax said. He scooped another spear off the ground. "Are you with me, lad?"

Isander was very white, beneath the spattering of dirt and blood that adorned most of the men now. He nodded though. The youth's two friends were still there as well, and Axylus, the big man streaming with blood. It ran on either side of the twisted white scar on his arm, making a grotesque pattern. Teucer leaned to drive his spear through a prone man's chest and straightened to nod.

More Greeks were fleeing in terror, and the Apollonians still churned their way forward through piles of the dead. Other Greek companies were trying to join the struggle, but they were kept at bay by archers and the racing Trojan chariots. Whenever a unit tried to approach it found itself flanked by the drivers, with spears thrown at exposed flanks. They had to stop, turn to deal with the new threat, and so they opened themselves up to the archers again. If it went on like this the Greeks would break soon enough. Ajax would not let that happen.

"You five come with me," he ordered. They did so, hurrying south towards the empty space where the chariots ran, and as they went Ajax explained what he wanted to happen.

Chapter Twelve

Sorrows

The chariot swooped down on the little group of men, swung around and slowed almost to a halt. Hector leaned out to snag a bunch of spears from one of the men, five shafts held together with a leather strap. He broke it and began to slide the spears into sheaths in the wall of the car.

"Horses are tiring," Heptolamus said. He was kneeling in the front of the chariot, hidden almost completely from view. It made him very hard to hit. "Two more runs and they'll be done."

"Good enough," Hector said. There were plenty more horses waiting east of Scamander, fresh ones. Every Trojan chariot would be able to fight until the soldiers couldn't throw anymore.

He didn't think it would come to that. The Greek breakthroughs were being torn apart, both here and further south. Apollonians armed with Mursili's iron weapons were tearing them to shreds. The new spear points sliced through Argive cuirasses as though they were paper, and the swords were even better. Hector had seen tough leather shields cut clean in half with one blow. He'd known how good iron was before, of course, from his time fighting for the Hittites in battles on their eastern border. But he hadn't thought Mursili could produce the same quality here in Troy, not for years. The little smith was a magician.

Men might say the same of Hector, when this day was done. His plan had worked just as he hoped, luring the Argives across western Scamander and into the killing ground between streams. Once they were there he'd unleashed the chariots and Apollonians, and now the invaders were being slaughtered. He grinned to himself and tied his helmet back on.

Heptolamus let the horses trot back towards the battle, giving them time to rest. It was further than it had been, the last time Hector came back to collect more spears. The Argives had retreated almost to the base of the earthwork by the ford. One block of them was holding together there, about a thousand men by the look of it, all huddled close together with their shields forming a solid wall. Trojan spears flung from chariots rattled against it and fell away. The Apollonians were forming up again, gathering new spears themselves from the bodies of the fallen, and the gods knew there were enough of them. Heptolamus had to weave his way past clusters of corpses to reach the fighting.

"Get in close," Hector instructed him. "Closer than before. I want to break this stand quickly."

His friend nodded, eyes on the ground as they always were. Ahead of them a small group of Argives edged forward from the mass, crouching so low they almost shuffled on their knees. That meant their shields left no gap for a spear to find. At the front was a rectangular shield, the height of a man at least, and Hector smiled again; he knew who that belonged to. Ajax was here.

Heptolamus had already begun to turn towards them, the chariot picking up speed as he urged the horses on. Hector plucked a spear from its sheath and hefted it, gauging the balance as he spread his feet against the rocking of the car. He braced, one hand on the chariot's rim.

There was no gap between those shields, but Hector's spear was tipped with iron, and his arm was strong.

They were barely ten yards away when he threw. Heptolamus immediately began to pull the horses left, taking them into a circle that would bring them around for another throw. Hector watched his spear fly true, straight into the shield beside Ajax's oblong one. The point burst through the leather and the man behind it twitched once and fell, pierced through the neck.

"Axylus!" someone cried.

By then Ajax was already bursting out of the group. Hector's eyes came back to him as the big man lunged, throwing himself forward with his spear held out in front of him. He was going to try to thrust the shaft through the chariot's wheels, a feat hardly anyone could manage without breaking an arm or several ribs. It ended a man's life as a warrior more often than not – by Ipirru, often it ended the life itself, then or a few days later. But Ajax was trying it. Hector had another spear in his hand but he wasn't going to be ready in time.

Ajax was. He'd timed it superbly. He rammed the spear through the nearside wheel and into the soft earth, then let go just as wood screamed and broken spokes flew.

Hector was airborne by then, throwing himself clear with a shout of warning to Heptolamus. The driver didn't seem to hear him. It might not have mattered if he had. The chariot slewed, horses screaming, and the car first tipped to one side and then hit something and was thrown into the air. It came down in a smash

108

of splintering wood with Heptolamus in the middle of it. Hector heard the crash but didn't see it, as he'd struck the ground with one shoulder and was rolling over his own spear. He felt it snap beneath him and the jagged end struck him hard in the hip, making him grunt. His head banged off the ground as he uncoiled from his roll onto his feet.

He found a man in armour coming straight at him, spear already thrusting to end his life.

But Hector had not won the acclaim of the Hittite king by being easy prey. He was drawing his new iron sword even before he was fully aware of the oncoming Argive, instinct and habit telling him of the danger before his eyes recognised it. He'd held onto his shield and took the man's spear point near the centre, where the bronze struts came together and made it strongest. The Argive snarled under his boar's tusk helmet – a noble, then, or at least a captain – and attacked again.

Hector chopped the head off the spear and cut across hard on the backswing. The blow slashed through the man's cuirass and the flesh beneath, dragging across ribs. Hector pulled it out and thrust, straight through the heart even as the Argive's eyes were still widening from the first blow. He convulsed, seeming to clench around the blade, and then Hector stepped back and the man fell, helmet rolling away from his blond hair.

Blond hair.

"Teucer!" Ajax screamed. He was just regaining his feet. Everything had happened so fast, with no time to think. Hector stared down at Hesione's son in dismay. Pain flared in his hip but he hardly felt it.

A few yards away Heptolamus lay in the wreck of the chariot. He hadn't moved. He never would again.

"Night fill your eyes!" Ajax bellowed. He lifted his great shield and started forward with murder in his eyes – not killing, not honourable combat, but sheer butchery. He was forced to stop almost immediately when a chariot raced by and someone flung a spear that went through the shield and stuck there. Ajax paused, cursing, to drag it back out.

Then the Apollonians were there, a full company of them driving head-on into the Argives. Ajax was forced back to his band of companions and then they were pushed into the larger mass of Greeks, which was hit a moment later by two more Apollonian units. The Argives roared in defiance, but they began to give ground even so. Ajax's swearing rose even above the din. An Apollonian fell to him, then another, but the weight of those iron swords was too much and he gave ground slowly, fighting for every yard.

Hector stared down at Teucer's body. It seemed strange, to have lost Heptolamus and not be grieving for him. Not thinking of him much, really. But this had been Hesione's son, and all that remained of her. Priam had dreamed of seeing him walk in Troy one day, marvelling at the walls and buildings as everyone did. Fate had snatched that hope away. Hector hadn't known him, hadn't realised who he was fighting, but that was the kind of trick the gods played.

"Hector?"

He turned to see Molion approaching. The tough captain had been with Paris in Sparta last summer, when the plan to force the Argives to bargain had begun to go so spectacularly wrong. He didn't look much like a sophisticated traveller now, stained with the blood and grime of battle just as they all were. "What is it?"

"I'm sorry," Molion said. "Troilus was killed by the river. I just heard the news."

Another grief. Troilus had never been a lover of battle, not the way Hector was, and the Argives. He'd given his heart to horses by the time he was old enough to toddle after them; Hector remembered their mother snatching the child out from under the hooves of an unseeing chariot steed when Troilus was about a year and a half old. But whenever he was unwatched Troilus went back to the stables. He was happy hauling water for the troughs, or forking out straw and dung, as long as he was near the horses.

Troilus. The only one of Hector's brothers close enough to his own age and size to play with, when they were young. This war was tearing their hearts to pieces, bit by bit. There wasn't much consolation in knowing that the Argives must be equally riven by sorrow. If the gods were kind – and they were sometimes, just as often as they were cruel or capricious – then soon the invaders would decide the loss was too great, and set sails for their home.

"Arinna will walk with his shade to the underworld," he said. "Did we bring his body back?"

Molion shook his head. "The Argives have it."

He looked down at Teucer again. The young man ought to be buried in Troy, really, as a reminder of what he could have been. He was Trojan as much as Argive, after all. But perhaps it would be better to exchange his corpse for Troilus'. A hard choice for Priam to make.

"Very well," he said. The Argives had withdrawn back over the earthwork now, losing all the ground they'd gained and littering it with their dead as they ran. "I need another chariot, and a driver. There's work to be done yet."

*

"They are breaking," Antenor observed.

Priam nodded. He'd had his chair carried out onto the balcony, so he could sit and look down over the Plain and the Bay and watch the fighting. "Hector said they would."

The Argives still had the advantage of numbers, by more than three to one. Hector said that didn't always matter. Once men were running they stopped caring about numbers, or strategy, and simply fled. The trick was to get them running in the first place and then stay on their heels, like wolves nipping at a cornered stag, so it didn't have the space to remember it could actually kill them.

He had got them running, it seemed. Helen had thought he'd wait until reinforcements had come: Maeonians and Carians from the south, and most of all Hittites from the east. Troy had sent its sons to fight and die for Urhi-Tešub often enough to have earned aid in return. Hector had won glory in those battles far away, places Helen had never heard of and would never see. But she'd heard of Miletos even before Paris had taken her there; memory of the disaster at that city still made Greeks blanch. It reminded them that whatever they took, the Hittite spear battalions could take back.

They had married one of their princesses to Lycaon, a prince of this city. Surely they would come. Surely.

They had sent an ironsmith too, and Mursili had proven a godsend. His iron spear points and blades were what had enabled Hector to plan and spring the trap. Helen had watched the Apollonians roar into Argives already weary from fighting, had seen them slaughter their way through invading companies like butchers chopping sausage. She could scarcely believe the

111

difference iron had made. The island between braids of Scamander was black with fallen bodies. Men moved among them, Trojans with minor wounds seeking out Greeks with more serious ones, and finishing them with the thrust of a spear.

A door opened behind her, then closed again. Helen took no notice at first. Servants were always coming in and out, silent except for the snick of the door. It was Hecuba's sharp glance which alerted her that this was no servant. She looked up just as Andromache did, from rocking her son in his crib, to see Laocoon crossing to the balcony. The tall man was even paler than normal. His head jerked once as he approached, a sign of tension or anger.

Priam had turned in his chair, alerted perhaps by a change in the air behind him. "What is it?"

Laocoon didn't go to him. He was a priest as well as a Seer, and so under the authority of the queen. He bent to whisper in Hecuba's ear. Helen watched her face grow old.

"What?" Priam asked again.

Hecuba turned to look at him. "Oh, my dear. Troilus is dead."

The king only stared at her. Nobody moved except Hecuba, who rose and went to lay a hand on her husband's shoulder. "There's more, and nearly as bad. Teucer was killed as well. Hesione's son."

"But I wanted to speak with him," Priam said. He sounded lost suddenly, a child in a dark and angry world. "I wanted… who killed him?"

"Hector did," Hecuba said. "Without realising who he was, until it was too late."

When Helen was a girl, her brother Castor had come home from training still clad in his armour, helmet still covering much of his face. She hadn't recognised him and had screamed half the palace down. How much harder it might be in battle, to take a moment amid the chaos to pause and let the brain understand what the eyes saw, she couldn't imagine. She was no warrior.

The king and queen were still talking, Laocoon and Antenor close to the chair where Priam sat with his head bowed. Grief in the moment of triumph; an old tale, though no less painful for that. Someone else would be sorrowing now as well. Helen stood and went quietly out of the door. Andromache turned to watch her go but said nothing, for a blessed change.

Helen went down the corridor and a flight of stairs, with a scene of Scamander painted on the walls on each side so she seemed to be walking in the water. Tamarisk and elm, with frogs and turtles half-hidden in the bulrushes, cormorants and geese paddling in the shallows. Two warriors followed her, both of them older men with a padding of fat around their middles. Men who could be spared from the battle, though she'd wager her jewellery that neither was happy about it. Along more corridors, and she emerged from Priam's palace into the wide avenues of the Pergamos, the citadel of Troy.

"A chariot, my lady?" one of the soldiers asked her. She shook her head and kept walking, faster now. Out through the West Gate behind the barracks and into the city itself, then down the main avenue towards the market. She turned off before she reached it, the guards still hurrying to keep pace with her and people noticing now, drawing aside as she passed with many a mutter and pointed finger. Helen didn't need to hear their mutters to know what they said: there goes the foreign queen who brought all this upon us. There walks the cause of it all.

There were few men in the streets, except the aged and the very young. Old men and boys, she thought, remembering a phrase of her father's. The women stood in tight knots, usually clutching their children, for comfort if a husband fell outside the walls. Several were screaming or weeping, those who'd heard bad news already, as Priam had. Most of that came from adjacent streets, out of sight, but Helen passed two sobbing women, one of them hardly more than a child. She wondered if the girl had lost a husband or a father, and supposed it didn't matter.

She stopped by a tavern and turned to face the two guards. "You'll have to help me from here. Where does Tanith live?"

They exchanged a worried glance. "My lady?"

"Troilus' lover. The Phrygian girl." They only stared at her, and Helen stepped forward until they were eye to eye. "You guarded the prince sometimes when he came to her, I'm certain. You know where she lives. Take me there."

The bigger guard took a pace back. "My lady –"

"Show me!"

They showed her. It was a neat little home just east of the springs, half of one of the oval houses the Trojans preferred. The wall was painted with a muscular man strangling an eagle, which Helen remembered was one of the myths of Phrygia, though she couldn't remember the hero's name. The son of some god or other, she thought. She knocked at the door.

It didn't open, but Helen thought she heard soft sounds from inside, as though someone was trying to be quiet. She opened the door and went in.

Tanith was sitting on the floor, her back against the far wall. Her eyes were red but dry; whatever crying she had done was over, at least for now. The gaze she lifted to her visitors was as blank as white wool.

"Helen." Her voice was empty too, drained of emotion. "You killed him, when you brought this war upon us."

She nodded. It was true. She had been deceiving herself, had believed two contradictory things at the same time; that the Greeks would never dare assail Troy for her, and that Menelaus would never let her go. It was the latter that had proved true. More accurately, she suspected, it was Agamemnon who would always hunt her, however many years went by. He had always been the courage his brother lacked, pushing Menelaus on or else taking action on his behalf.

But still, Helen had not for a moment thought the High King would rally the lords of Greece and come to Troy with war. The lesser kings were too fractious. Schedius and Ialmenus could hardly be in the same room without arguing, Leonteus hated Nireus, and everyone in Greece despised Telamon except his sons. But somehow Agamemnon had done it, and at the root of his achievement was the excuse Helen gave him when she abandoned her husband and fled from him.

"I know," she said.

"He was going to marry me," Tanith said. Her face crumpled suddenly and now the tears came, heavy silver drops that rolled down her cheeks and fell into her lap. "We were – going to live – with the horses."

She was sobbing by then, hardly able to speak. Helen crossed the room in two steps and gathered the other woman into her arms. For a moment she thought Tanith would fight, push her away with shrieks and imprecations, but then tension went out of the Phrygian girl and she wept against Helen's shoulder, clinging to her like a child.

She cried for a long time. Privately Helen doubted Troilus would have been allowed to marry the outland woman who'd stolen his heart; Troy needed her princes to marry noble women from other cities, tying them with bonds of family. The loss of Paris from Hecuba's plans was a heavy enough blow already. But Troilus would probably have kept Tanith as his mistress, a favoured lover given a home and moderate wealth, and most likely children as time went by. More than a poor girl had any right to dream of. And it didn't matter, because Troilus was gone, and Tanith had a right to whatever cherished beliefs helped her survive that sorrow.

"You're not alone," Helen said when the tears finally ended. "Not while I'm in Troy. I don't know if you want to stay here, Tanith, but stay or go, I'll make sure you're attended to."

The words sounded cold when spoken aloud. Tanith nodded though, and even murmured something which might have been thanks. Helen would take it as such. She rose and turned back to the door, where her two guards still waited in silence. Beyond them stood what looked like half the street, easily a hundred people, all trying to peer through the doorway without shoving or making a sound. Helen paused in the doorway. In the faces staring back at her she could see no hate, none of the flagrant dislike of before. No affection either, it was true, but perhaps the merest hint of respect.

I will take it as such, she thought grimly.

Rising shouts made her turn, towards the wall from which the cries had come. More townsfolk were lined there, crammed in with the soldiers left on guard. All of them were staring across the Plain towards the Greek camp. The crowd around Helen stirred, and a murmur carried one word back to her.

Fire.

115

Chapter Thirteen

Trojan Fire

"Bring fire!" Hector shouted.

It had come to this. All the martial might of Greece, driven back to the beach like frightened lambs. Agamemnon could barely believe it. There were three of them, four, for every Trojan in the field, yet the triumph of crossing Scamander had turned almost at once into this jostling, riotous panic. And now Hector stood with one hand on the prow of a Greek galley and cried for fire, despite all that the heroes of Greece could do.

It didn't make sense. Agamemnon had heard the words of the Pythia in Delphi, the prophecy she had made that promised him glory. *Troy's fate lies in the hands of the Greeks... Greece's name will ring down the ages, written in letters of fire.* Something like that, anyway. He couldn't remember exactly, and it didn't matter: Troy was supposed to fall. It had been promised.

He spoke a savage, maleficent oath against the gods who tricked men so. Several of the men closest to him paled beneath their helmets and drew a little away from him, as though afraid of a thunderbolt from above that would burn Agamemnon to a crisp where he stood.

It might as well happen, if he lost this battle. In defeat Agamemnon would have no authority, no power as High King. Only the rank, and titles meant nothing to men who ignored them. Kings in their *megarons* would laugh at him over cups of wine, or curse him in the name of all the dead lost in his futile war. All the force of his rule would be lost. Greece would fall back into the endless warring of former days, king set against king with no one to dissuade them, while on Olympus the gods shook their heads at the gullibility of men.

And it would be that way *forever.* There would be no more High Kings, no more slow knitting together into unity. Greece would squabble while Troy rose to greater power; while the Phoenicians spread along the shores of the Greensea and took all the land Greece needed so badly. While Egypt expanded and Crete rose from the ashes of Minos' fall. One day a conquering host would appear on the beaches of Greece, and it would all be traced back to now, to this day and this battle, when the fool Agamemnon had led his people to disaster.

It could not be allowed to happen.

He shouted for his men to form up. They did so without hesitation, an island of calm amid the buffeting mass of men. The Trojans were still pressing forward, men in the white and gold lacquer of the Apollonians at the front with iron in their hands. Greeks screamed and died. Behind the fighting line smoke rose from torches brought forward at Hector's call.

"Push!" Agamemnon ordered.

*

Fleeing men buffeted the outside ranks of Diomedes' company as they rushed by. Many were weaponless, spears and shields flung aside so they could escape more quickly. Some had thrown off their armour too. They shoved and fought each other as they ran, each determined not to be last, in peril of being run through when the chasing Trojans reached them.

They were cowards, and not worth worrying about, so Diomedes didn't. He watched the Apollonians instead, and saw them react to Agamemnon's assault.

They were excellent soldiers. As good as the Myrmidons, probably, and better than any others Greece had to offer. He saw their captains become aware of the advancing Achaeans, then shout orders that Diomedes was too far away to hear over the shattering noise of battle. But the Apollonians heard. Lines that had become ragged reformed, men falling into ranks with their shields locked together. Spears poked through where men still had them, swords where they didn't. Both weapons glinted like tin outside a bronze-smith's forge, but this was not tin.

Everyone knew the advantage iron gave on a battlefield. You only had to look at how jealously the Hittites guarded the secret of its forging, and how their spearmen hacked their way through enemies armed only with bronze. Egyptian and Assyrian armies had spent a century being slaughtered by an enemy with half their own numbers, because Hattusa had iron and they did not. Today the Apollonians had smashed Greek units into fragments, destroyed them like toy ships in a summer storm. But only half of that was due to iron. The rest was simple: good, well-trained men.

117

Agamemnon had courage. Whatever his faults as High King – and by Zeus of the Black Cloud, he had faults – Diomedes had to concede that. The Achaean wedge was driving straight at the heart of the Apollonian companies, Agamemnon right at the front in the ludicrous rainbow armour he was so proud of. He would try to shove the Trojans back, or at least keep them from the ships. And he'd fail. There weren't enough of them to do that.

"Rally!" Diomedes shouted. He was standing partway up a sand dune, so he could see the struggle at the front lines. It meant he could be seen as well, and he thrust his spear above his head to draw attention. "Rally to me, men of Greece! Stand with me!"

His own men were already there, the two hundred of them who had managed to hold together in the mad flight back from the river. Argolids, the best troops in Greece when counted man for man, except the Myrmidons of Thessaly. Diomedes would challenge any man who said different, no matter who he was. Hector if he dared, or even Achilles. But two hundred wasn't enough either. He sucked air into heaving lungs. "Rally, I said! By the crows of Apollo, are you all deaf? Or cowards? Gather to me!"

"Gather!" someone shouted, close beside him. Diomedes saw with surprise that it was Thenelus, his captain, so covered in blood that he was unrecognisable until he spoke. He'd lost his helmet somewhere and a swatch of his black hair had been chopped off, the blow somehow missing his flesh. Diomedes clapped him on the shoulder and got a wolf's toothy grin in return.

"Rally!" he bellowed again.

A galley caught fire with a sudden whoosh of air. It was some way behind the advancing Trojans, beyond Greek help now, but the sight still set Diomedes' mouth into a flat line. Ships were not supposed to burn here on this beach. The seeress in Delphi had promised the Greeks triumph, not disaster. As though to mock him a second ship burst into flame, then a third, both with a heavy *crump* that told him oil had been thrown onto a lit taper. Smoke began to rise from the burning decks.

Agamemnon's company crashed into the Trojans at a run, sheer momentum sending the Apollonians staggering back. Spears darted and jabbed. The men in lacquered armour seemed

118

to hesitate, weary perhaps after so much fighting. A fourth ship blazed up not far from them.

Then a voice rose above the din, crying out in a strange tongue to a god Diomedes knew. Apollo, lord of the sun and the Silver Bow, but known here in the east as Ipirru. That named the owner of the voice as a Trojan, and the volume meant it could only be Hector. The scourge of the Greeks until now, standing in their way at every turn. Diomedes looked but couldn't pick him out, even when he roared more encouragement. The line steadied.

Then another group of Trojans struck from the side, these ones in armour painted green and blue, like dragonfly wings. Agamemnon's troops were barged sideways. Now they had to fight on two sides and they began to give ground, fighting savagely but still being driven slowly south and west, towards the sea.

"Not yet," Diomedes said, mostly to himself.

Men were gathering around him now though. Some were those who'd been running moments ago, perhaps shamed by his example, perhaps realising flight would only result in a greater slaughter. Others came pushing up from the beach behind, soldiers from all the lands of Greece. He knew them by their leaders, if at all; men all looked the same for the most part, especially when covered in blood, sweat and dirt. Prothous struggled through the fleeing mass with about fifty men, and Leitus with twice as many moments later. The little king of Boeotia looked about to spit teeth in rage, but then he usually did, especially if someone mentioned his height. Menestheus of Attica brought a company which must have been through half the torments of Tartarus already, to judge by their split shields and mismatched swords, most of them notched.

"Still not enough," Thenelus said into his ear. Diomedes' own thought, spoken to him before his own tongue could give it voice.

Most Greeks were still fleeing, fighting one another as they struggled to reach their ships. That had to be stopped before they put to sea, and turned Cradle Bay into a wreckage of splintered hulls in their panic. Diomedes could see some kings and captains trying to stem the chaos, far back from the fighting, but without much success. Talking wouldn't halt the flight. Only seeing the Trojans driven back would do that, and Diomedes needed time to gather enough men – but not so much time that ships began to put to sea.

"They gulled us." He spat into the sand. Understanding of what Hector had done had come to Diomedes earlier than to most, but not early enough. "The Trojans lured us in, and when we took the bait they turned and slashed us apart." Hector's plan, he was sure of it. The Trojans had several good captains but Hector towered above them like Zeus above a mortal man. "Hemmed in like this we can't bring our numbers to bear."

Thenelus shrugged. "Then we have to hold them here, until the men from the southern end of the line have time to reach us."

"Troy won't fall if all we can do is hold them off," Diomedes said.

A roar to the side brought his eyes around. At the foot of the dune a large company of Greeks rushed by, heading straight towards Agamemnon's beleaguered force. "Who is –"

"Agapenor," Thenelus supplied. "Agamemnon's pet. He won't stand by while the High King fights."

Trojans appeared on the dune ahead of the Arcadian king, forty of fifty of them. Too few to present much of a threat in combat. But they didn't try to engage, instead raining a sudden shower of arrows down on the Greeks from above. Dozens of men fell before they realised the danger. Then the company split, half going up the dune towards their attackers and the rest continuing straight on, Agapenor in his boar's tusk helmet yelling useless orders for the rest of his men to come back.

Two Trojan units in red and black armour crashed into them. The Greek front ranks were actually driven up in the air, men lifted and thrown onto those following them in, and Agapenor's assault disintegrated. Diomedes saw the king slashing with his sword, keeping three Trojans at bay until the line around him collapsed and he was left alone among enemies. He jerked suddenly and fell out of sight. Diomedes cursed horribly.

"Rally!" he bellowed again, doing his best to imitate Hector's godlike shout, and then Thenelus touched his arm and pointed.

Ajax was coming. The giant looked like Ares himself in mid-battle, all blood and spattered gore: he had taken his vengeance for a father and brother lost, today. It wouldn't be enough, but then, blood could never wash away grief, however much you spilled. Only love could do so; *and never mind that now,* Diomedes told himself. Ajax had lost a corner of his oblong shield and the top bore a split six inches deep, but he had some three hundred men with him. It was time to throw the bones and let the gods decide.

"Welcome," he said, extending an arm which Ajax gripped in a slippery hand. Diomedes glanced around at the gathered kings. "You'll accept my command, for this one assault?"

"I don't see why," Prothous began. He was cut off at once.

"We will," Leitus said. He cut his eyes towards the bigger man, sensing him about to protest, and repeated, "We will! No time to argue. If your honour is bruised I'll fight you in single combat when we can, but for now, Diomedes leads us."

Prothous glowered at him, but finally he gave a short nod. On the other side Menestheus straightened from a crouch, still trying to catch his breath, and signalled agreement.

"We drive straight at the Apollonians," Diomedes said. "Just to the right of where Agamemnon is fighting. There's no time for proper planning, so just hit them hard and keep pushing on, whatever happens. Ajax," he added, turning to the big man, "when we get close, you and I have to kill Hector."

"Hector?" Ajax said, and in his eyes and voice was something Diomedes recognised at once as fear. His mind flew back to Delphi, and Ajax vomiting on the stone floor of the Pythia's cavern, all his courage gone. Diomedes had never thought to see the big man that way in battle. It was best to pretend he'd noticed nothing, so he raised his voice to a shout. "Come, men of Greece! There is *kleos* to be won!"

The soldiers roared, shaking their spears at the sky, and plunged down the side of the dune in a torrent.

*

Another Argive ship caught with a whoosh and a billow of black smoke. He wasn't sure how many that made now: eight? Ten? A fraction of the total, irrelevant really… except the invaders were fleeing in terror, their whole mighty army humbled by the smaller band of Trojans who now drove gloriously against them.

Hector slid away from a thrusting spear and hewed downwards, severing the shaft. A pivot on one heel and Mursili's magnificent iron blade cut through the cuirass and pierced the man's heart. As the Argive fell Hector kicked him back into the next man, trying to lunge over the top, and then killed him too with a quick chop to the neck.

He was very tired. The spill from a racing chariot would have killed many men; luck was always a part of any fall. It had left Hector nothing worse than bruises but they ached now, and his muscles rebelled at the thought of another effort. But on the dunes Paris was marshalling the archers, so arrows fell steadily into the Argive host. Below him the Scamandrians had arrived, meeting a Greek attempt to counterattack and throwing it backwards into the heaving mass of their own men. Hector grinned and roared a challenge, exulting as the Argives before him fell back in dismay. Ash from burning ships had begun to thicken the air, flakes falling on hair and shoulders, a pyre of Argive pride.

Troy could win this war here, right now. The thought was already in Hector's mind when a big man emerged from the cringing Argives in front, spear steady in front of him, a boar's tusk helmet on his head above rainbow armour.

Agamemnon. Kill him and the war would be over on the instant. Ipirru of horses had truly smiled on his Trojan children today, and Pallas Athena who chose the victors in battle, and Tarhun, and all the myriad gods and goddesses of Ida. This was perfect. Hector laughed and went to meet the Argive ruler.

His laughter faded as Agamemnon's spear rammed into Hector's shield, sending a shock up his arm. The High King was bulky but moved well, and he was too shrewd to overreach and let his spear be cut through. Hector parried and slashed, watching Agamemnon's moves, learning how he timed his strikes and when he withdrew. Beneath his tusk helmet Agamemnon's eyes were narrow as he did the same, gauging his enemy.

Except he wasn't, Hector realised. That slitted stare was the result of fear, not calculation. His spear was pulled back early because Agamemnon was in terror of him. Everything changed in Hector's mind. He was very tired but his brain knew how to read fighting men; he could do it in his sleep, probably. The next time the spear darted forward he surged to meet it, turned it with his shield and then cut through the shaft with one blow. Before Agamemnon could draw his bronze blade Hector was on him. The High King stumbled back, catching a fearsome blow on his own shield, panic now clear in his eyes.

Someone else sprang into the attack. Hector saw him from the side of his eye, recognised the danger with whatever small part of his mind watched for it while he fought. He cursed and turned to meet the new assailant, a slender man wearing a cuirass and helmet in plain black. A Myrmidon, then. Hector had thought they were all away raiding.

One exchange, and Hector's weariness was forgotten. It had to be: the Argive was very good. All his focus was on this man, this one combat. Other Trojans came up around him, but he was only dimly aware of Molion, the tough captain, and Hyrca from Mount Ida, dismounted from his chariot now and fighting with the spearmen. He saw Agamemnon falling back, into the shelter of his personal guard and out of reach, but it didn't matter. Nothing did but the man he faced.

The man was a dancer, full of leaps and pirouettes, as hard to pin down as a drunken memory. But Hector's brain worked as it had with Agamemnon, gauging and calculating, and one time when the Myrmidon came around from a spin he found Hector's blade waiting. The iron all but severed his sword hand and then swept back as he gaped, before he could even scream, and smashed through flesh and bone just where the shoulder met the neck. The man tried to clutch the wound with his flopping right hand, and keeled over in silence.

More Argives seemed to spring out of the sand where he had stood. Suddenly they were everywhere, Greeks in battered leather cuirasses, shields dented and swords notched. Hector cut down the first onrushing enemy almost before his brain realised there was a threat – and then he found himself facing two men in boar's tusk helmets, and he knew them both.

Ajax half crouched behind his tower shield, striking from behind its shelter with heavy thrusts of his ash spear. Diomedes, his silver armour no longer gleaming, was faster on his feet, an always-moving phantom Hector couldn't hit without turning his back on Ajax. Twice he came close, sure the second time that he'd drawn blood, only to find the Argive had been just quick enough. Then Ajax stabbed from the other side and Hector was forced to back up. He snarled and steadied himself, nearly catching Ajax with a blow that would have opened his throat if it hadn't clanged off the broken top of the shield.

Then Pandarus was there, smashing his way through to Hector's side with two dozen of his green-and-blue lacquered

Idaians behind him. Diomedes saw him coming and backed away to gain room, setting his feet solidly among the fallen bodies.

Pandarus paused, turning as well to face a new threat. A slender man in a helmet of tusks, with an unremarkable face Hector was sure he should recognise. He couldn't place it though. The newcomer ducked lithely under Pandarus's spear and rammed his sword through the Trojan's thigh, so hard the tip came out the other side. Pandarus lurched to the side, suddenly pale. The Argive gave his sword a savage twist and yanked it out, and so much blood followed.

They had filched a bottle of wine when they were twelve and drunk it down by the strand, so naïve they didn't realise wine should be watered. Hector had been helplessly sick and Pandarus had to help him home. They sneaked away to pay for women in the town two years later, reed girls teaching two boys their first lessons of the bedroom. They learned the spear together, visited the smaller towns together on a succession of sunlit days, boys growing into men in a world they thought would last forever.

Pandarus toppled backwards onto the dead bodies, sword falling from slack fingers.

And then horns began to blow on the dunes, Trojan signals of an approaching threat. Hector squeezed his eyes shut for just a moment, trying to fight down the bitter bile that rose in his heart. A moment ago the war had seemed all but over, the Argives in helpless retreat. Now his friend was dead and the horns were blowing, more every moment it seemed, and though Hector couldn't see the danger he knew he had no choice.

He looked at the man who'd killed Pandarus and knew him, this time. Odysseus, who had been at the failed parley before the Scaean Gate. He'd needed Helen to explain who he was: none of the Trojans had known. She said Odysseus was clever. She hadn't said he could fight so well.

"Get the body," he rasped to the men beside him. They didn't need to be told which one. Hector stood guard until Pandarus's corpse was carried away, and none of the three Argive kings moved to prevent it.

124

Chapter Fourteen

If The Gods Were Kind

That night the kings gathered in Agamemnon's tent. Those who were left.

Three rulers had fallen in a single day. Thalpius, killed at the earthworks, and later Agapenor in his suicidal attack on the Apollonians. The third was Schedius of Phocis. He was killed by Trojan chariots on the grasses between braids of Scamander, but in the chaos of near-disaster none of the other lords realised at the time. It was when he failed to appear at the meeting of kings that a herald was sent to find him, only to return with news that he could not be found.

Odysseus sat with his back against one of the stone pillars. He was exhausted, too tired to feel hunger, though he made himself nibble at cheeses and olives. His body needed food even if his stomach didn't want it. He chewed without tasting, fighting to keep his eyes open.

"You won a good deal of glory today," Menestheus said. He was clad in a *chiton* of plain blue, probably the first thing he'd laid hands on after taking off his armour. Bruises poked out from both sleeves: one of them covered his arm nearly to the wrist. "*Kleos* like few of us have won in this cursed place. Shame you couldn't recover his armour."

"Bind my tongue if I care," Odysseus said.

Menestheus looked at him from the side of his eye. "The other kings are talking about it, you know."

That was more interesting, or should be, but Odysseus couldn't make himself bother. Nestor would have been contemptuous, ready with a caustic remark that any Greek who only respected a man for killing wasn't much of a Greek at all. It was too much effort to summon such a reply now.

"Starlings murmur together," he said, meaning that gossip held no interest for him just now. This time it was Thersites, standing as usual a pace behind Menestheus, who glanced at him. The storyteller said nothing though. He said nothing far too often. Men who guarded their tongues were often the clever ones, and not to be trusted.

Except that if one did not trust the thugs, the old-world Greeks who revelled in violence and respected a man only for the blood he'd spilled, then who was left? Only the clever ones, the men who could think. Who watched and listened while bronze wheels turned in their minds. Men like Nestor, Odysseus himself, Diomedes much of the time… and men like Thersites. Crippled, hardly able to wrestle a child let alone a bear or wolf, and yet under it all a mind like polished marble, full of fugitive glimmers and gleams.

By Zeus, he was tired.

The heel of a staff rapped the wooden floor, three times.

"As the High King summoned, so have you come," Talthybius said. It was always a surprise to hear such a sonorous voice coming from the Herald's thin chest. He held his staff in one hand, and the silver-inlaid sceptre in the other. "Grief to my heart to tell it, five kings are missing. Nestor of Messenia fell and is replaced by his son, Thrasymedes. Do we accept him in his father's place?"

Odysseus spoke his assent, watching the kings as they did the same. He'd have taken it amiss if anyone had denied the right of his best friend's heir. Thrasymedes was not his father – he lacked the wit, for one thing – but he had the right to rule. The young man looked satisfied as he stood to bow his thanks.

"Telamon of Salamis fell in battle," Talthybius said. "Do we accept his son Ajax in his place?"

A louder murmur for that, although *fell in battle* was an exaggeration worthy of the most outlandish tales. Telamon had been stoned to death and drowned while being lowered in a net from the side of his ship, killed like a pig in a trap. Fates alone knew if it was rocks or water that had killed him in the end. The kings let it pass though: for Ajax's sake, Odysseus thought. The giant man had lost a father and brother in a matter of days. A little compassion was merited.

It seemed Odysseus' brain was still working, despite the exhaustion of his body. He sighed and sat up straighter.

"Thalpius of Elis –"

"I think," Menestheus broke in, "that we can dispense with the names. We know who went to Hades' halls."

He was standing, one hand extended to be given the sceptre. It was unheard-of. The High King always spoke first, and then only when his Herald had finished the formalities. All the kings roused themselves from their weariness to eye the king of Attica. Agamemnon began to get to his feet.

126

And Talthybius handed the sceptre to Menestheus. Then he turned and went back past the stone pillars, making his message obvious: he would not interfere. Agamemnon's gaze on his back was hard with anger, but before he could speak Menestheus stepped forward.

"I have much to ask today," he said. "Many doubts about this war, and how it is being fought. Even about whether we can win. But before it all," he added over a sudden murmur, "I have one question, and I insist upon an answer. *Where was Menelaus?*"

Silence fell. Agamemnon sat slowly back down again. In his chair to the High King's right Menelaus looked up from thought. His face was flushed and he looked tired, but it was the weariness of a man whose nights are troubled, not of one fresh from the field. His bare arms bore no bruises.

"Night filled the eyes of two kings the day we landed," Menestheus went on. "Three more are walking the road to the underworld today. A prince of Salamis was killed, and by Raging Ares, enough men went to Hades to keep that black god sated for a year. They died fighting a war in Menelaus' name, for the return of his wife. And yet on the beach I never saw him, and today the same. If he fought I know nothing of it. *Where was he?*"

The last words were hurled like stones. Menelaus' head snapped back and his brother glowered furiously, but neither spoke. It was Idomeneus who rose and put out a hand for the sceptre.

"Accusations don't help us now," he said when he had it. He'd gained respect from the kings today, hurrying back from his place in the south of the line to turn the Trojans back just in time. No one interrupted him. "But Menestheus is right that we need to reconsider how to win this war – and win it we will. I'll not let us slink away from this plain like whipped dogs."

Another king stood; Prothous, the boastful king of Magnesia in the north. He took the sceptre and said simply, "Where was Menelaus?"

Leonteus of Pieria, grim and unsmiling as he always was. "Where was Menelaus?"

"Where was Menelaus?" This from Nireus of Rhodes, who had hated Leonteus for years. Odysseus couldn't remember the two men taking the same side before. "Why didn't he fight?"

"Where was –"

127

"All right!" Menelaus bellowed suddenly. He was on his feet, face as red as his hair. "I was unwell. Would you have me face the Trojans on weak legs? No man can be blamed for sickness."

"He can if it came out of a wine jug," Diomedes said. "You've had your nose buried in a cup since your wife fled. The gods know you have my sympathy, king of Sparta. But by Ares' teeth, if you won't run your spear like other men, you betray those who fight for you."

"Have a care," Agamemnon warned. His tone had taken on the petulant edge it always had when he felt angry, or thwarted. "There are some things I won't allow to pass."

Diomedes looked at him contemptuously. "What will you do, High King? Send me home? Kill me? Greece has lost enough kings today."

This was becoming dangerous. It was one thing for the kings to argue: they did that all the time, whoever held the sceptre. Odysseus sometimes thought there were more hatreds between Greeks than in all the rest of the world. But the derision in Diomedes' voice was more than that; it was an insult to the High King, and a challenge. Agamemnon's authority was under threat here. If he lost control of the lesser kings the army could disintegrate on his beach, and if it did then war would follow soon after in Greece itself, king against king. That had always led to ruin, before. Ithaca was too remote and unimportant to suffer the worst of it, but trade would collapse, and the islands relied on that.

Nestor would have said there was another thing to consider, one even more important. Greece was edging towards unity, slowly and with many false starts, but making steady ground. It was only together that they could match Egypt, in the long run, or Assyria further east. The great powers rose in cultures that were whole, not splintered into pieces. Greece either learned to imitate them or it would be swallowed by them, one day soon or late.

Odysseus sighed and pushed himself to his feet. He saw Thersites glance over again and ignored him.

"What will *you* do, Diomedes?" Agamemnon shouted. "Sail home and abandon Greeks on this beach? Argolis borders my lands of Achaea. I promise you, if you leave us you will never know peace while I live. Not a day of it!"

"He may not fight alone," Ajax growled.

"Treason!" Idomeneus pointed a finger at the big man. "You swore oaths, king of Salamis, and your father did before you. Have the courage to stand by them!"

Ajax surged to his feet, hand grappling at his belt for a sword that wasn't there. Other kings were standing too, shouting words lost in the tumult. Leitus and Ialmenus were nose to nose, exchanging snarls that would turn any moment into blows. Menelaus half-fell back into his chair and took a long pull from his cup.

Odysseus came up to Idomeneus and plucked the sceptre from his hand. He went into the centre of the circle and threw it hard against the deck with a ringing crash. When the echoes died away the room was silent, and every eye was on him.

"I don't think we need the sceptre anymore," he said lightly, "since nobody seems to care who holds it in any case. Sit down, my friends. Sit, and think who has driven us to such desperation that we fight among ourselves."

"He did!" Nireus said, gesturing at Menelaus. "He –"

"Sit," Odysseus repeated, and Nireus sat, looking surprised. But if Idomeneus had gained respect for his rush to help the beleaguered defence, Odysseus had won glory when he killed Pandarus on the sand. Ithaca had always been nothing and it was still nothing, but its king had achieved something no one else had been able to, and dealt a heavy blow against Troy. On a day filled with disaster, that deed shone like sunlight after a storm.

He waited for the first king to speak, making a wager with himself as to who it would be. He was wrong, in the event.

"Hector," Carystus said finally. Despite all the shouting around him his celeste eyes were calm, but then, the king of Euboea had always been a mediator, able to find common ground in the thorniest of disputes. That called for a certain amount of insight, Odysseus supposed. "It's Hector who is doing this to us."

"Hector," someone else said, and then a third voice agreed. Nireus nodded unwillingly. "Yes. Hector."

"One man," Odysseus said. "Greece has its own heroes, but they're falling like wheat before Hector and his Apollonians. Iron is part of it, but most of the reason is simply Hector. Today he leapt out of a crashing chariot and killed the man who attacked him as he fell. Is there any man here who believes he could have done the same?"

129

It was Diomedes who replied, the man Odysseus had thought would name Hector first. "I might be able to, if the gods were kind. But give my body to the dogs if I'd want to try. And I don't think there's a man in this army who could say more."

"I can!" Ajax shouted. "Hector might have you all whimpering like women, but he does not frighten me!"

"Good," Odysseus said. "Then tomorrow you can challenge him to single combat, friend Ajax. Because we need to kill him before he soaks the whole plain with Greek blood. Will you do it?"

Ajax stared at him with hate in his eyes. Not hate for him, Odysseus thought, but for Hector, who had put him in this terrible position. After a long time Ajax shook his head. He looked down at his feet and said nothing.

"I believe," Diomedes said thoughtfully, "that Hector is too good for me. When we fought him today he was already weary and bruised, yet Ajax and I together couldn't defeat him. He's the best I have ever seen." He looked around at the kings. "Except one."

"Except one," Odysseus echoed. "Achilles."

There was silence. The rage seemed to have gone out of the room now, replaced by a grim understanding of the challenge they faced. Well, it was about time. Troy had always been too strong to fall easily or soon. Too many of these kings had thought glory would fall into their hands like a gift sent down from Olympus; a golden apple, or an enchanted helmet. They had learned better now. Perhaps it was not too late.

"Achilles does as he pleases," Agamemnon said. "He listens to orders and then follows his own will. No, Peleus, you know it's true. Your son is a magnificent warrior. But he disrupts any army he's part of. That's why I sent him to sack the lesser cities. It's a task he can achieve without causing trouble."

"We need him," Odysseus said.

Agamemnon shook his head. "Not that much."

"Then perhaps you'd prefer to challenge Hector yourself," Odysseus said, smiling to take the sting away. "No? I don't blame you, High King. I wouldn't like to face him either. But the truth is simple." He looked around the room again. "We can never take Troy while Hector remains to defend it. And there isn't a man here who can face Hector in battle and win. The only Greek who might be able to do so is Achilles, and therefore we

130

need him here to change the course of this war. Or else we might as well hoist sails and make for home, before more men are butchered in a war we cannot win."

Ajax made as though to speak and then did not. Nobody else challenged the claim. Odysseus turned back to Agamemnon.

"Send for Achilles." He addressed the High King directly now, like a penitent making a plea. "Tell him he can do as he pleases, attack where he likes, as long as he hunts Hector for us. Set him after the prince of Troy like an eagle after a rabbit. It will offer him the *kleos* he craves, and as for the rest of us, we may then win this war."

There was silence for a moment, and then someone began to stamp his feet in approval. He'd barely begun when others joined him, and soon the whole gathering was hammering on the deck, showing their support. Agamemnon studied Odysseus and slowly, reluctantly, he nodded.

*

Nobody was talking much. Men sat around their fires in desultory silence, some of them eating, some dozing, but most just stared at the blazes. Isander knew what they were seeing in the flames; the catastrophe that had struck the Greeks today, and the far worse disaster that had barely missed them. That last most of all, perhaps. It was what Isander had seen, in the nightmare that brought him out of a single hour's sleep.

Ships aflame all along the beach. Trojans rampaging as they chose, killing left and right, with no one able to strike back at them. The remaining Greeks were gone into the night or fighting each other for places on the remaining galleys, swimming out amidst thrashing oars in their desperation. As many sank in the black water as were cut down. Isander had dreamed he was one of those men, scrabbling at a hull until the water took hold of his legs and dragged him under, only the splash of oar blades to be seen as he sank. And then not even that, and the pressure on his chest became a killing pain and he came awake with a scream lodged in his throat and his arms raised, as though in a final effort to claw back to the surface and take one more gulp of air before he died.

He hadn't tried to sleep again. Soldiers had to learn to rest when they could, he knew that, but it was a trick that evaded

131

him. He could eat though – another thing all soldiers were meant to do whenever the chance was there. He roasted slices of mutton over the fire and ate them slowly, burned but not really cooked, and tried to think of nothing at all.

Gorka *was* asleep, a mounded shape at the edge of the firelight, but Nikos was awake. He roasted his own meat and didn't speak, for once. He'd hardly said a word since the mayhem of the afternoon. Hector had almost *beaten* them, in the gods' sweet names! The massed armies of all Greece, more men than any army brought together before; and they were the best, the finest fighting men in the world. Egyptians might claim that title, or Hittites, even Assyrians far away, but that was just boasting. The Greeks were best. Everyone around the Greensea knew it, in their hearts.

Hector had almost beaten them.

Someone at another fire stretched, then stood and walked out of the light. Hunched figures all around turned their heads to watch him go. It was the most movement there had been for hours, half the night maybe. Isander couldn't remember the last time he'd heard the murmur of voices, much less a laugh or jest.

Hector had beaten them. There was no *almost* in it. He'd thrashed them utterly, and only weight of numbers had saved Greece from oblivion. That and blind luck, or the kindness of the gods: whichever your heart believed. And what preyed on the mind, what had all these living men as still and silent as the dead, was the knowledge that he could do it again tomorrow.

He looked around at a footfall, loud as crashing waves in that eerie quiet.

"Don't get up," Socus said. Stubble made a shadow around his jaw and there were dark smudges under his eyes as well. He moved like a man ready to collapse. "I only want a brief word."

Isander ignored the instruction, rising so he could bow. "My lord."

As he straightened he saw a grimace on the older man's mouth. "I suppose I'll have to get used to that, won't I? People bowing to me." He looked directly at Isander. "I never wanted to be king."

"I know that," he said.

"I loved Thalpius. He was an easy man to admire, a good man to follow." Socus shook his head. "I know what he'd tell me. Here on this beach we don't have the luxury of picking a

132

king at our leisure. The soldiers need leadership, and I'm best placed to provide it."

"I'd agree with that," Isander said.

This time Socus nodded. "So would I. That's why I took the crown. Anyway, I'm king, and I have news for you. The prince of Troy you killed has been returned to the city, in exchange for Teucer's body. The armour you won went with him."

That was bitterly unfair, and Isander drew breath to argue.

"However," Socus went on, "the two men are of a size, and Teucer's armour has been awarded to you instead, on Agamemnon's order. To the displeasure of Ajax, I might add. He's very angry with you."

"He is more than that," someone else said, and Diomedes stepped out of the darkness.

Isander bowed again. He hoped he covered his surprise at the Argolid king's appearance; Diomedes seemed to have aged ten years. His forehead bore creases Isander was sure had not been there back home. *And what would I see, if I had a bronze mirror before me? Is my face the one I wore when I left Greece to begin this war?*

He doubted it. Perhaps Meliza wouldn't know him, when he came home again. If he ever did.

"Ajax is livid," Diomedes said, breaking into his thoughts. "He threatened to fight you for possession of his brother's armour. All the other kings opposed him, though. A soldier's right to the body and goods of those he kills is too important to deny, even once. Half the men on this beach would sail for home at once if we took that opportunity away."

Isander felt the stirrings of anger, even so. He'd been lucky to kill Troilus, he knew that, but it had still been done at risk of his own life. That was the bargain every soldier struck. You risked an eternity in Hades as a grey shade, in return for a chance at wealth, and perhaps also *kleos,* the glory that might mean your ghost walked the Fields of Elysium when death did come. To achieve it you needed luck, and a god smiling on you, but you took the risk.

Now Ajax had tried to take away fairly won spoils. The giant was terrifying, a force of nature in a man's body, but Isander would fight him rather than surrender what he'd won.

"Be careful," Socus advised. "I don't think Ajax will defy Agamemnon's explicit order, but all the same, keep a few men of your company with you at all times. Which reminds me. This is your band now. I'm naming you to replace Axylus as company captain."

Isander stared at him. "Me?"

"There's no one better," Socus said, then added, "until you're killed or maimed, anyway. Get some sleep."

He turned and went back into the night. Diomedes made to follow him and then paused, looking back at Isander over his shoulder. "You've the makings of a fine warrior, young man. Should you survive to see Greece again you might become a captain to reckon with. But if you want to do that, watch out for Trojan arrows. Men who got no more than a scratch are dying tonight. The enemy is using poison on its barbs."

Back in Elis the recruits had been taught to wash arrow wounds as soon as they could, and thoroughly, because of poison. Bandits used it even if armies rarely did. That the Trojans had begun to added another horror to this war. Isander had heard the whine of arrows throughout the day, and he shuddered to think that any one of them could have scraped his skin and ended all his thoughts of wealth and *kleos* for good.

He would stay well away from archers, if he could. He'd keep back from Hector too, though the admission shamed him. Perhaps there really was a fine warrior in him, but he doubted he'd ever be able to match the heir of Troy as he'd been today. He doubted anyone could.

An idea wormed into his mind at that, a name murmured so softly he was hardly aware he'd thought it.

Achilles.

Chapter Fifteen

Moments

The letter spoke of pirate raids, and forces gathered to repel them. Women for the most part, and old men, all taught how to use bow and arrow so they could kill the raiders from a distance. Penelope's prose was matter-of-fact, plain words with none of the ring and dash of heroic speech, but the meaning came through clearly all the same. Ithaca was under threat.

Nearly all her fighting men were away, clinging to this sandy shore on another continent.

If they were home this would never have happened. If *Odysseus* was home his mere presence would drive the pirates away; the gods knew Ithacan kings had punished them often enough. It was Laertes, Odysseus' father, who had begun to sail into pirate bays and ravage them there, taking the fight to the raiders for the first time. Odysseus had done the same, and when he left he would have sworn there wasn't a reaver's nest within thirty miles of his islands. Now they sailed within sight of the coast, unchallenged, seeking a weak place to strike.

Despite all that, Odysseus found his eyes straying down the parchment, to the paragraph tacked onto the end of the letter like an afterthought, something of little importance;

Telemachus is well. He fell and cut his head a week ago, playing with a wooden sword and pretending to be his father. I had to make him stop so I could clean the wound; he said warriors did not stop in battle. He's not yet two years old. You would be proud, I know.

Proud? He was filled with such joy it was suffocating. But there was fear too, because Odysseus wasn't there to protect his son as he grew. And there was despair; *what is it we do to our sons, in this world we make?* Not yet two, and Telemachus wants to be a warrior. Odysseus looked up at the stars, tilting his head back so the tears would run down inside his throat and not be seen.

He was sitting some distance away from the campfires, and the ships beached beyond them. Most of the men were awake, even though the night was old. Days like the one they'd survived

135

left wounds on the mind and heart that kept sleep away, until they scabbed over. They never truly healed. The men who lived to see their homes again would remember this beach, and the furious press of Trojan soldiers, until they died. Perhaps even beyond death. Who really knew?

Because he was alone, the voice when it came startled him.

"I'm sorry," Thersites said. "I was just walking to clear my mind. I didn't realise you were here."

Odysseus looked at him. Hollow-chested even in the dark, those misshaped shoulders hunched forward, one leg out to the side to balance the bad foot. An excuse for a man, really. And that was the voice of the old Greece speaking, a place where a man was judged by the strength of his sword arm and nothing else. A place of endless war and ruin. Nestor would be ashamed to know Odysseus had such thoughts.

A mind like polished marble, Odysseus had thought of the crippled man earlier, in Agamemnon's tent. *Full of fugitive glimmers and gleams.* One of the few who watched and listened and *thought,* with ideas turning like bronze wheels in their minds.

"I'll leave you alone," Thersites said.

Odysseus lifted a hand. "Wait."

He didn't particularly like the man. Didn't trust him much either, though that might just be because Thersites was so clever. Odysseus had met few men who could match his own brains, and he tended not to put too much faith in them. Perhaps it was just fear of being out-thought. He didn't know, and it didn't matter. Not now, in the aftermath of disaster.

The Greeks needed Achilles. They might need cleverness even more, and not even know it.

"Sit with me," Odysseus said.

Thersites raised his brows, not bothering to hide his surprise.

"Please." Odysseus gestured to the sand beside him. "We should talk." *And I will not speak more unless he sits, not if all the Greeks here die for it. I am not going to beg.*

Thersites came over, dragging his club foot awkwardly behind him. He had to position his body carefully before he sat, making sure he didn't overbalance and fall. It was hard not to shrink away. Old women and priests in Greece sometimes said that physical infirmity could be passed by a touch, so one should always stay away from cripples. Odysseus supposed he must have believed some of that, as a boy, and the distaste had never left him.

What we learn as children never wholly leaves us. My son is not yet two and he's playing with swords.

He didn't want to think about that, in case it brought the tears again. "We have a problem."

Thersites nodded. "If Hector kills Achilles, this war is over for us."

That was true enough. "Achilles can win that battle. Have you ever seen him fight? He's a match for Hector."

"A match," Thersites agreed. "Perhaps no more than that. I'm not a gambler – I've never met a man who won more than he lost from the odds-men at the Games – but if I were, I would still not risk a coin on that contest. Not even a bent one."

That was how Odysseus saw it too. Not that he was going to admit it. "We can't affect that, in any case. It will be decided between the two of them. But there's another issue that we *can* address."

"The city," Thersites said.

Odysseus had started to feel as though the other man was half a step ahead of him. It was time to change that, see how smart Thersites really was. "How do you see the problem?"

The storyteller's fingers wandered across the strings of his lute, producing a soft whisper of sound. "I keep coming back to the same difficulty. We can't throw a cordon around Troy, and starve the city out, because of those woods to the east. They're a tangle, all hillocks and underbrush, and visibility is very bad. One archer could kill ten men and slip away. There are a hundred paths through and none can be seen from a few paces to either side. It would take half the army to control that, and supplies would still find a way through, some of the time."

"Troy also has springs inside the walls," Odysseus pointed out. "They'll never be short of water."

"And I expect their granaries are full. A siege might last years, with terrible losses all the time and no guarantee of success. In short," Thersites said, "laying siege would not work."

Odysseus agreed, as it happened, and for exactly the reasons Thersites had laid out so succinctly. That had often happened when he talked with Nestor. All at once he missed the old man with a sharpness that cut him inside, missed him *terribly,* the way a man will grieve for his father when he dies. Or for a son, still alive but far away, growing up without his father to watch over him.

Telemachus needed a land to rule, when his time came. It was another reason why a siege here was impossible; the Greek armies couldn't afford to be away much longer. If there were pirates in Ithaca there would already be raiders on all the coasts, and bandits venturing out of the hills to raid and steal. By autumn that would be worse. In a year's time half the kingdoms of Greece might have been taken by outlaws.

The eastern sky had begun to turn pale. Odysseus had been awake all night, and though deathly tired he still wasn't sleepy.

"We can't tunnel under the walls," Thersites went on. "I heard that Leonteus did something like that, at a town north of Pieria. He had his men dig right under the wall. Is it true?"

"He dug two tunnels," Odysseus agreed. "One collapsed, and a lot of men died. But the other held up, and Leonteus' men appeared inside the town with no warning at all. It wouldn't work here, though."

"No. Dig down six inches on the Plain of Troy and you hit water." Thersites stroked the lute again. "Unless we can persuade Nereids and water sprites to fight for us, tunnels are impossible. So are siege towers, because most would bog down on the Plain, and the rest would reach the foot of Troy's hill and stop there, unable to manage the slope. Either way, they'd be useless."

"Which leaves?"

"Assault," Thersites answered. "It's the only option left – and it would also be useless, because those walls are just too high."

They were more than merely high, they were monstrous. The main wall was twenty feet high, with another rising out of the back of it which added another fifteen feet. Anyone who did gain the first parapet would still find arrows and stones raining down on him from above. All that was without the overtopping towers, without the even greater wall of the Pergamos in the north, the inner citadel of Troy. And the whole structure stood atop a steep-sided hill a hundred feet high, every inch of it a killing ground.

Greek losses would be appalling before they even reached the wall. And for what? Thersites was right. Assault would not work.

"Agamemnon didn't consider this," Thersites said. "Did he? This army was created to smash Troy and make Greece supreme on the Greensea, but he never gave much thought to getting men over that wall."

Odysseus' brow creased. "Greece is already supreme on the Greensea."

"Oh, my friend," Thersites said. "Really? Egypt is the dominant power in our world. We forget that because Egypt doesn't care about us, or anyone else. The people there are too wrapped up in their pyramids and temples, their own stories of how special they are. Descended from gods with the heads of falcons or bulls, chosen to be civilised where other cultures aren't much more than barbarians. But don't let those tales blind you, Odysseus. If ever Greece wakens Egyptian anger, her armies will cross the sea and stamp every one of our cities into the dirt."

That was true, actually, though Odysseus didn't like being reminded of it so bluntly. He looked away, watching for the sun to peek over the rim of the world. There was fog again this morning though, rising off the braids of Scamander and from the Plain itself. The towers of Troy poked out of it like lonely islands, the wall below shrouded from view.

He frowned. There was a thought there, something he should have recognised but which his weary mind couldn't hold.

"I wonder," Thersites said beside him, and trailed off.

Odysseus turned to him, grasping at the words. "What?"

"Just a thought," Thersites said. He sounded doubtful and lapsed into silence again. Odysseus was about to seize his coat and shake the man when Thersites spoke again.

"I'm thinking," he said slowly, "about fog."

*

The messenger finished speaking.

Antenor did nothing for a moment. He had stood here for many years, right where he was now, just to the left of Priam's cedar wood chair on the dais in the throne room. Kings had come to bow to the lord of Troy, rulers from small provincial cities and sometimes from rivals; Ephesus in lovely Maeonia, Halicarnassus above its bay, poor ravaged Miletos. Twice a prince had come from Hattusa, bringing the praise of the Great King of the Hittites, gratitude and honour offered to a king who was lesser but still mighty.

Merchants and mendicants, mariners and messengers and magi. All had been escorted into this room of panelled diamonds in blue and gold. All had knelt on the polished floor. Some were welcome, others not, but all had been allowed to speak, and most had been permitted to leave.

Antenor didn't think any of them had brought such dire news as the herald still waiting for an answer. He dismissed the man with a gesture and turned, moving slowly as though age had finally caught him in its swollen hands. Behind the statue of Tar-Suteh in the corner of the room was a small door, used for access by the king and his advisors. Antenor went through it and down a hallway, his boots the only sound. A little later he emerged into the open air beside the wall of the Pergamos, higher even that that of the city itself.

Two soldiers flanked a doorway ahead of him, armour lacquered in the green and blue of the Idaians. That was a new thing, a practise adopted – at Antenor's suggestion – only after the Argives had taken the beach. He didn't really believe the Greeks could sneak a killer into Troy, but a wise man never assumed too much. The men watched him as he went by but didn't move, and Antenor started up the stone steps beyond, climbing inside the wall. He emerged on the parapet, with the roofs of the oval houses of the town below him on the left. Another pair of guards stood by the entrance to Ilos' Tower, the highest in the city. Antenor passed them, ascended a coil of winding stairs and came to a door, which he pushed open without knocking. He hadn't knocked for twenty years.

Priam was sitting by the window. The shutters had been thrown back so he could look out over the Plain of Troy, and of course he was looking west. Towards a sinking sun and the Argive camp, with the ships packed behind like seals basking in the sun. Sometimes at night, when the city was quiet, Antenor lay awake and listened to timbers creak in the sea swell. So many of them that the sound carried across five miles, like ancient bones scraping in tombs, and Antenor couldn't help but feel afraid.

Beside him in his bed on those nights was his wife of a lifetime, daughter of one king of Thrace and sister to another. Raised among that warrior people, Theano wouldn't curse him for cowardice, or upbraid him for feeling fear. She'd simply sigh, as though disappointed by a child, old enough now to know better. And so Antenor concealed his fear, buried it beneath smiles and false confidence, until it broke out of him at odd moments and he had to breathe deeply until it passed.

Moments such as this.

"What is it?" Priam asked from his chair. He hadn't moved, not even to turn his head. "Tell me, my friend."

The king had lost a son today. The Argives had handed Troilus' body back, in exchange for the corpse of Teucer of Salamis. The son of Hesione, the last link Priam had to his lost sister, and he had come at last to Troy only to die there beneath the walls of what should have been his home. A son killed, a longed-for nephew killed and then lost anew. Two griefs. The gods alone knew what this man must be suffering now.

Antenor swallowed. He walked into the high room, poured wine into a cup, and downed it unwatered.

"Tell me," Priam said again.

He put the cup down. "A messenger has come. From the south. With... bad news."

"Am I to drag words from you one at a time?" the king asked. Still he hadn't turned his head. "What news?"

"Pedasos is burning," Antenor said. "Argive raiders came in the night. Myrmidons, the survivors say. King Crethon is dead."

"Then now we know where Achilles went." The king's voice was flat, almost uninterested. "You warned me to expect this. I knew I was wise to keep you as my advisor. Is that all?"

"Lyrnos has been sacked," Antenor said. He had to swallow again. "And Thebe-under-Plakos. Most of the coast of Cilicia is burning. Eetion... Eetion has not been seen since."

"Ah," Priam said. "Our allies are being stripped from us, then. And those which remain unharmed will wonder; should they continue to side with their liege-lords of Troy, when we so clearly cannot protect them? Or should they wipe their hands and deal with the devils of Greece?"

"One of those others has already decided," Antenor said. "That's the last piece of news. Chromis of Mysia sends regrets, and says he cannot leave his land undefended while Argives raid his neighbours. He wishes us all good fortune, of course."

"Of course," Priam said. There was a wryness in his tone that told Antenor he was smiling. "Clever Chromis. Cyme is the next city down the coast from Thebe, and he knows it. Well, I can't blame him."

141

"We helped *him* when he needed men to sweep bandits out of the hills," Antenor said bitterly.

"The Argives are more than mere bandits. And the sea is wide, my friend, and we cannot sail it safely. There's no sweeping these raiders away. It's not the same thing."

"We helped Chromis, and now he refuses to help us."

"Not the same thing," Priam said again. "Pour me a cup of that wine, will you? Then sit down. I'm too tired to keep guessing at your expression while you stand behind me."

Antenor poured again, two cups, and this time he watered both. His head had begun to spin from the first. He walked over to the window and set them on a table, then sat beside the king he'd served all these years.

"I don't know how I should feel," Priam said. "One son killed, but the others live. Three of them came back alive today. Now I hear cities have fallen, friends died, and yet Troy still stands. Half of me weeps, the other half sings."

Antenor said nothing.

"We won a great victory yesterday. Storytellers will still sing of that battle when our grandchildren are old. Argive kings fell like wheat. Agapenor was Agamemnon's staunchest ally, you told me, except for his brother. Well, Agapenor is dead now, among others. Yet the Greeks still hold that beach. Hector burned a dozen ships but hundreds remain. You see?" He picked up his wine, sipped it. "I feel elated, and yet I grieve."

"My boy was out there too," Antenor said. "Helicaon saw the Myrmidons before, in Mysia. Do you remember?"

Priam nodded. "Three years ago. He was driving a chariot when the Argives came ashore and was able to escape."

"Killed two of them doing it, mind." He couldn't help smiling. "Helicaon has spent his life trying to match Hector, and he never could. He's good though. But my heart couldn't rest until I saw him come back through the gate. He's bruises all down his left side, but he's all right. Until the next time."

Priam smiled wanly. "Yes. Sorrow and joy, both together."

They sat in silence, sipping their wine. Across the Plain tiny figures moved, busy with one task or another, but fewer than on days before. Most of the Argives seemed content to stay in their tents and rest. That was good; they had been taught a lesson yesterday, by a far smaller Trojan force. This city was not ripe for the taking. Their mood must be darker even that that of Troy, the elation of survival mixed with a lot of sorrow.

Still, the mood here was grim, and would be worse once news of the sacked cities spread. Any large city relied on its vassals for security, just as they depended on it for the same thing. Take that away and anyone would suffer.

But none of it mattered if the Argives couldn't breach the walls. That was the point Antenor's mind kept coming back to, in its endless calculation of chance and balance in this war. The Greeks couldn't get over the walls. They might parade outside, encircled the city even, but they would have to do it for *years* before Troy could be taken. Not even the regiments of Egypt would be able to stay that long. The Argive kings, never more than one insult away from blood feud, certainly could not.

And then? Finally the Greeks would give up and sail home, perhaps all together, perhaps one king and his men at a time. Troy would still be standing, if at terrible cost. She might have lost her allies but alliances could be remade. Her wealth may have gone but the Trojan Road would reopen, horses could be sold again, and the coffers would fill. In twenty years Troy would be rich once more, mistress of Troas, in control of the road to the Euxine Sea. In fifty, she might be a power to rival Minos in days of old.

But that was yet to come, if Tarhun chose it so. Tonight Troy was alone, abandoned by her allies and clients, and there was a prince's pyre to light when the sun went down. Sunset; the most propitious time of day, when light met darkness. *Joy and sorrow,* Antenor thought again.

Priam was trying not to think about that, but Antenor had known him a long time, and he recognised the signs. Such as sitting in this room alone, gazing over the Plain, as Priam had done so often when full of pain. Hecuba came here when her husband stayed too long, or Antenor did when there was urgent news, as today. Hector too, in recent years, but nobody else. There were advisors but then there were people the king trusted, and few enough of them.

Antenor would tell Andromache of her father's death in Thebe. It wasn't a duty he relished, but it had to be done, and it would spare Priam the task. That was much of a councillor's role; easing the burden on a king, if possible without his ever knowing it had been done. But there were limits to it. Some

143

duties could not be passed, however much the heart might wish it so. Outside dusk had begun to draw down, shading the Plain in grey.

"It's time," Antenor said.

Priam nodded. "I know."

The two men stood, leaving their cups of wine on the table for the servants to clear. They went to the door and started down the stairs, the king first, to light the funeral pyre of a prince.

Caesura

Men claim the gods are fickle. We say their favour flits from man to man or cause to cause like a swallow chasing flies, now darting here, now darting there. The oldest tales are full of men supported by one god and opposed by another, immortals fighting over the destiny of one man until Zeus of the Black Cloud intervenes and decides the issue. Or when the Fates choose, as they do in the end for everyone, men and gods alike.

The Plain of Troy saw a slaughter of kings and heroes such as Greece had never known. Soldiers fell in their thousands: the funeral pyres burned for three days, and only stopped then when there was no more wood. And hidden amidst of it all, known to no one at the time, the truly significant moment was the first conversation of a minor king, a peasant almost, and a storyteller too frail to fight.

Odysseus didn't trust me at first. I knew that, and he admitted it later, back home in Ithaca. I think it was my rank, or lack of it, which unsettled him: he was enough of an old-style Greek for that. Odysseus had no difficulty accepting cleverness in a king like Nestor or Menestheus, but he did with a bard, a low-born *aoidoi*. He overcame it in the end. That spoke well of him.

He always said Nestor was the cleverest man he ever knew. For myself, I disagree. I met Nestor several times, and while I agree he was intelligent, he was no match for Odysseus. The pupil outshone the master, when it mattered. But Odysseus loved that old man like a father, he wouldn't hear the words, so I stopped saying them. I was too glad we were talking at last, making our slow and careful plans, to risk it all.

I wasn't the only man who learned to trust the king of little Ithaca. Sometimes he and I would have bare time to meet before a herald arrived with a summons from Agamemnon, calling for Odysseus' advice. All the kings listened when he spoke. They had called him *chorikos* for years, the peasant, king of a few rocky hills and the sheep which grazed them. Now they listened to his counsel. He'd speak leaning against one of the pretentious stone pillars in Agamemnon's pavilion, while the kings sat in their circle in the middle of the room, attentive to him while he stood apart from them.

I saw the significance, even if they did not. Greeks of the old type indeed, men with large muscles and little brains.

145

Odysseus returned from one such meeting to announce that Achilles seemed to have vanished. He'd suggested a ship be sent to Scyros, where the young firebrand had retreated before when he was tired, or enraged. Idomeneus had actually asked what cause Achilles had to be angry.

"Well, let's see," Odysseus answered. "He allowed himself to be persuaded to join the war by promises of glory, and then was sent away to fight at the fringes while others carried on the fight for Troy. Cause? I can't think why he might be furious, can you?"

It was a mark of how differently the kings saw Odysseus now that nobody objected to this open ridicule. A few men even laughed. And of course the ships sent to Scyros *did* find Achilles there, he and his Myrmidons taking their ease among the forests and glades, enjoying cups of wine and the company of Temple women. Odysseus had been right again. His reputation rose a little more. Agamemnon began to say that Troy had Antenor but he had Odysseus, and of the two the Greek's wits were the sharper.

Menelaus was dispatched to Scyros to bring the wayward prince of Thessaly back to the fold. I thought it foolishness, myself. Word of Menelaus' failure to join the spears in the desperate fight on the beach would have reached Achilles by now, and he'd been contemptuous of the man's bluster. But Odysseus said it was all right. Achilles would be further incensed by the insult, and that made him more likely to sail to Troy and spill out his venom at the High King.

Meanwhile Greek soldiers circled Troy and ventured into the wooded hills east of the city, to cut the paths that led to Dardanos and Tereia. What followed was what Odysseus and I had expected to follow. Arrows flew out of the brush to take men in the throat, the thigh, the belly. Sometimes a single shot and then nothing, while the Greek company huddled behind their shields and waited for an onslaught. Other times one arrow would be followed by fifty more, leaving a dozen men dead or injured. Survivors spoke of Hittite soldiers seen through the foliage, and of other men more like Trojans in appearance but without the lacquered armour. We learned later they were Maeonians. Somewhere in that tangle of undergrowth lurked Sarpedon, king of that fell people, the man who'd killed king Peteus of Attica

146

twenty years before. Menestheus' eyes were grim when he was told.

Several regiments vanished entirely, presumed ambushed, and finally Agamemnon ordered the men withdrawn. Nearly five hundred men had been killed by then, and not a single Trojan confirmed dead. It was as we'd thought. Troy could never be cut off, and so would never starve.

Men's eyes began to look west, out to sea. Sarpedon was here and Troy was as strong as ever. The Greeks needed Achilles and they all knew it.

Odysseus and I went on working, not immune to the mood of the army but staying apart from it. Much like Odysseus among the kings. We realised that if the Hittites and Maeonians were here it wasn't in large numbers, which meant that Achilles' raids on the coast had worked. Troy's allies were keeping their strength back against the risk of attack.

We made our plans, discarded them, made them anew. I sailed to Lesbos to examine a sheer cliff of basalt, black and wet from sea spray. Two days later I was in Cradle Bay again, back with the army, when ships with black hulls were spotted sailing from the west, sails furled against the incessant north wind that turned the Greensea to whitecaps.

Achilles had arrived.

Chapter Sixteen

The Challenge

There was no dramatic landing, as there had been at Aulis. The Myrmidons didn't leap over the prow of their ship as it beached, to land in perfect formation on the sand. They simply drove the ship hard onto the shore and climbed down rope ladders, wearing black chitons and no battle gear at all. In the middle of them Achilles went unnoticed at first, just another fighting man splashing his way to the beach.

Once on the strand he was impossible to miss. Achilles stood tall amidst his soldiers, crowned with a shock of hair like corn in the sun. Men oriented themselves to him as well, his own troops and others, sensing the aura of the man before their eyes recognised who he was. By the time the fifty Myrmidons were ashore they were surrounded by a thousand soldiers, then a moment later by five thousand, all pushing forward to try to grasp his arm and welcome him to the battle for Troy.

They paused when they saw the fury etched into his face. A couple of times men further back tried to start a cheer, but both stuttered and died. Back in Aulis the adulation had been spontaneous, a great roar from countless throats, as the black-hulled ships made their way up the Euripus Strait. But Achilles had been full of pride then, accepting the worship of the men. Not now.

And then the army had been filled with hope, the promise and expectation of glory. Now they were tired, mourning fallen friends and lost comrades. They just wanted to go home alive. Glory could look after itself.

Isander spoke of that to Nikos, and his friend snorted. "Easy for you to say. You won your *kleos* when you killed Troilus by the river. How does that new armour suit you, by the way?"

It suited him very well. Teucer's cuirass fit Isander with no need even to adjust the straps, and it was real quality – hardened leather with a sheet of hammered bronze over the top. The round shield was heavier than he was used to so he planned to keep using his own, but the helmet was lined with boar's tusks and was very fine indeed. Wearing it, Isander felt half a lord and half a fraud.

148

He'd seen Ajax once, bellowing abuse at some poor soldier who'd had the misfortune to find himself in the wrong place. Ajax did a lot of shouting now his brother's armour had been given to a common soldier. Isander had seen him yelling and backed away, glad to escape before Ajax noticed him and was swallowed by rage.

Command of a company suited him too, though Isander would never have thought it would. He was not the same man he'd been back home, in Elis, before the army sailed. Perhaps Nikos was right, and it was his success which had changed him, but Isander didn't think so. It was the war which had done that, the two bloody battles fought on the beach and Plain of Troy. The slaughter, the sudden death which came in an instant, leaping from man to man and leaving only cooling flesh behind… that would change any man.

Hope and glory, turned to tiredness and sorrow.

So he watched Achilles and his Myrmidons land, with more ships nosing into Cradle Bay behind. He studied them as they started along the strand, calmer than the youth he'd been, an older, wiser man. When Gorka cleared his throat and asked what he thought they should do, Isander thought for a moment before he said, "We follow. What else?"

He knew where Achilles was going, of course. Every man on the beach knew that. They surged around the black-clad men as they walked, jostling and calling their hero's name, but no more tried to break through the cordon of Myrmidons around their leader. Achilles wasn't armoured but he did have a sword at his belt, and his expression would have cracked stone. None of the soldiers wanted to get too close to him in that mood. The crowd went on swelling until it spanned the beach, a mass of heaving men all the way from dunes to the water's edge.

Achilles went straight to Agamemnon's ship, and the pavilion which stood on the deck. And there he stopped, his men a solid phalanx behind him. The throng halted too, forming a great circle that enclosed the Myrmidons and the pillared entrance to the tent. Someone shouldered through it near the ship, a big man with a black beard, and Achilles' hand shot out.

"I see you, Schedius," he said. "There's no point trying to scuttle inside so you can watch the fun. I'm not going in."

The king of Phocis turned, heavy brows drawing down. He didn't like being spoken to that way, Isander could see as much, but he saw Achilles' face and paused. "Not going in?"

"Tell Agamemnon he'll have to come out if he wants to speak with Achilles," he said. "The days when I heeded his call are done. I came this far. Now he must come the rest of the way."

"I am not your herald."

"Then pick out a man to take the message for you. But don't try my patience, Schedius, not today. Tell him."

Schedius stared a moment longer, then turned and went past the two blank-faced guards and up the ramp. The whole crowd exhaled at once, Isander included. Afterwards the silence was so complete that he could hear the rush of waves on the shore.

"This may break Agamemnon," Nikos murmured. "Achilles isn't even a ruler, but he makes the High King come to him? There might be blood before this is over."

Isander put a hand on his friend's arm to quiet him. He agreed, as it happened, and to judge by his tight nod so did Gorka. But some things were better said later, in private, or else not said at all. He would not have thought so, six months before. *An older, wiser man.*

Footsteps sounded on the ramp, and Agamemnon came out into the sunshine and the breeze.

Other kings followed, but Agamemnon stopped in the entrance and they couldn't get by without pushing. Isander recognised a couple, though their faces were shadowed; Diomedes, who everyone knew, and short Leitus at the front, as ever looking ready to snarl. Just to one side was Odysseus, arms folded on his chest and that strange storyteller beside him, Theritus or something like that, hunched over his own hollow chest. Crippled he may be, but he seemed to appear among the kings whenever he chose.

"So," Achilles said. Rage bubbled in his voice. "The Lion of Achaea can conquer only a strip of sand, without Achilles."

Isander was looking at Agamemnon then, and he saw utter hatred flash across those thick features before it could be masked. There was no mistake. Agamemnon would nurse those words as a mortal grievance all the years of his life, even if the Fates spared him and he lived on and on into great old age. They might poison his soul – if he had one – and still he'd hold them

150

close around his heart. Achilles had made an eternal enemy today.

And he didn't care. That was obvious as well, to everyone watching. Achilles wasn't merely angry, he was eaten up by fury. It came off him like heat, baking into the Greeks gathered round. Isander, near the front, began to wish he'd hung back. Nikos was right. Blood might be spilled here.

"Have a care," Agamemnon said. There was rage in his voice too, the anger of a man unused to being defied. "I would not forgive that tone from a king, and you don't have a crown."

"I have something better," Achilles snapped back. "I have something the High King can gain from no other man. *I can kill Hector.* Or did you call me back for a different reason?"

Gulls cried above, but the beach was utterly quiet.

"I thought not," Achilles said. He was still stiff with anger, a bad-tempered boar which might charge at any moment. "I will do it. Tomorrow I'll challenge Hector to single combat, with the war hanging on the outcome. He wins, and the Greeks sail home. I win, and the Trojans hand Helen over, and half their treasury beside. Will you honour those terms?"

"Show respect," Agamemnon began.

He was cut off by Achilles' laughter. "Spare me your bluster Will you honour them?"

Agamemnon glowered, lips twisting. "I will honour them."

"Then know this. And let all men know," Achilles added, raising his voice. His words carried over men's heads and out to sea. "I do not do this for the High King. I don't care if Greece wins this war or Troy does, it's no matter to me. I fight for my own name and my own causes... and I fight for Patroclus. For the memory of my friend, who was cut down while I fought elsewhere, sent from the beach of Troy by the pride of a fool.

"And after I have killed Hector the bards will sing that this was *my* war – my glory, my victory. If they remember the name of Agamemnon it will be as an afterthought. The man who tried to keep Achilles from the fight and failed, the man who tried to win without him and failed. Perhaps we should put that on his tomb, do you think? *The Lion of Achaea; he was all roar and no teeth, and had to call on stronger men in his need.*"

"Show respect!" This time it was Leitus who snarled the admonition. "You go too far."

151

Achilles turned that ferocious glare on him – and then, surprisingly, he inclined his head. "I always admired your courage, king of Boeotia. Very well then; I'll withdraw. But remember my words, and his," he nodded toward Agamemnon. "He promised to honour the terms. If Hector kills me the Greek army sails home." A sudden smile pulled at his lips. "But he won't kill me."

He turned and led his Myrmidons into the crowd, which parted for them like soft soil before the plough. Some of the troops followed, a great mass that surged away down the beach. Others remained near the pavilion, Isander and his friends among them. He kept his eyes on Agamemnon, watching the purple shade fade slowly from the High King's face.

"Achilles didn't fight elsewhere while Patroclus was killed," Gorka said. He spoke even more rarely these days, perhaps affected in his own way by this war, and now when he did the words were much too loud. "He was on Scyros, remember? Menelaus found him there."

That was true, actually. Isander had been so caught up in Achilles' fury that he'd forgotten where the Myrmidons had gone, after sacking Pedasos and Thebe-under-Plakos. The heir to Thessaly had given up raiding Troy's allies, perhaps out of weariness but more likely because he felt aggrieved by his treatment, and he'd done what he always did when he needed to clear his head; retreat to the warm welcome of the priestesses of Scyros. His mother had belonged to a temple there, or so rumour claimed. Achilles seemed to find a haven in those forests that eluded him elsewhere.

But the realisation that he hadn't been fighting changed everything. Achilles had gone to Scyros to nurse his ego – to *sulk,* in fact, while men fought and died here at Troy. Isander wondered suddenly whether Achilles had a new woman. He was known for abducting them from his raids, losing himself in their touch, and then growing bored of them weeks or months later. There were even rumours of a temple high on the Scyros slopes which was full of those abandoned conquests, tossed aside like broken greaves. Every time Achilles vanished it seemed to turn out that he was in love again.

It felt like treachery, harbouring these thoughts about the hero of every soldier's dreams. Isander couldn't help it though. He was no Odysseus, able to spin a plan out of spider silk and fading dreams, but he wasn't a fool either. Achilles was as proud and full of bluster as Agamemnon. *I don't care if Greece wins this war or Troy does,* he had said, as though all the blood spilled and friends fallen mattered not at all. But while Agamemnon could never say that, Achilles could. He was their hope, the finest warrior in Greece.

Whether he was the finest in the world, Isander supposed they would find out tomorrow.

*

Hector was naked, face down on a bench with his arms crossed above his head. He looked more like a sculpture than a living man, perfectly proportioned and every muscle cleanly defined. Two women massaged oil into those muscles, kneading with strong fingers to take away the stiffness.

"Let me take the fight for you," Aeneas said.

Hector's left shoulder was the yellow of a healing bruise, darkening in the middle to something close to black. There was an ugly stain on his hip too, where he'd rolled over his own spear as he escaped the chariot wreck. His shield arm – the left, again – was dotted with overlapping bruises the size of a man's thumb, in clusters at the top of the bicep and above the wrist. Both places where the shield rubbed in combat, as a man moved and absorbed blows.

Well, every man in Troy had injuries like those. It was the shoulder and hip that concerned Aeneas. There weren't many men who could leap from a crashing chariot and not break bones; fewer yet who could shrug off the impact and keep on fighting. Hector sometimes seemed more than a man, more than mortal, a half-god like so many Argive heroes. But laugh at Death too often and he marked you for his own. Hector had mocked him enough.

"No," Hector said.

Aeneas had expected that. He sat on a stone bench, trying not to let his worry show. "Mind telling me why?"

"You already know why." Hector grunted as fingers dug in beneath his shoulder blade. "The challenge was to me, not you. If I avoid it the men will wonder why. They'll say I'm afraid – in whispers, no doubt, but they'll say it. We can't afford that.

153

Troy's morale is wavering, my friend. I must not allow the army's will to waver as well."

"It will collapse if that man kills you."

"I'm relying on you not to let it," Hector said. "If we speak honestly, we both know neither Paris nor Lycaon can inspire an army. Lycaon tries, and he's a good brother, but…" He shrugged. "And Pandarus could have done it. Gods' teeth, it's only been a few days, and I miss him."

"So do I," Aeneas admitted. He leaned back against the wall.

It was hard to believe that Pandarus was gone. He'd been the third member of their triad, as the three boys grew into men. Hector of Troy, Aeneas of Dardanos, and Pandarus of Zeleia: young men with dreams, wrestling and racing together, dicing in taverns, buying a woman for an hour in an upstairs room. So many shared memories. Life went on, new memories were added to old, but Pandarus was not part of them. He never would be.

"I'm not saying I expect to lose," Hector said after a moment. "How do you read it, Aeneas? In truth, now. Don't flatter me."

"Achilles is the best in Greece," Aeneas said. "You're the best in the east. I can't decide it."

"Then I –"

"But you're carrying injuries," he went on, interrupting. "Achilles has been razing towns, not fighting in the savagery we've had here. I think the longer the fight lasts, the better his chances become."

"So I need to win quickly."

"If you can."

"Against Achilles?" Hector laughed wryly. "It's not likely. The man's too good to be played for a fool."

"Then let me take the fight for you."

"No," Hector said again.

Aeneas might have argued further, but the door opened behind him before he could speak. He sat up straighter, turning to see who had come past the guards. He thought it would be Priam, or else Hecuba, perhaps even Creusa come to plead with her brother. It was none of them.

"Let me take your place," Paris said.

Aeneas stared.

"Leave us," Hector commanded. As the two servant women withdrew he rolled from the table, outwardly agile as ever. Aeneas knew how well he could conceal pain though, and wasn't

154

fooled. Perhaps Paris was. The younger man's face was white as the fleece of a Mount Ida sheep.

"So, you've found your courage," Hector said when the three of them were alone. "Good for you, brother."

"I found my courage before this," Paris replied. "I've led the archers, and led them well. Don't deny it."

"I won't. The bowmen are as brave as any; I've seen them stand while chariots race down on them. And you've done well. But commanding archers isn't the same as fighting hand to hand. Achilles would chop you into meat. That's the plain truth of it, I'm afraid."

"And he won't do that to you?"

"Perhaps he will. Or perhaps I'll do it to him. But I have a chance, Paris, while you would have none." Hector wound a towel around his waist and sat on the bench. "Every time I've gone into battle I've known I could die. You feel every beat of your heart, every pulse of blood, because it might be the last. A spear can come out of nowhere, or an arrow or sword. In every moment you know that, and you ignore it too."

"You have to," Aeneas put in, "or the fear will choke you."

He'd been raised in the places of Troy, as much as in his own father's Dardanos. Aeneas was a brother to these men in all but blood, yet Paris didn't even glance at him as he spoke. "But this is my fault. Troilus is dead for my mistake. Nobody else should die for me."

"No," Hector said. "But thousands already have, not just princes of Troy. This is where the path has led, brother. I won't shrink from it now."

"If Achilles kills me the war will be over." Paris still refused to give up. "Father will hand over Helen and the Argives will leave. They promised us that. Thousands more Trojans won't have to die."

"Nor will they die if I kill Achilles," Hector answered. "Paris, did you think I meant that *your* path led to this? The road you chose when you took Helen away, and married her? I didn't. I meant *my* path, my way in life. I'm a warrior, a captain of men. Soldiers have faced me knowing they would die, and they've died, so many of them I can't remember their faces. That's what I chose. And I will not now cower away, or let another take the fight in my place, because I might not win. It will be as the gods

155

will it, and I'll trust in Pallas Athena as so many men have done when they came before my spear. If it's my turn to die, so be it."

"You put Troy at risk with your *so be it,*" Paris snapped.

He stumbled then, reeling back against the wall. It took a moment for Aeneas to realise that Hector had hit him; the man's hand had moved too fast to see. Only with the flat of his hand, but the force had still been enough to almost knock Paris down. The younger prince steadied himself and stared at Hector in surprise.

"I hit you harder before, when you didn't appear on the battlefield," Hector said. "Remember? This was a minor insult compared to what you did that day. But it was you who put Troy at risk, brother, when you abandoned Antenor's plan for the sake of your own passion. Don't ever put the blame on me."

"But that's the point," Paris said. "The fault was mine. I should be the one to face Achilles."

"Perhaps. But the gods have never been fair to mortals. Listen, now. Lycaon will be heir to Troy, if I do fall. No, listen!" His voice became a crack, as it so often did on the battlefield. "He will need both of you. I trust you to be the strong shoulders he leans on. Listen to each other, help each other, and with Tarhun's blessing Troy will still survive."

"Of course we will," Aeneas said, before Paris could speak. "But if you do your part, it won't be necessary. Kill this Greek and we can all go back to how things were before."

"I doubt that," Hector said, smiling.

So did Aeneas. Whatever happened tomorrow, or after, neither Troy nor Greece would ever be what they had been before the Argive army sailed. Aeneas had seen the smoke from Greek funeral pyres, he could guess at how many dead had been carried to them from the Plain. The Argive kingdoms would be decades recovering from their losses. Troy was wounded too, hundreds of her men dead and several ally cities little but ashes, the others keeping their distance until they saw who would emerge victorious. Her own power might not recover in Aeneas' lifetime. Perhaps not at all.

He was afraid, even so, that the worst was yet to come. On this he agreed with Paris, which wasn't a thing he could remember happening before, but the youngster was right. Paris should be the one to face Achilles, and when the Argive butchered him – as he would – Helen would be handed over to

Menelaus, and the invaders would sail for home. One death, traded for the lives of many others, and better Paris than anyone else.

Hector was going to risk all that on the gamble that he could kill Achilles. Even if he did it might not make a difference, because Agamemnon was more snake than lion, and his word was not to be trusted. He might see Achilles fall and continue the war regardless. And if Achilles won, and it was Hector who fell, Troy would seem to the Argives to be leaderless, bereft, ripe for the taking at last. Why would they even think of taking Helen and sailing away?

Hector was looking at him, he realised. "You think I'm a fool."

"You've always been a fool," Aeneas said. It was an effort to make his tone light. "It's thinking with your muscles that causes it."

Hector was surprised into the bark of laughter. "I'm going home to my wife and son. You'll be with me in the morning?"

"I'll be with you," Aeneas said.

Chapter Seventeen

Onto the Plain

The air was heavy, dense. Eudorus could feel it, even here by the shore of the Greensea, where the night breeze ought to have cleared it away. But this wasn't the haze of smoke or men's sweat, hanging over a crowded camp. It was the tension of expectation, thousands of soldiers longing for morning to come.

Because Achilles was here. Eudorus had seen it happen too often to take much notice of it now.

A figure approached, picked out by the glow of stars and a dozen glimmering fires, and that Eudorus did take notice of. He leaned on his spear and watched the man come closer. The newcomer was limping too badly to pose any threat, assuming the limp was genuine, but Eudorus wasn't about to be fooled by a trick like that. He watched until the figure resolved into someone he knew.

"Mind if I sit down?" Thersites asked. "I've been awake all night, and my leg is howling at me."

Eudorus nodded at the sand, and the storyteller sat, massaging his thigh. After a moment Eudorus sank down beside him. You weren't meant to sit on guard duty, but he'd been doing this for a long time and knew how to stay alert. Besides, they were deep inside the Greek camp, near the middle of the long row of ships. No assassin was ever going to reach this far.

"Why have you been awake?" he asked.

"Writing." Thersites grunted as his fingers found a hard point in the muscle and dug at it. "I like to get everything down while it's fresh in my mind, so I remember it as it happened. And my friend, a *lot* happened yesterday."

"I noticed," he said.

Most people avoided Thersites, if they could. In truth he didn't help himself, with his wily cleverness and a lacerating tongue to go with it. He made men feel slow and clumsy, and for a proud fighting man to be made to feel so by a cripple was… difficult for them. But usually they avoided him for his disabilities, more than anything else. A whole clutch of them, foisted on a single man by some cruel god; the hollow chest, stopped shoulders, and club foot. It was a wonder Thersites could clamber out of his own bed.

Eudorus didn't mind him though. The best friend of his childhood had grown up crooked, his once-hale body taking on a twist of the spine and then a curve too, hunching him over. Glaucus had developed a biting wit too. It might be something that went with infirmity, a way of challenging the limitations of a weak body.

Glaucus was named for a sea-god, once a mortal man, who had gained everlasting life by eating a magical herb. If such things existed they were beyond the reach of all but the most fortunate of men. Eudorus' friend had mocked the wrong man and been killed in a tavern when he was seventeen, which had put an end to all his challenges.

"I don't suppose I could speak with him," Thersites said. He nodded towards the large tent some way towards the sea, in front of the black prows of the Myrmidon ships. He didn't name Achilles though. There was no need.

"He's sleeping," Eudorus said.

A cry carried through the air, the soft tone of a woman. A woman in passion, at that. It seemed to come from the tent.

Thersites raised his eyebrows.

"Well, he's supposed to be sleeping," Eudorus amended. "It's just... you've heard of Briseis?"

Thersites nodded. "There are rumours of a woman he took from Pedasos. A priestess, isn't she?"

"She was. A Bride of Apollo," he agreed. "Though she says it the Trojan way; Ipirru. Achilles spared the other priestesses when she agreed to come with him. It's the kind of thing he does. He falls in love easily."

"Lust, not love," Thersites said. He caught sight of Eudorus' frown. "No, I don't mean an insult. But love lasts longer than Achilles' dalliances. He picks women up and forgets them a month later. You know he does."

He conceded that, reluctantly. "But it's still love, while it lasts. The rules aren't the same for him. He's just..."

"Achilles," Thersites nodded. They shared a smile, and another cry came to them across the sand.

Eudorus found he didn't want to listen to that. He wished the gulls would call, or the *Meltemi* blow so the surf roared louder on the sand, but neither happened so he spoke instead. "What's the plan for tomorrow?"

"For today, now," Thersites said. He nodded towards the eastern sky, where the stars had begun to fade. "The plan's as you'd expect. The armies will march out to confront each other on the Plain, between the braids of Scamander. Achilles and Hector will face each other between them." He rubbed his leg again. "The orders are for nobody to interfere, no matter what happens. Agamemnon wants this fight seen to be fair."

"But you doubt it?"

"I'm a cynic," Thersites said wryly. "Two armies that hate each other will be drawn up together on the Plain. I don't need to be a Seer to know how easily things could go wrong."

That was how Eudorus saw it too. He'd have the Myrmidons ready to step in, whatever orders the fool in the rainbow armour saw fit to issue. One hint of trouble and he'd throw a ring of bronze around Achilles, whether it was an arrow fired by a too-nervous archer or a spear flung out of sheer tension. Ugly things happened fast when armies got too close. Maybe it was the gods meddling again, but Eudorus thought it was probably just human stupidity.

"I think," Thersites said, "that plan is the most complex idea Agamemnon could come up with if you gave him a week to consider alternatives."

"Careful," Eudorus warned. "There are always ears to listen in a campsite, and tongues to tell their tales."

"Agamemnon faces worse troubles than my little doubts," Thersites said. "You really have no doubt at all that Achilles will win, do you?"

That was the way with the little man. One moment idle talk, the next a knife of words driven right into you, past all your deceptions and deceits. Glaucus had been the same. Sometimes it seemed cripples could see right into the thoughts of ordinary men.

"Not one," Eudorus said.

It was plain honesty. Eudorus had never seen Hector fight, but he'd heard the stories, and he thought the Trojan was probably the second best warrior in the world. Better than Diomedes, better than Ajax even with that bulwark of a shield he carried around as though it was nothing. Better than any prince or captain from Egypt or Assyria. It was no wonder the easterners spoke of him as the finest fighting man in the world.

But he was no match for Achilles.

160

He wasn't merely mortal. Eudorus was sure of that. His mother had come from Scyros, an island where half the priestesses were said to be descended from sea-nymphs, the daughters of Nereids and men. Hardly any had ever left, before Thetis met Peleus of Thessaly and married him. That meant their lines bred back into each other, generation after generation, like horses on the ranches back home. Eudorus had spent enough time around the wranglers to know that sometimes a long-hidden trait would reappear, for no reason they could tell. Often it was stronger than ever before.

He thought that had happened with Achilles. Something in the man harked back to the pure Nereids, handmaidens waiting on Poseidon deep under the sea. They weren't quite gods, perhaps; a half-step short of Olympian grace and power. But they were a long bowshot more than human, and whatever that difference was – speed, poise, balance – Achilles had in himself.

"No doubts at all," he said. There was a sound behind him and he turned, to see Achilles standing at the flap of his tent in a kilt and shirt, the sort of clothes a Trojan might wear. His hair was mussed but otherwise he looked the same as always, except for a fire in his eyes that was obvious even in the not-quite light before dawn.

"Ready the men," Achilles said. He turned and went back inside, and by then Eudorus was already moving.

*

A horn blew.

At once the lead companies began to march out of Troy. Crescas was too far from the front to see for himself, but he could hear the tramp of booted feet, and the calls of captains to their men. There was no cheering though. The people of this city had cried their heroes' names often enough, and seen them come back laid on a shield. That couldn't be borne again, not today. Not with Hector. Men and women lined the main avenue and watched the soldiers leave, but they held their tongues.

The group ahead stepped off. A moment later the captain called an order and Crescas felt his feet begin to move.

He was going to battle. To a battlefield, at least, where two men would batter each another and one would fall, one rise, and a war would end. Except the Greeks were not to be trusted, they

161

never had been, and no one in Troy knew that better than Crescas the Argive.

They still called him that, even in this war. But he understood now that to the Trojans he was *their* Argive, a western barbarian who'd shown the sense to change allegiance and the cleverness to build a life here. A business, a wife, a daughter. Employees, even.

"Just keep your nerve," Bienor said beside him. One of those employees, his face little more than seams piled on top of a neat beard. The ship captain looked peculiar in a cuirass, even a simple one of leather stretched over a frame. He hefted a bow in one hand. "That's all."

"You've told us that twenty times," Eteon said. He looked at his boss for support. "Hasn't he, Crescas?"

"Let him tell us twenty more, as long as it helps," he answered.

Plain old Crescas, going to war. A sailor, later a trader and marketeer, with a bow in his fist and only a passing ability to shoot it. Going to war, and taking along the men who worked for him, and had become friends. Against the *Greeks;* his own people, once, and if you measured by blood and birth, they still were. It was said that nothing in the world bound more tightly than ties of family, and yet here he was, ready to risk his life against his kin.

He marched down the sloping street and under the Scaean Gate, with the stables on his right and the battlement above. Then turn hard left, where the road ran between two towering walls of stone, and twist back to the right as it came back out into the morning's bright sunlight. And there was Hector in his chariot, with Paris on one side and Lycaon on the other, the three sons of Priam letting the army see them as they passed. Nobody spoke though, not one soldier raised a cry of greeting or praise. They walked by and on down the switchback trail that descended the hill on which Troy stood without a word.

As though Hector is already dead, Crescas thought. He tried to squash the thought but it resurfaced, more bitter than before. *As though his shade is beyond hearing the words of men, and the army knows it.*

The lead companies had already reached the bottom of the hill, and forded the river Chiblak where it ran past Bramble Hill. Outliers had been posted there since morning, to ensure that the

Argives couldn't hide a force out of sight and then ambush the Trojan force as it came by. But the land was empty, as far as Crescas could see, and he supposed it really must be because the army went right on marching, beyond Bramble Hill and then westward, to cross the nearer branch of Scamander where bulrushes pushed the elms and tamarisk aside, marking the ford.

Six chariots rolled by, each with its driver and rider, and a minute later six more. The foot soldiers stood off the road to let them past, then formed their units again and went on. Ahead Crescas saw the white and gold of the Apollonians, grievously reduced now but rearmed with Mursili's iron points. Once he caught a glimpse of the Hittite company as well, five hundred little brown-skinned men in armour of rigid leather, treated in some way he didn't know.

They were barely across Scamander when an order was called and they turned downstream, walking now behind a thick line of companies taking their positions. Trees lining the bank threw shade over them. They walked until they came to a place where the land was a little higher and they stopped.

A snapped-off half of an arrow lay in the grass not far away, though there hadn't been much fighting in this part of the Plain. A little distance from it was what might have been a finger, before the insects got at it.

"Look," Eteon said, nudging him. "The Maeonians."

"Did you think you came here to gawk?" the captain demanded. He was a wiry fellow called Caletor, with a bow somewhat larger than any of the men carried. But then, he probably knew how to use it better, too. "Shut up and check your strings. We're going to do this right."

Eteon was right though. Sarpedon and his men made up the two companies immediately in front of them. The king wasn't in view – he must be down the front somewhere – but the bulls painted on their shields identified them. Without that motif Crescas wouldn't have thought them any different from Trojans, but now his attention was drawn to it he noticed subtle differences; the shape of a nose, the jut of a jaw. He was glad to have them here, however they looked. Troy had suffered terribly. A thousand southerners might tip the scales their way again, if the Greeks went back on their word.

Crescas realised, with a dull ache in his heart, that he expected them to. It was what Greeks did.

And he hated them. They might be his birth people, but he loathed them the way water sprites detested fire, or as Cerberus hated the living who came to the gates of Hades. He'd never been a fighting man, never wanted to be, but now he wished he'd trained and fought all his years, just so he could hammer life from as many Argive bodies as he could and turn them into corpses, rotting to pieces on the grass with no one there to bury them.

He swallowed, aware his heart was beating too fast. *Keep your nerve,* Bienor had said, and it was good advice. Crescas checked his bowstring and the hang of his quiver, then checked them again. When he looked up the Argives were pouring onto the Plain.

They came in a swarm, regardless of where the fords were or how thickly the trees clustered at the banks. Crescas swallowed again when he saw how many they were; their numbers seemed greater, now he was down in the pastures with them. They must have formed their line west of the river's braids and then simply marched across, a great block of men that stretched from near the Bay of Troy for two miles southwards. Chariots rolled ahead of them, pulled in the Argive way by only two horses, and bowmen came behind.

"Be easy," Caletor said. "But be ready too."

The Greek host kept coming. They moved at a walk, not hurrying, but it still felt like a headlong charge to Crescas. Around him Trojans shifted in unease, measuring the advancing force against their own. Men twisted to look back at the walls of the city, the only haven they had.

Captains ordered their men to stay calm. Caletor told his company to be easy again.

The Argives stopped, perhaps a hundred yards away. After a moment two chariots rolled out from the ranks, one bearing a figure in rainbow armour, the other one in black.

Two more went to meet them. Hector in his white-plumed helmet, and beside him Paris wearing a leopard-skin cuirass.

*

"So," Achilles said. "The man all Troy relies on."

Hector ignored him. It was theatre now, as much as anything. He and this other man were going to fight, they all knew it, but

164

there would be a degree of posturing before spears are unsheathed. Sometimes what you said, or didn't say, could have an effect. He addressed his words to Agamemnon. "You will honour the terms of this match?"

"I have said I will," the high King replied. In the other chariot Achilles scowled at being ignored.

"You will take Helen and leave these shores?"

"I answered you. I do not see the need to do so again."

"Even if I fight in his place?" Paris asked suddenly. Hector checked the urge to look at him in surprise. His brother had asked this before, but that was in private, not before the Argives. Paris was a fool, of course, ignorant of the ways of warfare. This spear had been thrown. Its course was set now.

"You weren't challenged," Achilles said contemptuously. "And you're too much a coward to mix with the fighting men. Be quiet while your betters are talking."

"Coward?" Paris repeated. "Let us talk of that, then. I am here, and offering to fight you, Achilles. And where is Menelaus? This war is fought in his name. Where is the king of Laconia?"

Silence from the Argives.

"How many men have died for him?" Paris asked. He'd always had cleverness, and now he'd found courage from somewhere he was going to speak his mind, it seemed. "Has he fought at *all* since you attacked us, or is he too sodden with grief and wine? No wonder his wife fled. She left him for a better man."

"Bind your tongue!" Agamemnon swore. "My brother will still be ruling in Sparta when your bones are picked clean. You farmyard whelp! This war is your doing, the result of your own acts. If you were any kind of man you'd have offered to fight days ago!"

"If your brother was," Hector said, "he would have fought at least once. Starting days ago."

Agamemnon flushed almost as bright as his patterned armour. It was hard not to laugh. The man was such a peacock, with all his dreams of bright glory but little substance beneath the finery. And his brother was worse, a drunk and a coward, exactly as Paris named him. The sons of Atreus had not become the leaders they promised to be, when they were boys.

165

"These are words," Achilles said then. His voice was harsh and it changed the mood in a moment. "Prepare yourself for death, prince of Troy. In the name of my friend, whom you slew."

"I've slain a lot of friends," Hector said. "I don't see what makes yours any different. Or you."

"You will," Achilles said. He turned his chariot and drove back towards his own lines, already shouting for his weapons.

Words had made no difference. Hector hadn't really expected them to, but you tried, when you could.

"Go," he said to his brother. He stepped down from his chariot and handed the reins to Paris. His spears were propped in the car and he took them down, hefting them for weight as he always did. "Tarhun be with you."

"Hector," Paris said. His lips twisted.

"Go." He smiled this time, to take the sting away. "This wasn't all your fault. Antenor and our father misjudged too. It happens, Paris. Men make mistakes. All we can ask is that we aren't disgraced by them." He thrust the spears into the earth beside him. "Go. It is time."

166

Chapter Eighteen

The Overbearing Shield

The two men advanced. Both wore helmets with a white crest, and swooping cheek guards that hid their faces. Both were tall men, bulky across the shoulders, graceful, strong.

But it was easy to tell them apart. Achilles' armour was golden, Hector's lacquered in the blue and gold of Troy. Every man in both armies would be able to see which of them fell.

Isander thought that was dangerous, actually. This combat was meant to end the war, one way or the other, but it could easily lead instead to another bloody, desperate melee. The Greeks had not done well in such fights before. Looking at the two armies an observer might think they were certain to win the next, such was their advantage in numbers, but Isander's eyes wandered to the iron-armed Apollonians, and he wondered.

Then Hector threw a spear, and the thought flew apart in his mind.

Achilles crouched, one leg bent and the other extended behind him. He didn't even try to dodge. The spear rang off his shield and landed in the grass, but he didn't glance at it. His attention was all on Hector. Then he straightened, lifted his own spear, and threw.

It flashed across the gap to Hector – who braced exactly as Achilles had done, seeming not to even watch the shaft. It struck his angled shield and looped away harmlessly. Then Isander understood: the two men had gauged the spears' flight early, taken their positions, and then studied one another from behind the rims of their shields. Looking for clues to how the opponent would move, how he positioned his body, or perhaps something Isander hadn't thought of. *Probably* something he hadn't thought of. These were the two best fighting men in the world.

They pulled their second spears from the ground, hefted them, and started towards one another.

Hector moved easily, seeming relaxed, but Achilles walked on stiff legs, stalking like an angry cat. It was the first difference Isander had seen between them. And it was Achilles who burst into sudden motion, whiplash-quick, darting forward and right to strike at Hector's flank.

The Trojan wasn't there. He had stepped aside and jabbed back as his enemy passed, but Achilles was twisting away before the blow was properly begun, and Hector's thrust met only air. Isander's senses were straining towards the two men, yet even so it had all happened so fast that he almost missed it.

A soft murmur ran through the armies, and then a gasp as men remembered to breathe. Hector looked at Achilles and nodded, as though to himself. Achilles stared back and bristled.

The fight began again.

*

Aeneas was thinking of swallows.

Troas was crowded with them in summer, especially along the coasts. The low, wet Plain of Troy teemed with the insects on which swallows fed, attracting them as soon as they came north from wherever they spent the cold season. But catching insects was hard. Swallows flickered left and right as they flew, picking mites too small to see right out of the air.

Like the spears of Hector and Achilles, faint shadows that were never still, so the eye couldn't settle on them. Dart and flit, nudge and jab. The fighters were trying to manoeuvre one another, not even attempting to land a serious blow. Aeneas had spent a lifetime fighting, and he knew.

He had never seen Hector fight so well. Growing up there had been three of them, all closely matched although Hector was always a little ahead. Hector, Aeneas and Pandarus, a trio of young men who dreamed of being heroes, and who wrestled and fought with spear and sword as they learned how to be men. Aeneas had been perhaps a shade faster than the other two, Pandarus a whisker stronger, but it was in Hector that speed and power came together best. The other two had beaten him, on occasion, but they had lost far more often.

Had they fought the Hector who faced the Argive now, Aeneas doubted they would have won at all. Or even lasted one minute, come to that. Hector was perfectly balanced in every moment, always moving, shifting places and positions so Achilles never had a set target to aim at. And yet with all that, every scintilla of his skill, he was still not winning.

"Come on," someone muttered, further along the line. The heavy accent meant it could only be Sarpedon, standing at the

front of his companies, but Aeneas didn't glance away from the fight. "Kill that thick-skulled Argive so we can all go home."

Nobody else responded, or seemed to hear. Both armies watched in near silence, broken only by the occasional sigh of breath as though all the soldiers had remembered to exhale at the same time. They hadn't even begun to creep forward, though that usually happened during a single combat as men forgot themselves and edged up for a better view.

Someone was praying. Aeneas knew the royal line of Troy well enough to recognise Paris' voice. It took his focus for an instant though, and he nearly missed it when Hector broke Achilles' spear.

*

Achilles had jabbed again, as he had done twenty times already. This time Hector shifted *towards* the thrust, bore down with his shield, and the spear which clanged off it buried its point in the earth. A moment later Hector stamped a booted foot on the shaft and split it clean through. He was rising from his crouch at once, pulling back to gain space.

Not fast enough. Thrasymedes watched as Achilles let go of the spear and drew his sword in one movement, and incredibly he moved towards Hector instead of back. A diagonal slash missed the Trojan prince by inches and forced him off balance, making him stumble, his shield shifting away from his body. When the reverse cut came he could do nothing but block with his own spear, which Achilles hacked through a foot above Hector's grip. Three feet of ash thumped to the earth.

Achilles slashed again, but Hector had his balance back now and avoided with ease. They stood a few yards apart, both breathing hard.

Thrasymedes could never have done that. Not either part: Hector's beautifully timed deception, or Achilles' instant, brilliant response. Heracles aside, he didn't think there had ever been a man who could have done; not Perseus, not Jason, not even Theseus who his father had known.

His father had been killed by this man. Hector had flung a spear that took Nestor in the throat, fulfilling the prophecy Calchas had spoken back at Aulis. *The first man ashore shall ascend to immortality:* die, in other words. Thrasymedes ought to

169

hate Hector, really. He had done, in the days since, but he didn't now. It was impossible to watch such courage and skill and still hate.

"Time to end this," Achilles said. The only words spoken by either man since the fight began, and they carried. There was blood on his thigh, from a wound Thrasymedes couldn't see. It didn't seem to slow Achilles as he started forwards again.

*

Never anyone as good. In all these years, all these battles, never anyone as good as this.

Hector has expected that, of course. Everyone around the Greensea has heard stories of Achilles for years now. They feared the Myrmidons, the black ants who brought fire and slaughter without warning, but they admired their leader, almost in spite of themselves. You could laud a man for his skill and still hate him. Or fear him.

Hector isn't a man given to fear, and he feels none now. But he does recognise that he is losing.

Achilles is too good. There have been stronger men – a black-bearded Assyrian at Emar, for one, half a foot taller than Hector with a chest like a bull's. But he was slow, and Hector had ducked under a blow that would have cleaved a tree in two and thrust his spear up into the man's gizzard. There have been faster men too, such as an Argive raider in Maeonia years ago, all dance and dodge until Hector cornered him by a wall and impaled him to it. And Aeneas, of course, who has always been near as quick as thought. But there has never been someone who is both, and whose mind flashes even faster than his hands. There is no surprising Achilles, no fooling him. Hector even thinks the Argive foresaw the move that cracked his spear; not in time to prevent it, but in time to turn defence into attack and shear off Hector's shaft in return.

Achilles rams into him, all his weight behind the overbearing shield. Hector is thrown staggering backwards. His boots dig into earth made soft and sticky by Scamander's water. To those watching he might seem as much in control as ever, but Hector knows different.

He feints an overhand blow and then hurls himself at Achilles, striking the Argive with his shield just as he himself was struck. Achilles is knocked backwards, but he never loses his balance as Hector did. He expected the riposte, accepted it even, willing to gamble everything on his own strength and stamina. He will exchange strike and counter-strike until he wears Hector down. It will happen. All that is needed is time. Never anyone as good. In all these years.

He takes a gash to his shoulder, a whipped cut that comes over the top of his shield too fast for him to react. That will hasten the end. It isn't too serious now, but every time he lifts the shield the cut will open wider, and blood will run from his body taking his strength with it. He's already weary. Perhaps some of it is the effect of previous days of fighting, and especially that tumbling fall from the chariot Ajax had broken with a driven spear. But only some of it, and anyway that's a part of any battle. No use complaining.

Achilles' sword lances into his leg just above the knee, into the thick muscle there. Hector lashes a reply and is gratified to see it crash into the side of Achilles' golden helmet, leaving a dent. Achilles is jolted sideways. But he shakes his head and comes again, grinning now, no doubt feeling in that last blow a lack of power that tells of fatigue.

Bit silly to guess what Achilles is thinking. He should focus on his own fight, his own technique.

Except it doesn't matter now. Hector knows he's going to die here, and that's all right. Troy will be saved by it. Sometimes that is the task of a prince, to give his life so his people can be made safe. His father will hand Helen back, to face whatever punishment the Argives have planned for her, and the invaders will sail away. There will be grieving families all over Troas, sons and fathers lost, but the war will be over. No more will die. And the royal line of Troy will have suffered alongside the commoners, with two princes killed but two left alive. A fair price to pay, to escape the ruin of this war.

He parries a thunderous overhand and thinks of his wife. Andromache, whom he loves. Has always loved. And the son she gave him, little Astyanax, who will grow up with no memory of his father but who *will* grow up, a prince of Troy, happy and proud in his strength.

He parries again, then a third time. Those big, down-swinging blows are doing what he feared, making him raise his shield so the wound in his shoulder is pulled ever wider. There is quite a

171

lot of blood now, and he can't put full weight on his wounded left leg. He retreats again. Absorbs another hammering impact and backs up further.

Thinks of something he can try.

When the next attack is launched he takes it not on his shield but his sword, hurling himself left to do so. And then he spins, coming around on Achilles' right where that looping blow has left him exposed, Hector's shield about to be driven with all his remaining strength into the Argive's vulnerable side.

He feels the sword bite deep into his armpit, behind his shield. He isn't really sure how that happened, and it doesn't seem to matter. The right side of his face is wet and he can smell earth, the rich black soil of Scamander, where the horses run. He can see Andromache, wearing the deep blue gown he gave her, beads sewn into her hair as she smiles.

It is not Andromache, he realises, but another woman. One who shines, and holds out arms into which he goes with a small sigh.

*

The Trojan line stood silent. Across the field the Greeks were cheering, but Aeneas hardly heard them.

He watched Achilles pull off his helmet and toss it aside. It bounced on the grass and rolled to a halt. The Argive used a foot to push Hector over on his back and looked down at him.

Paris was white and staring. Aeneas made his way towards the prince, walking on legs that felt numb and unsteady, like a new-born foal's. Not one Trojan made a sound as he moved. He climbed the little slope to the archers and came to a halt beside Paris.

"Honour the terms," he said. "Give Helen back, and end the war."

"What?"

"You must honour the terms," Aeneas said again. Paris' eyes were shocked, empty of thought. "To honour your brother, and his death."

His death. That was too large a truth for his mind to hold and Aeneas' mind shied away from it. First Pandarus and now Hector, the friends of his life, brothers of the soul. What did you

172

do, when such men were taken from you? How were you supposed to find joy?

"Send a herald," Paris said to the man beside him. The words were jerky, as though pulled from his throat with a fish hook, one by one. "Bring my – bring my wife from the city to –"

Around them the army murmured suddenly, a rising surge of anger. At the same time the Argive cheering broke up uncertainly. Aeneas turned, seeking the cause of it as one hand went to the sword hilt at his shoulder, and he saw Achilles had brought his chariot over the Hector's body. For a moment he thought it must be to bring the corpse back to the Trojans.

Then Achilles spat, full in the dead man's face.

"What's he doing?" Paris asked.

Aeneas couldn't reply. He watched the Argive pull a rope from the chariot and begin to tie it around Hector's ankles.

"Achilles!" Paris shouted. He took a step forward. "We will honour the agreement made. Hand my brother's body back for burial."

Achilles ignored him. He finished tying the rope and started back to the chariot.

He was going to drag the body. It was a thing Argives did sometimes, when they sacked a town. The captured king would be bound and hauled around the walls, until the stony ground smashed his body into pulp. It was a sign of contempt, meted out to lord who had hidden inside the walls rather than come out and fight. A humiliation, done in public. But it wasn't done to men who fell in combat. Aeneas thought he was going to be sick.

"Archers ready!" Paris called. Bows creaked as they were raised. "Stop, Achilles! There was an agreement. Show honour!"

Achilles began to tie the rope to the chariot.

"All we can ask is that we're not disgraced by our mistakes," Paris said. That made no sense at all, but Aeneas had no time to dwell on it. Paris lifted his voice again. "I warn you, for the last time. Stop this!"

Achilles stepped into the car and reached for his reins.

"Loose!" Paris ordered.

Arrows flew, two hundred of them arcing into the space between the armies. The range was very short. Achilles reacted to the snap of strings by throwing himself out of the chariot and down, but there were too many shafts, and too little time. Arrows thunked into the wooden car and the earth around it. Two struck

173

the nearside horse and it went down, leaving the other screaming as it fought to stay upright in the traces. And five, then ten found Achilles, some skidding off his helmet, others piercing his cuirass. One went through his leg and pinned it to the black earth, and he gave a shout of fury.

The Argives roared, and a moment later they were pouring across the Plain. No order was given that Aeneas heard. The whole host simply charged, a black mass of men rushing down on the outnumbered Trojans. Aeneas threw himself back towards his own men, yelling back over his shoulder as he went. "Sound the horns, Paris! We have to retreat!"

Horns blared from his Dardanians even before he reached them, and Aeneas blessed whatever god had given sense to his heralds in that moment. Other notes sounded up and down the line. The Trojans and their allies began to withdraw, pulling back across the Scamander.

Hector's body was lost. That was a bitter cruelty, one the heir of Troy had not deserved. There was no help for it though. He had been a friend, and Aeneas wished he could have brought him back for burial, but his duty now was care for the living. For all of them; there was no one now but him to take command of the Trojan forces. He ran back down the retreating line, buffeting his way past soldiers until he found those in the white and gold of the Apollonians, the iron tips of their spears shining. Aeneas saw a captain and grabbed him by the arm.

"Get to the ford of the Chiblak," he snapped. The Argives were closing the gap already. "We need time to get inside the city. Buy it for us."

"We will do that," a deep voice said. He turned to find Sarpedon there, a big man with creases on his brow and hair gone grey at the temples. "My Maeonians have not bled yet in this war."

"You don't need to –"

"Against the Argives we all have reason for vengeance," Sarpedon said. "And Hector was a nephew of sorts, through my sister. Allow us this."

He was Hecuba's brother. Aeneas had forgotten that, in the rush of events. He hesitated, even with the enemy rushing down upon them all, and then nodded once. Sarpedon crammed a helmet on his head and smiled like a wolf in the dark.

174

It was a long way back to the city. Aeneas turned and began to run.

Chapter Nineteen

Stand or Fall

Achilles sat up. Arrows stuck out all over his cuirass but none had gone deep, and he broke them all away with a sweep of his arm. He reached down to snap off the arrow in his calf and pulled the shaft through, wincing. There was another in his ankle which he broke as well, but when he tried to pull it he went suddenly white.

"The barbs are caught on bone," a man with a pointed beard said. He knelt by Achilles and probed the area with gentle fingers. "I'll have to cut flesh to free them. You won't be walking for some days."

"I need to ride a chariot right now," Achilles said. "Men are fighting."

The man shrugged. "Try, then. You'll collapse at once, and the effort will grind the barbs against bone so recovery takes longer. Which would you prefer?"

Achilles scowled at him and said nothing. After a moment a pair of Myrmidons came forward to help him stand. He kept weight off his left leg, which also had a gash across the meat of the thigh, left by Hector's sword. There was a lot of blood. The physician would need to clean it before he dealt with the arrow.

Metal crashed and boomed from across the Plain. The Greeks had caught the fleeing Trojans, and it seemed there would be battle again. Odysseus had hoped that was over. He had ordered his men to begin loading the ships for the journey home, once the duel was finished. That wasn't going to happen now.

He looked at Achilles. "You betrayed the agreement."

"Don't lecture me," the younger man said. "He killed Patroclus. I won't forgive him for that."

"Forgive him?" Odysseus shook his head. "You've spent a lifetime raiding around the Greensea. In war men die, as Raging Ares has decided. Don't pretend not to understand this."

"I told you not to lecture me," Achilles snarled.

Another man came up to them then, surrounded by soldiers and clad in rainbow armour that shone in the sun. Agamemnon held the sceptre of the kings, and it brought silence.

"You really shouldn't," the High King said to Odysseus. "Lecture him, I mean. He just killed the great hope of Troy. Now the city will fall."

He shook his head. "The great hope of Troy is her walls."

"Which you and Thersites say you have plans for," Agamemnon answered. "Is my trust in your word misplaced?"

"We shall see," he said, with a one-shouldered shrug he knew was characteristic of him. "But there's such a thing as honour. When Achilles spat in Hector's face he mocked the gods."

"The gods are with us," Menelaus said. He'd been standing half behind his brother, so Odysseus hadn't noticed him until now. "We war with the blessing of Zeus. The oracle at Delphi said so."

"No she didn't," Odysseus said wearily. "But I'm pleased to see you've joined us today, my lord of Laconia, and sober too it seems. Perhaps you might chase down some Trojans for us."

"Watch your tongue –"

Odysseus had already turned back to Achilles. "I don't agree with what you tried to do to Hector's body. It sits ill on you."

"I don't care," the other man said.

"And that's your failing." Odysseus gestured to the bearded man. "Listen to Deiochus, here. Nestor thought he was the best physician in Greece. Learned his craft in Egypt, and there are no better doctors in the world."

He turned away and went to join his soldiers, waiting patiently for him to lead them. They were very few now, barely half the number who had sailed from Ithaca in the spring, though the losses hadn't been as severe as that might suggest. A hundred men were absent, together with some colleagues from western Achaea and Locris, mountainous lands all. Few in the army knew they were gone, and fewer still knew why. Odysseus, Thersites and Agamemnon, that was all. Not even Diomedes had been told.

Odysseus had thought the fighting was over. Perhaps that had been more hope than expectation, more wish than solid truth. But this morning he'd been ready to sail home to his wife and son, whoever won the challenge between the two armies. He yearned for Penelope, the feel and scent of her, but his whole body seemed to long to look upon Telemachus again.

Not to be allowed, it seemed. Not yet.

"Come on," he said to his men, and started towards Troy.

*

Most of the Trojans had got across Scamander before the
Argives caught up. The river was shallow along much of its
eastern braid, offering plenty of fords. The bank was high
though, a levee built by the silt of flood after flood, and there
defenders turned to give battle. Pursuing Greeks were cut down
as they scrambled up the bank. Arrows fell among those behind,
and any man who fell wounded into the river was trampled
underfoot and drowned.

But Scamander was too long, and the Argives too numerous,
for the defence to hold. Wise Trojans dealt a handful of blows
and then fell back, hurrying to the narrower confines of the land
south of the river Chiblak. Those who delayed too long were
soon surrounded. Aeneas saw three, then four such groups, the
largest of more than a hundred men, fighting in a circle while the
barbarian westerners howled around them.

He didn't order an effort to save them. It would have been a
waste of men, and to no purpose. By selling their lives so dearly
they bought time for the others, still flying north towards the city.
Aeneas looked for the Maeonians and couldn't find them in the
morass of men.

Someone snatched at his arm.

"He's still out there!" the soldier yelled. Aeneas knew him
but the man's name wouldn't come. "At the river!"

"Who is?"

"We can save him!"

"Who?" he bellowed. He pried the man's hand loose. "What
are you talking about?"

The soldier blinked, as though surprised to realise he hadn't
explained himself. Aeneas had him placed now; he was Periso, a
man from Zeleia out towards Mount Ida. A Trojan by blood, and
a charioteer in the days when there were still horses for
everyone. "Lycaon. The prince! He's out by the river."

Aeneas turned to look, heart lurching. He was close to
Bramble Hill now, with the Scamander two hundred yards west
of him. Too far to go. *Priam will lose another son. He will have
only one left alive.*

And that one was Paris, a seducer of women but not a man fit
to be king. Even Creusa said so, when they were alone. Aeneas
had held her when she grieved for Troilus, and now it seemed

178

she would lose two more brothers in a single day. He shook his head like a dog ridding its ears of water. Best make sure she didn't lose a husband too.

"There's nothing we can do," he told Periso. "Get back to the city."

"But he's –"

"Do you want to die? Then go!" Aeneas thrust a finger out towards the battle. "Go, and by the time the sun goes down your soul will be walking the road to the underworld. But you can't do anything there. Do you even know which group Lycaon is with?"

"No," the man admitted.

"Then it's futile. And he might be dead already, in any case." He rubbed his eyes. "Now get moving. Unless you really do want to see the underworld tonight."

Periso nodded miserably and started up the road. It wound past Bramble Hill and towards the Scaean Gate, the horse entrance where the chariot animals were kept. It was already thick with Trojans, streaming all the way up to the doubled wall which hid the gates themselves. Some men had continued around the city rather than face that clogged portcullis, heading for the Dardanian Gate on the east side or the Attarina Gate facing the sea. That was good, as long as they moved fast. And as long as Sarpedon could hold the ford.

Aeneas found him there at last, with his two companies of Maeonians. Nearly a thousand men, all with that charging red bull painted on their cuirasses and shields. They were standing aside to let the Trojans pour past them, but close enough to block the ford quickly when the Argives appeared.

"We're ready," Sarpedon said, before Aeneas could speak. "You chose a good place to make a stand, Dardanian. The river here is narrower than Scamander, but the banks are steeper and the water runs deep."

"Just don't stand too long," he said.

Sarpedon shrugged. "Against the Argives the choice is simple. Stand, or fall. They allow nothing else. My men came here to make a difference in this war. Every one of them has lost family to those raiders. They all volunteered. This seems as good a place as any to leave a mark."

"You mean to die here."

"I mean to make a lot of Argives die here first," Sarpedon grinned. "Tell my sister the queen that I died well, Aeneas. The

179

gods watch over you in the days ahead, my friend, and see you through to light."

There was a roar from behind Aeneas, away to the south. A hundred-throated beast was dying there, while its conqueror bellowed victory at the sky. He didn't turn to look. "Why would you do this?"

"For the same reason your Dardanians have fought here," the big man said. "For the same reason Danel is bringing an army from Miletos to aid Troy in this war. The Argives have to be stopped, Aeneas. Otherwise they'll reduce the shores of the Greensea to little but smoke and ashes, and the only people left alive will be Greeks and their slaves."

"The Hittites have stopped them before."

"The Hittites sent five hundred men," Sarpedon said. "Ten years ago they would have sent an army large enough to bury the Argives under the bodies of their own dead. They have fallen, and you know it. The cities of the coast must look to their own defence now."

He was afraid that was true, actually. Or at least, that there was enough truth in it to make it impossible to deny. There wasn't time to argue in any case. That roar came from behind again, closer now, and this time Aeneas looked around. The press of men hid whatever was happening from him, but further back the trailing edge of the Trojan army seemed to be fighting to escape from something. He could hear the shouts, feel the sudden pressure of panicked men.

"The Argives are here," Sarpedon observed. "Tell my sister, Aeneas. Don't forget."

"I won't," he said. They clasped arms and then Aeneas went on, up the road towards Troy. He was on the slopes of the city itself, above the level of the Plain, before he could look back and see what was happening behind him.

*

The ford was narrower than most, hardly wide enough for a chariot to pass, and it looked as though the banks had been cut away to allow even that much. Willow and elm grew out of underbrush on both sides, above banks that dropped away to the water below. It might have been designed to provide a last defence before the walls. Knowing Hector, it probably had.

The hero was dead, but he could still hurt the Greeks.

Odysseus sheltered behind the sideways branch of a tamarisk tree and peered down at the fight. A company of Greeks had driven across and engaged the defenders, leaving two dozen of their number felled by arrows in the water. The bodies were washing away, but slowly; the Chiblak was lazier than Scamander. Greek archers were trying to return fire, but the cover on the south bank was sparse, as though it had been cut away. Hector's work again, most likely. The Greek archers kept being driven below the ridge.

A soldier slithered up to the branch on his belly and squinted through a gap under the branch. Half his face and helmet was wet with blood. A good helmet too, covered with boar's tusks, and the armour was exceptional. Odysseus thought he had to be a lord, but a moment of study told him his mistake; this was Isander, and the armour poor Teucer's.

"Is your company here?" he asked. Isander jerked a thumb over his shoulder without looking around. "Good. I want you to take it to the left and try to force the bank. Can you do that?"

"Someone tried it before I got here," Isander said. "He lost fifty men to arrows trying to clamber up the bank. See where the grass was scraped off? The earth breaks up faster than a man can climb."

"Then go upstream," Odysseus said. "Try there."

Isander shrugged. "Why bother? Mud is mud. It'll be the same there. And besides," he added, before Odysseus could interrupt, "I answer to the new king of Elis, Odysseus, not to you. And Socus has told me to wait."

"Wait?" He blinked. "If we keep hitting those Maeonians head on we'll be here all day, and the Trojans will be safe inside the walls by the time we're through." A thought occurred to him. "Wait for what?"

"For *him,*" Isander said, and pointed.

It was Ajax. He was impossible to mistake, with his size and that huge oblong shield he carried. He came through the gathered Greek forces like a spear through flesh, his Salamid soldiers massed behind him in a spreading wave. As his head turned Odysseus thought he saw hatred gleam in the shadowed eyes, just as they focused for a moment on Isander. There had been no lessening of the bitterness there, then.

The Salamids came to the edge of the river and just jumped straight in, shields up against the hail of arrows that rattled against metal and stuck in leather, and sometimes in flesh. Men went down, some dead and others wounded, but whichever it was they tripped others coming behind. The ford became a mass of struggling men, easy targets for the Trojan bowmen.

"Idiot," Odysseus muttered.

Ajax kept going, his reduced band at his back. His tower shield had been repaired with a plate of bronze across the split top, inelegant but effective. He reached the Greeks already fighting and pushed right through them, to lead his men into the Maeonians at a crashing run. From half behind the branch Odysseus saw the defenders' line bend backwards, and a big man sprang forward to bolster it.

"Ares teeth!" he exclaimed. "That's Sarpedon, I swear it is!"

Isander turned his blood-streaked face to look. "The king?"

"That's him. He killed Peteus of Attica when I was a boy. Bind my tongue, I can't have been more than six years old. He's a –"

A good man, he'd been about to say, before he bit the words back. Describing an enemy that way was not a good idea now, with so many Greeks dead and so many more grieving for them. But it was hard to think of Sarpedon as an enemy. Odysseus had only spoken to him two or three times, but he liked the man.

He watched as Sarpedon reached the front of the line, and came face to face with Ajax.

There was no finesse to their battle, none of the grace and technique shown by Hector and Achilles on the Plain. Ajax and Sarpedon simply hit one another as hard as they could, taking it in turns to hammer blows against shield and cuirass as though they'd agreed a rota. The men on either side let them be, perhaps afraid to come within range of those blows. Odysseus could hear the impacts even over the roar of battle, and the noise of hurrying men and water.

"Is that man going to *win?*" Isander asked. He was a captain now, but bloodied or not, he still sounded like an awestruck child.

"No," Odysseus said. Sorrow was a weight on his shoulders. "Twenty years ago, perhaps. Even ten. But not now."

A piece of shield spun away, Sarpedon ducking under the sweep that had severed it. He crashed his sword into Ajax's side but the giant's armour withstood the blow, and Ajax didn't seem to feel it.

"It makes you sad," Isander said.

The lad showed perception, to see that. He might be one of what Nestor had called the new Greeks, able to fight but capable of thought as well. Odysseus nodded. "Some of the people on the other side in this war were my friends, once. I'd hoped some would be left for me to share a cup of wine with again, when it was all over."

There was a pause, and then Isander said, "I don't think very much will be left at all."

Ajax absorbed another huge blow on his oblong shield, turned slightly, and brought his chipped blade down in an overhand blow that caught Sarpedon on the shoulder and smashed the bone into pieces. The Maeonian king staggered, his body bent out of shape. Ajax stabbed him through the belly and hit him in the face with the tower shield, pulverising his features and throwing his body back into his own soldiers.

"I don't think so either," Odysseus said.

Ajax howled his victory and plunged forward, right into the heart of the Maeonian company. He struck right and left as he went, with shield and broken sword alike, hacking men down before they could do much more than notice him. His men drove after him, widening the gap he made. All at once the Maeonian ranks shivered, men looking at one another in fear instead of determination.

Odysseus had seen that happen before. He knew what it looked like, even when faces were hidden by helmets; it was a set of the shoulders, something too in the angle of the head. He slithered down the back slope and beckoned to Arion, waiting a dozen yards back with the remaining Ithacan force gathered behind him.

"We're going to force the river," he said when the young man joined him. "The archers will have seen Sarpedon fall, they'll know the defences can't last much longer. My bet is they'll fire one shot and fall back."

"And if they don't?" Arion, ever the realist, asked.

"Then we'll fall back ourselves. Get the men ready. Tell them the bank is slippery, they'll need to boost one another up."

"You might be able to use another company," Isander said. He used a handful of leaves to wipe blood from his helmet and crammed it back on. "Gives you twice the chance."

"So it does," Odysseus said. He couldn't help but be impressed by the young man. "Downstream of my Ithacans, then. And Isander?"

The lad turned, waiting.

"If Ajax troubles you, let me know," he said.

Chapter Twenty

Lost Heroes

Archers broke away from the riverbank, running back towards the city. A moment later Aeneas saw Greek soldiers emerge from the brush along the levee, just downstream of the ford. One group pursued the bowmen, though their armour meant they had no chance of catching them. Keeping them running was enough. The other unit turned upstream, and fell on the flank of the Maeonians still trying to defend it.

Beset on two sides, the southerners collapsed quickly. In moments the remnants were retreating to the east, along the line of the Chiblak. It was only quarter of a mile to the first hills, and their sheltering carpet of shrubs and offspring trees. They might even make it.

Aeneas looked over his shoulder. The road into Troy was still packed with soldiers, waiting their turn to pass through the Horse Gate. The city's entrances had been built narrow to make it hard for attackers, but now it was working against Troy's own people. They needed time.

Then he looked down the hill, and realised they weren't going to have it.

Aeneas had seen Ajax throw himself on the Maeonian phalanx, then into the heart of it. He ought to have died then, surrounded by enemies while his men fought to catch up. But he hadn't, and now he burst towards Bramble Hill, his company again running a few steps behind. He was impossible to miss with that great oblong shield. Aeneas had seen it up close, an experience he didn't ever want to repeat.

He glanced at the men waiting to enter Troy. Checked the distance to the onrushing Ajax.

"Dardanians to me," he called. He made his voice languid, almost bored, as though he felt no unease at all. "And a few Trojans wouldn't go amiss either, if some are willing."

"I'll come," someone said. Crino was a soldier from the upper Simois valley, south of Dardanos. A man Aeneas knew, at least a little. Crino indicated the band of a dozen or so who half surrounded him. "We all will."

"As will we," said another man Aeneas recognised. Molion was the captain who'd captained the troops in Sparta last summer, under Paris' leadership. He wore the red and black lacquer of the Scamandrians now. A hundred men in the same colours stood behind him.

"Good enough," Aeneas said. "We need to buy some time for the men to get inside the walls. Ajax down there is going to try to stop us. We have to bloody his nose for him."

"A pleasure," Molion said.

They went down the hill. *An experience I never want to repeat,* Aeneas thought wryly. Sometimes you didn't get the things you wanted. Hector was dead, Trojans were in danger and soon they would begin to panic, with the Argives approaching and the Scaean Gate still blocked. Fear had a way of turning into ruin very quickly. It had to be averted, which meant stopping Ajax or at least delaying him, and Hector couldn't do it anymore.

So Aeneas would have to. He wondered if the Fates were already sharpening the knife that would cut the thread of his life, decided it was a pointless thought, and ignored it.

Ajax's men were well ahead of the Argive army, which was still swarming across the river. The ford was as much of a choke point as the Gate. That would stop the mixed Trojan force from being surrounded, at least. If they were quick. Aeneas slowed and signalled the men to form lines.

He saw the moment when Ajax recognised him. Under the helm of tusks the giant's eyes went wide, and his mouth twisted into a snarl. He redoubled his pace, dragging his men along behind him like a chevron of geese.

Troilus had fallen in the second battle. Hector was dead now, Lycaon almost for a certainty. There had been enough sorrow for Creusa. Aeneas prayed she would not have to suffer his loss as well. Not today.

He breathed deeply, holding himself to a walk. Ajax could win a battle in the first onslaught if you met him head on; the man would trample right over you. So he couldn't be met that way. But he had to be met, and stopped, immediately. Otherwise this sally was for nothing. Aeneas remembered when they had fought before – only a handful of days ago, incredible as that seemed. He thought about how Ajax had fought today, the headlong rush, the use of that tower shield to batter and crush.

He shouted, and his makeshift company broke into a trot, then a run as the two forces closed.

186

Ajax was still out in front. Aeneas ran straight at him, on flat ground now, earth as soft as any on the Plain.

They came together. Ajax wedged his shoulder behind his oblong shield and rammed it forward.

Aeneas kicked his feet out ahead of himself and went down on his back, letting go of his spear. He slid in the damp grass, through the gap Ajax always left between the bottom of the shield and the ground. The Argive was an unusually tall man, he just couldn't get down as low as he should. As Aeneas slithered past he stabbed upwards with his sword, taking the big Greek in the groin. Ajax shrieked in utter dismay.

Still sliding, Aeneas pulled the sword out and used the last of his momentum to regain his feet. He turned just as Ajax fell. There was a horrendous amount of blood. The giant was still trying to get up, but strength was pouring out of him and he fell back. The advancing Trojans streamed past him, crashing into the suddenly hesitant Argives a few paces further on.

"Coward's trick," Ajax managed. His voice was a moan.

Aeneas shook his head. "No son of Telamon has the right to call me coward, or any Trojan. If he had returned Hesione none of this would have happened. His sons are shades, and I can't make myself sorry."

Ajax was already dead by then. He lay on his back with the tower shield beneath him, skin white as spring clouds and the grass beneath his legs stained black. There was no point taking his armour. No man in Troy was large enough to wear it, or would want to try.

The Argive troops were falling back. Without their leader they seemed abruptly aware of how far from the main army they were, and retreated with as much haste as they could manage.

"Crino," Aeneas said. The soldier had taken up a place nearby, guarding Aeneas from a spear in the back. "Have a horn sounded. We've won the time we needed. Now we turn for Troy."

The man nodded and hurried off, searching for a herald. He must have found one because moments later a horn sounded one long, mournful note, and the ragbag company reformed around Aeneas. They were fifty yards back towards the city when Molion caught up with Aeneas, helmet missing and his hair matted with blood. With the crimson of his lacquered armour it

187

made him look like he'd stepped straight out of a butcher's yard, which Aeneas supposed he had.

"It isn't mine," the captain said, when Aeneas gave him a questioning look. "An Argive fell against me after I cut his throat, and sprayed blood all over me. Never mind that, though. I saw what you did to the Argive. Any time you need men, my lord, or have a task that wants doing, you ask the Scamandrians."

There was a chorus of agreement, and Aeneas allowed himself a weary smile. Hector was dead, and yet the war wasn't over. Now it was Aeneas who would have to lead the fight against the Greeks. He felt very tired.

They went on up the hill, and through the Horse Gate into Troy.

*

His leg hurt like half the torments of Tartarus. Achilles wasn't sure it should, actually. He'd been wounded before, everything from scratches to cuts half an inch deep, and none of those injuries had flamed like these. Came of the arrows going so deep, he supposed.

The physician had been right, bind his tongue for it. If Achilles had tried to drive a chariot he'd have collapsed before the horses were up to speed. He kept wishing he was good enough with a bow that he might limp along behind the army and shoot a Trojan or two, but he'd never learned. The greatest warrior in Greece killed his enemies up close, not loosing arrows from a hundred feet away. He wouldn't be able to bear the shame if he started now.

He drank from a wine cup and glowered at the doctor's bent back. Deiochus was writing on a square of parchment, at a desk placed by the tent's narrow entrance. It meant nobody could come or go except right past him. Achilles might be able to slip under the canvas – if his leg was working, he might – but every soldier within sight would immediately cry out in delight, and Deiochus would be out of the tent and fussing before his patient managed three steps.

He scowled and drank more wine, not watered.

Footfalls outside announced visitors before they pushed the flap aside and stepped in. Deiochus looked up sharply but held his tongue when he saw who it was. Agamemnon still wore his rainbow armour, and Diomedes his cuirass of shining silver, though both were lightly stained with mud. Eudorus was with them, and he was as clean as a girl still wet from her bath. Achilles drained his cup and set it aside.

"The Trojans escaped into the city," Agamemnon said. "How soon can you be up and fighting, Achilles?"

"When I say he can," Deiochus cut in. "For a normal man I'd say he would need a month, minimum, to recover from the ankle wound. But this is Achilles. He might be capable in two weeks."

"That is ridiculous," the High King snapped. "This is a war, and an army needs its heroes."

The physician shrugged. "You may dismiss me, or send me home, but while I am responsible for this patient then my word carries weight. He rests for two weeks – and perhaps more, as I may decide."

"He means it, too," Achilles said. He might have found Deiochus' intransigence amusing, had it been another man lying on this couch with a throbbing ache in his leg. As it was, he had something else to concentrate on now. "He'd have made a good soldier, with his stubbornness."

"My path went a different way," Deiochus said. "And you're a fine one to speak of stubbornness."

Achilles elected to ignore that. "How did the Trojans manage to get away?"

"They defended the Chiblak ford," Diomedes said. "Sarpedon held it long enough for the army to slip away. Ajax killed him, and drove the Maeonians off, but it was too late."

"Good for Ajax," he said. "He's worth three of any of you. Of all the Greeks, he's the only one I'd follow."

"He's dead," Agamemnon said.

The words were blunt, delivered without any attempt to soften the blow, and the glint of malice in the High King's eye said he'd spoken them that way on purpose. To embarrass, or humiliate. It worked, to some extent. Achilles muttered a hasty prayer to any shades which might be loitering around, excited by a mention of the dead.

So Ajax was lost. That meant the whole line of Telamon was gone, killed in this war. The father in a sling by his ship, being lowered to the beach like a fat cow. Teucer killed by Hector on the Plain, and now Ajax cut down beyond Scamander. "How did it happen?"

189

"Aeneas," Diomedes said quickly, before Agamemnon could speak. "He slid in under that tower shield and stabbed Ajax in the groin from beneath. A clever trick, I suppose."

"I suppose," Achilles agreed. Blood was roiling in his head, hot and thick. "I will kill him for it. I give you my oath."

"That's more like it!" Agamemnon exclaimed. From just behind him Diomedes shot the vulgar High King a look of loathing, quickly masked. "You'll be on your feet and itching to fight in a few days, I'm sure of it."

"Two weeks," Deiochus repeated, unperturbed by this burst of enthusiasm. "As I told you."

Achilles swallowed wine. His head was pulsing as badly as his leg now. He wanted nothing better than to be able to sleep well, then rise in the morning and drive his chariot out to Troy, to challenge Aeneas as he'd challenged Hector. And to kill him, of course: that was inevitable when Achilles fought. But he thought Aeneas would be less willing to come out and face him, in truth. The Dardanian would stay safe behind the walls of Troy, and might even order the archers to fire as Paris had done. A craven thing to do, but cowards suffered torments in Tartarus if they weren't punished before.

Ajax was dead. There was something that needed to be said about that. Achilles concentrated and said, "I will kill Aeneas for this. I swear it."

The two kings looked at him, and then Deiochus was beside the bed, touching a hand to Achilles' forehead. He frowned and took the wine cup away, then pressed fingertips to the wounded man's wrist. The frown deepened.

"What?" Agamemnon demanded.

"Fever," the physician said bluntly. "A high one, and it's come on fast, which worries me. I wonder…"

He trailed off, and there was a long pause before Agamemnon said, "Wonder what?"

"The Trojans poisoned their arrows before," Deiochus said. "I wonder if they did so again?"

Agamemnon and Diomedes turned to look at the patient. Both their expressions were suddenly blank, the guarded looks of men keeping their thoughts concealed. Achilles had never been good at reading such marble faces, but these were so obviously worried that he would have laughed, except that he coughed instead. A moment later he spat up a thick wad of spittle and wine in a dark mass that dribbled over the sheets.

"Out of my sickroom," Deiochus ordered, pointing with one hand. Achilles saw the two kings retreating through a haze of darkness, and then everything went away.

*

He came back to himself in the night, very weak, and at first he thought the gloom meant he was dead.

Then he heard faint sounds, the clink of plates at campfires and the wash of waves on the sand, and understood that he was still alive. Besides, if he was dead the shades of men he'd slain would have surrounded him, and borne him away to paradise in the Elysian Fields. He should have remembered that, but his head felt light and heavy at the same time, as though it had been stuffed with wool until no more would fit.

His leg burned. With an effort he lifted his head to look down at it.

"I have cut infection away from the wounds," Deiochus said, from a wicker chair beside the bed. "That opened them wider, but there was no help for it. I also bled you while you slept. How do you feel?"

There was enough candlelight for him to see the arrow wounds, which were visibly larger. Deiochus had packed them with lint and left them open, the way surgeons sometimes did. There was a smell of hot wine, used to sear wounds, but under it was another, ranker odour.

"Infection?" he asked. His voice was a croak.

The physician nodded. "The Trojans used poison arrows."

Not just cowards but treacherous ones, then. "Don't worry yourself. My mother blessed me with all the arts of the island temples when I was a babe. I'll be healthy again in no time."

"My experience has been that prayer and blessings only work when allied to good medicine," Deiochus said dryly. "Look at the sword cut on your thigh and tell me how healthy you'll be."

He did. The slash had turned green at the edges, and fingers of discolouration reached down to his knee and were stretching towards his groin. When he prodded it with a finger the world wavered and he thought he was going to faint.

191

"The poison has sunk too deep for me to stop," Deiochus said. "It's in your blood now. Left to itself it will spread throughout your body and kill you."

"So cut the wounds wider," Achilles said.

"I can't. There are major veins close by, and in any case the infection has gone beyond those specific areas. The only thing I can do now is amputate the leg."

Achilles turned his head to look at the man. His eyes hurt, every part of him hurt, but he refused to let that master him. "If you try to take my leg I will kill you, physician. Believe it."

"If I don't, you'll almost certainly die."

"If you do, I will live as a cripple," he said. "Mighty Achilles, hopping around the village on his crutch! It won't be. If this is when the Fates cut my thread, then I accept it. Understand me, Deiochus. Crippled or no, if you saw off my leg I will kill you as slowly as I can manage."

The Messenian pursed his lips. "Then drink this, at least. It tastes foul but it might help, a little."

The concoction did taste foul, and it coated Achilles' throat like slime and made him want to cough. But he tasted poppy in the mix and drowsiness overcame him too quickly. The last thing he remembered was Deiochus lowering him back down on the pillows.

When he woke again the tent was lit by several lanterns, placed on tables and the floor. He could only see a haze now, vague shapes and colours that blurred and swam whenever he blinked. His leg throbbed but it didn't hurt anymore. It seemed too much effort to look down and see why.

Briseis stood by the side of his bed, looking down at him with a tremulous look on her face. Behind her someone was sitting in a chair; it took a moment of squinting for Achilles to realise it was Odysseus. That meant the slightly twisted man beside him must be Thersites. There was no sign of the physician.

But on the other side of the bed stood Peleus, Achilles' father. He wore an expression of mingled pride and love and grief, which puzzled Achilles for a moment. Why grief? Then he understood; the doctor was not here, but his father was. Death was coming for him.

He turned his head to look at Briseis. "You shouldn't be here. This isn't a place for women."

"I want to be here," she said.

Achilles shook his head. It hurt amazingly and he stopped, breathing carefully before he spoke. He couldn't inhale properly without pain, dozens of knives in his chest. "Go. Or I'll have you carried."

She went, straight-backed and proud. Of all the women he'd known, all those abducted outlanders and seduced Greek girls, he thought she was the bravest. Perhaps that was just because she was the last, though. There would be no more, he understood that now. But his thoughts kept drifting away, however he tried to clutch at them. He was very tired.

She was beautiful, Briseis. As lovely as a goddess, and he'd tell those proud Olympian women as much, if ever he saw them. He thought he might. There were few heroes who'd done more than him, achieved such glories, in all the history of Greece. Heracles of course, and perhaps Perseus, who had been so favoured by Athena in his fight against the Gorgon.

"Father," he said. His voice was weaker already than when he's spoken to Briseis. Peleus had known Theseus, he'd be able to answer a question. "Was I a greater man than him?"

"A greater man than any I've known," Peleus said.

Achilles frowned. He hadn't named Theseus, he realised, but fathers knew what their sons meant sometimes, just as mothers did. Anyway, the gods might be here in this room, easing understanding with the aura of their presence. He turned his head with an effort.

"Odysseus," he said.

The Ithacan king rose and came to his bedside. "I'm here, Achilles."

"You're planning something," Achilles whispered. "You're always planning something. Tell me what it is."

"We think we can get over the walls," Odysseus said. "Thersites and I. We've been talking."

His eyelids were heavy. "The walls?"

"Fog hides the Plain on some mornings," Thersites put in. "When the *Meltemi* doesn't blow, which isn't very often. But at those times, the walls are shrouded in cloud."

"So?"

"So they can't see what we'll do to them," Odysseus said. "Peleus, you must not breathe a word of this. Not a murmur. If a Greek is captured the Trojans might learn what we intend."

"Then it wasn't in vain," Achilles said.

193

"No. It wasn't." Odysseus hesitated. "And courage is never in vain. You can be proud, Achilles."

He closed his eyes and let sleep steal over him again. As he drifted off he thought he heard Thersites whisper in his ear; "You are the best of warriors, Achilles. You proved it in this war, and I'll tell it so when I speak my tales."

But that may just have been his imagination. He felt his breathing slow, and then sleep took him once more. He died an hour before dawn, in a tent surrounded by deep circles of soldiers, standing in silence in the dark.

Chapter Twenty-One

The Pyre

There had never been a time when she couldn't speak her mind to Aeneas. Be easy with him, relaxed, laughing at some minor jest that would have meant nothing to anyone else. But now Creusa sat across the table and watched him eat, and could think of nothing to say.

He had gone away from her today, to some inner place where she could neither follow, nor reach him there.

At that, she was luckier than poor Andromache, left alone with her infant son when Achilles killed Hector. Andromache wasn't even from Troy, she'd lived here less than two years, and had few friends. Royal women rarely did. That was why Hecuba had tried to involve her with Helen, when Paris brought the Argive woman here from Sparta and started all this misery. There had never been much pleasure for Andromache in Helen's company, and there would be scant comfort in it now. If Helen even offered.

Poor Tanith was bereft too, Troilus' Phrygian lover from the stables. She could never have married her prince, of course, but women like her were kept as lovers sometimes, tucked away in a house behind the palace, or outside the wall of the Pergamos. Eshan was widowed, the Hittite wife of Lycaon, left alone in Troy to listen to rumours of the fall of her homeland, if she could hear them above the crash of bronze in battle.

There was grief all around, among common folk as well as the lords and princesses of Troy. Sorrow for the dead, and yet here was she, fretting because she couldn't think what to say to a husband who was still alive and whole. Creusa knew she wasn't pretty, but she'd never been a fool. She left her seat and went around the table to sit at his side, resting a hand on his leg as he stripped a chicken carcass to the bone.

She didn't speak. When speech escaped her then she let it leave, and waited until it came back. Or until Aeneas spoke. And if that took long ages of the world she would endure them, seated here with her legs curled under her like a cat, until her bones crumbled and nothing remained but her spirit.

She'd never really believed, when she first began to love this man, that he might come to love her too.

She had known him before that. Aeneas had all but grown up in Troy, a close companion and trusted friend to Hector, with Pandarus usually close by. Dead now, those latter two, leaving only her husband. But in those days they had been young, and laughter was never far away while they fought and hunted and fought again, emerging always with grins of triumph or congratulation.

Aeneas had just been a friend of Hector's. Not someone she expected to pay attention to her. She'd stolen glances at him though, this tall Dardanian with the quick hands and even quicker smile, and the pause for thought before he spoke. That she observed especially: among all the boisterous youths and boastful men, Aeneas always made time to think.

Creusa, born with straggly hair above a farmer's plain face, noticed such things. She had thought a hundred times that when women missed out on looks they gained cleverness instead, an idea that collapsed when you looked at Hecuba or Andromache, who had both. It persisted though. As for Aeneas, he had looks and wit both, but men often did. The rules for them were not the same.

One day when she was seventeen she'd been reading in the gardens when he walked by, and he stopped at her bench to talk.

After that they seemed to encounter each other every day – in the streets, the gardens again, the *megaron* or the temples. Even once in the market in the lower town, where Creusa had been trying to decide whether she was brave enough to wear a lapis necklace she thought was far too ostentatious for her. Aeneas had admired it, placed it around her neck, and then cajoled and persuaded her into buying it despite her fears. That night, lying alone in bed, she'd relived the touch of his fingers around her neck and shivered… and because she was Creusa, a thought had come to her.

Because she was Creusa, she spoke it to him, next morning when they met on the city walls.

"You didn't just happen by, that day in the gardens," she said. "Did you?"

He smiled at her. "No. I thought you'd realise that."

"Then why were you there?"

"To talk to you," he'd said, as though puzzled by the question. "Why else would I be there?"

But she hadn't been able to believe it, not truly, in her heart. He couldn't have walked along that path simply to speak with plain Creusa. Not handsome Aeneas, the darling of Dardanos, adored almost equally by the Trojans who put him nearly on a level with Hector himself. Adored by half the women of the city, too, who would fall at his feet in return for a smile. He could have any lover he wanted. Why would he bother with her?

Then he'd come to tell her he wanted to ask her mother if Creusa could be his bride, if she wished it. She said yes without really being aware of what she was doing, or saying. And it wasn't a game, some cruel joke: he actually did it, went to Hecuba and asked. A month later they were standing under the Palladium, the wooden statue of Athena that guarded Troy against conquest, their wrists tied with cord while the priest spoke words that bound them forever.

The world offered glories, sometimes. But then later it gave horror instead, such as standing on a wall and watching the man you loved, and would always love, rush over the ground to meet an enemy bigger and more savage than any man should be. He'd survived, thanks to the gods, and felled Ajax with a single clever blow. But next time might be different. Next time she might be the wife sobbing for the empty place in her heart.

"I think," he said now, speaking for the first time all evening, "that Troy is doomed."

His hand was resting on her shoulder. She'd been so caught up in memories that she hadn't felt it there, or noticed he'd finished his meal. She heard his words but made no sense of them.

"I hope I'm wrong," Aeneas said. "By Tarhun, I hope I am. But I don't think the Argives will stop."

She found her voice. "But they can't get over the walls. And they've lost so many men already."

"That's why they won't stop. They've paid a higher price than they thought possible. Agamemnon and his advisors believed they could sail here and sweep us away in one assault, then dictate terms to a beaten Troy. Argive soldiers stationed in the Pergamos, most likely, and their traders allowed free use of the Trojan Road and access to the Euxine Sea." His hand moved to her neck, then back to her shoulder, a restless movement not mirrored in his voice. "Now the Plain is soaked in their blood, and they can't redeem their pride except by conquering."

197

"That makes no sense."

"No," he agreed. "But there's a kind of madness in the Argives, I think. A lust for glory taken so far that they abandon all else, forget anything but the hunger for greatness. This *kleos* of theirs." He snorted. "Fame won in battle, undying, a name to last forever. But no victory is forever. They sacrifice everything in pursuit of a dream they can't win."

She thought about that. Creusa had always been capable, not a woman much given to panic. His hand moved on her shoulder, now resting still, now stroking down her hair the way she liked. That made it hard to think, actually, but she tried to ignore it.

"Then this isn't about Helen anymore," she said at last. "It's only victory they're interested in."

"Yes. I think so."

"And no more allies will come to help us."

"No."

The Maeonians had already left, driven east along the Chiblak by a mass of Greek spearmen. They'd lost more than half their numbers at the ford before then, as well as their king and captain. Another grief for Hecuba to bear, along with the loss of three of her sons; Sarpedon had been her cousin. The Hittites had withdrawn into the eastern hills, willing to patrol the countryside but not join the defenders now hemmed into Troy itself. Not that there were enough of them to matter. Troy had bled for Hattusa whenever the Great King called, but little help came down the road when it was Troy in need.

Pedasos and Thebe-under-Plakos had been sacked by the Myrmidons. No help could come from those cities, or from Lyrnos and Thermi, whose kings lay sleepless in fear of a similar assault. The Mysians hadn't come, perhaps afraid of the same thing. An army might march from Miletos, where people had learned to hate the Argives in fire and slaughter. But it couldn't come for weeks yet. Miletos was the length of the Aegean away.

Troy was alone.

"We've already lost," she said. "Even if they set sail tomorrow, it will be a generation before Troy is what it was before."

"Yes," he agreed. His hand tightened on her shoulder. "My love, I want you to go to the slopes of Ida. I'll send soldiers to guard you. But I want you out of the city in the morning."

She glared at him fiercely. "I will not leave you."

198

"You will do as I say," he replied, quite calmly. "I've never commanded you, Creusa, not once since we were wed. But I'm ordering you now. Go with my cousin Leos to Mount Ida, and wait there until I come to you. If the city falls, its royal line must survive. That's the only chance for Troy to rebuild."

"But –"

"Creusa," he said. He leaned and kissed the top of her head. "I can't bear the thought of you here when the Argives break in. Please, do as I say. I love you too much to lose you."

It was that which disarmed her, as it so often did. The renewed surrender of his heart, so unexpectedly given, so hard to believe she really held. She leaned her head against his knee and fought to hold back her tears.

They sat that way for some time before his hand on her shoulder went from resting to caressing. It was often that way with them. Any proximity, any touching or shared strength, led to something more intimate. They made love on the divan by the dinner table, still half-clothed when they both cried out within seconds of one another. For that time Creusa forgot the grief for her dead brothers, Hector so impossibly strong and Troilus so handsome and careless, and most of all her twin Lycaon, like the other half of her soul. Forgot the sorrow, and the fear that all she'd endured was no more than a taste, a foreshadowing of what was to come when the Argives broke through the wall.

Later, lying in bed with her husband sleeping lightly beside her, Creusa's tears did come. She made no effort to stop them but she did weep in silence, and beside her Aeneas slept in peace.

*

"What will you do after the war?"

"Same as I did before it," Molion said gruffly. "Breed horses and train with the Scamandrians." He looked to his right, over the parapet towards the Argive camp. It had become a habit with him, something he did every few seconds even when there were buildings or trees in the way. Take two steps, look to check on the Argives. Hand over coins, check on the Argives.

"I want to find a wife," Hyrca said. "And learn to sail a galley. Travel the Road to Priapos, and the Euxine Sea beyond it. You know, it's strange how few Trojans have ever been there."

199

"Why bother?" he asked. "The world comes to Troy. We've no need to go searching for it."

No need, and Molion had never felt the desire either. The journey to Greece last summer had been the first time Molion left Troas, and he hadn't enjoyed it much. He'd avoided seasickness, unlike half the soldiers, but he didn't like the movement of the deck under his feet, and he hadn't slept well in the bays they found either. There was never any telling who else might be aground in the next headland, or whether island outlaws might be lurking atop the cliffs and waiting for the seamen to fall asleep. It was safer here in Troas, where the land was familiar and the roads patrolled. Molion saw enough danger as a soldier without going looking for more, thank you very much.

He didn't seem to be very good at small talk. Usually his sentry duties were shared with other men from his company, soldiers he knew well and who knew him too. They wouldn't have asked him silly questions about after the war. But Hyrca and Periso weren't Scamandrians. They fought for Troy though, and casualties had been so hideously high that men from different companies found themselves pitched together now, sharing duties. Who knew, by the time the war was over there might be so few Scamandrians left that these two would be asked to join.

"What about you?" he asked, making an effort. "What will you do when the war's over?"

Hyrca shrugged and smiled. "Find a wife. Learn to sail. Travel the Trojan Road."

"Go home to Zeleia and raise a family," Periso said when Molion turned to look at him. "Though I'll have to teach Anteia to cook first. Give the woman a skillet and she turns ham-fisted in a flash."

"He looks half-starved, doesn't he?" Hyrca asked ironically.

"I've been eating well at the camp fires," Periso said, not abashed in the least. "Back home I always used to buy from street vendors, and I suppose I'll have to again."

"A soldier's pay doesn't buy many pies."

"I won't be a soldier," the other man said comfortably. "I'm going to raise sheep. There's good grass on Ida."

There was, though it was already heavily grazed by whole flocks of sheep. And by herds of horses now, driven up before the Argives landed so they would be safe. The bloodlines had to be protected at any cost, especially from the Argives. If the stock spread across the world Troy would lose one of its main sources of wealth. And there were no outlaws on Ida these days, none of the bands that had raided and stolen with impunity for time out of mind. The spread of Troy's people, and her power, had seen to that.

But if finding space for sheep would be hard, it should be easy for Hyrca to find a wife. So many Trojan men had fallen that women would outnumber the survivors three to two, or perhaps more. Maidens would all but fight each other over who had claim on an eligible man, and there would be a lot of children born to unwed mothers in the years to come. Molion wasn't married, and he wondered whether he should bother, or just enjoy the favours of a string of women with no husband. He shook the thought away. It hardly mattered, unless the war could be won.

He glanced over the battlements, to where the Argive camp fires were beginning to flare.

A servant came up the steps with a platter of food, sliced meats and fruit with a pitcher of ale and three cups. The soldiers ate and drank in silence for a while, watching night settle on the Plain of Troy as stars came out above. The *Meltemi* had died away, for a mercy; it would have been very cold atop the tower with the north wind blowing. Mist began to rise from the wet soil.

The lords said the Greeks could never take these walls. Molion believed it, had grown up believing it, because there was nothing in the world to match them. Any soldier worth the name would look up at them, craning his neck, and die a little inside at the thought of assaulting them. Sitting atop them he should have felt safe. He no longer did.

The lords said the walls were impregnable, but they had said the Argives would exchange Helen for Hesione, too. They'd told the soldiers that Agamemnon could never bind the quarrelsome Argive kings into a single army, and then bring them across the sea to Troy. They'd said the Hittites would come anyway, and smash the Greeks even if they did somehow make it across the Aegean. And they had been wrong, every time. The Argives were here and the Hittites were not, and so many men were dead. Soldiers from Troy itself, from Zeleia and Bunarbi, Dardanians,

Maeonians. Pandarus, Troilus, even mighty Hector himself. So many things had happened that Molion once thought impossible. He thought the walls would hold. He thought they would.

"Look," Periso said.

Molion didn't need telling. A yellow glow had appeared by the coast of Cradle Bay, in the Argive camp four miles away. The fog was thick enough now to hide all the campfires and at first he thought the whole camp must be ablaze, perhaps caused by a carelessly spilled amphora of olive oil too near a flame. He'd seen that happen once, on the campaign with the Hittites; three men had lit up like old wood, and staggered around screaming until a clear-headed captain ordered spears thrust into them.

But this blaze didn't spread. It brightened until Molion couldn't look at it anymore though, and he understood.

"It's a pyre," he said.

Hyrca nodded. "Someone important must have died. One of their kings, probably."

"If we're lucky it might be the high chief himself," Periso said.

It might be. There had been no rumour of plague in the Argive camp, but there didn't need to be: there was always disease. Thousands of men eating together and voiding their bowels in shallow trenches invited it. When contagion came it did so quickly, sweeping through the tents as quickly as the wind. Or the explanation might be simpler; perhaps a king had taken a wound that became infected, and finally took his life.

It didn't matter. The death of any Argive lifted Trojan hopes, if only marginally, but the death of a king – which this surely was – could turn the war. It could be the blessing of Tarhun, favouring his chosen people of Troy. With that Molion suddenly knew who had died, was *certain* of it, as though the gods had reached down and given him the knowledge as a gift.

Paris' archers had used poison on their barbs. The pyre was for Achilles, wounded on the field and now walking the road to Hades. A moment ago Molion had been morose, hardly able to think of a life after the war, but now he felt his lips stretch in a smile.

"You two keep watch," he ordered. "I'll take word of this to Aeneas."

202

With that he hurried away, to the stone steps that ran down the outside of the tower to the wall below. They were precarious in the dark and he went carefully until he was on the parapet, when he picked up speed again. He turned right and went down another flight of stairs, and near the top descended into the fog that rose to meet him, wreathing the walls in a shroud of white that reduced visibility to the length of an arm.

Caesura

It was Achilles who had died, of course, though the Trojans were not certain of it. Not that night.

Most of the army had gathered around the pavilion before the last breath left him. They stood in silence, unarmed, Achaean next to Pierian next to Argolid, kings and common men alike. The sea was only a faint rustle on the sand, quieter than men's breathing.

Agamemnon ordered the tent taken down around the dead man's bed. All that long day soldiers passed by, then took a timber from a broken-up ship and carried it to the pile that would become a pyre. Many returned to walk past the body again, to carry a second plank. It was allowed. Even Agamemnon understood that the army needed to see before it believed.

Then it needed to grieve. Men wept together, prayed in small groups and gatherings of a thousand. If the Trojans had come on them just then the Greeks would have been routed, unarmed as they were, and still in disbelief. How could Achilles be dead? It didn't seem natural, like a fish hatching from a cuckoo's egg. He had seemed more than mortal. Every ordinary man had thought he was greater than that, halfway to godhood.

The Trojans could have swept us away with half her forces. A quarter of them. Greeks would have fled, unable to summon the will to resist. They would have waded into the waves and drowned in despair, not caring. But Troy too was licking her wounds. Hector had died, and Sarpedon. Losses almost as great as Achilles and Ajax. There were enough dead to crowd the road to Hades while those heroes walked it.

Hector's body was laid face down at the base of the pyre, bound hand and foot, with no coin under his tongue for the ferryman. His only way to the afterworld would be as Achilles' servant, for all time. Odysseus thought that was ungracious, a bitter way to treat a brave and decent enemy, and he said so – to Agamemnon. The High King invited him to say as much to the soldiers, if he felt so strongly. Odysseus held his peace.

He sorrowed for that decision, in the years which followed the war. So did I, usually when night was drawing in and the wind was cold, and I felt death's touch a little closer to my ageing skin. But I don't blame him, or curse myself. If we'd